HUCKLEBERRY FINN

MARK TWAIN

Huckleberry Finn

abridged

A Purnell Classic

OTHER TITLES IN SERIES

SBN 361 · 03540 3
First published in this edition 1976
by Purnell Books, Berkshire House, Queen Street, Maidenhead,
Berkshire
Made and printed in Germany

CONTENTS

EXPLANATORY

In this book a number of dialects are used, to wit: the Missouri Negro dialect; the extremest form of the backwoods Southwestern dialect; the ordinary "Pike County" dialect; and four modified varieties of this last. The shadings have not been done in a haphazard fashion, or by guesswork; but painstakingly, and with the trustworthy guidance and support of personal familiarity with these several forms of speech.

I make this explanation for the reason that without it many readers would suppose that all these characters were trying to talk alike and not succeeding.

THE AUTHOR

CHAPTER I

Civilizing Huck–Miss Watson–Tom Sawyer waits

You don't know about me without you have read a book by the name of *The Adventures of Tom Sawyer;* but that ain't no matter. That book was made by Mr. Mark Twain, and he told the truth, mainly. There was things which he stretched, but mainly he told the truth. That is nothing. I never seen anybody but lied one time or another, without it was Aunt Polly, or the widow, or maybe Mary. Aunt Polly–Tom's Aunt Polly, she is–and Mary, and the Widow Douglas is all told about in that book, which is mostly a true book, with some stretchers, as I said before.

Now the way that the book winds up is this: Tom and me found the money that the robbers hid in the cave, and it made us rich. We got six thousand apiece–all gold. It was an awful sight of money when it was piled up. Well, Judge Thatcher he took it and put it out at interest, and it fetched us a dollar a day apiece all the year round–more than a body could tell what to do with. The Widow Douglas, she took me for her son, and allowed she would sivilize me; but it was rough, living in the house all the time, considering how dismal regular and decent the widow was in all her ways; and so I lit out.

I got into my old rags and my sugar-hogshead again, and was free and satisfied. But Tom Sawyer he hunted me up and said he was going to start a band of robbers, and I might join if I would go back to the widow and be respectable. So I went back.

The widow, she cried over me and called me a poor lost lamb, and she called me a lot of other names, too, but she never meant no harm by it. She put me in them new clothes again, and I couldn't do nothing but sweat and sweat and feel all cramped up. Well, then the old thing commenced again. The widow rung a bell for supper, and you had to come to time. When you got to the table, you couldn't go right to eating but had to wait for the widow to tuck down her head and grumble a little over the victuals, though there warn't really anything the matter with them–that is, nothing only everything was cooked by itself. In a barrel of odds and ends it is different; things get mixed up, and the juice kind of swaps around, and the things go better.

After supper she got out her book and learned me about Moses and the Bullrushers, and I was in a sweat to find out all about him. But by and by she let it out that Moses had been dead a considerable long time; so then

I didn't care no more about him, because I don't take no stock in dead people.

Pretty soon I wanted to smoke and asked the widow to let me. But she wouldn't. She said it was a mean practice and wasn't clean, and I must try to not do it any more. That is just the way with some people. They get down on a thing when they don't know nothing about it. Here she was a-bothering about Moses, which was no kin to her and no use to anybody, being gone, you see, yet finding a power of fault with me for doing a thing that had some good in it. And she took snuff, too; of course that was all right, because she done it herself.

Her sister, Miss Watson, a tolerable slim old maid, with goggles on, had just come to live with her, and took a set at me now with a spelling book. She worked me middling hard for about an hour, and then the widow made her ease up. I couldn't stood it much longer.

Then for an hour it was deadly dull, and I was fidgety. Miss Watson would say, "Don't put your feet up there, Huckleberry," and "Don't scrunch up like that, Huckleberry—set up straight," and pretty soon she would say, "Don't gap and stretch like that, Huckleberry—why don't you try to behave?" Then she told me all about the bad place, and I said I wished I was there. She got mad then, but I didn't mean no harm. All I wanted was to go somewheres; all I wanted was a change, I warn't particular. She said it was wicked to say what I said; said she wouldn't say it for the whole world. *She* was going to live so as to go to the good place. Well, I couldn't see no advantage in going where she was going, so I made up my mind I wouldn't try for it. But I never said so, because it would only make trouble and wouldn't do no good.

Now she had got a start, and she went on and told me all about the good place. She said all a body would have to do there was to go around all day long with a harp and sing, forever and ever. So I didn't think much of it. But I never said so. I asked her if she reckoned Tom Sawyer would go there, and she said not by a considerable sight. I was glad about that, because I wanted him and me to be together.

Miss Watson, she kept pecking at me, and it got tiresome and lonesome. By and by they fetched the niggers in and had prayers, and then everybody was off to bed. I went up to my room with a piece of candle and put it on the table. Then I set down in a chair by the window and tried to think of something cheerful, but it warn't no use.

I felt so lonesome I most wished I was dead. The stars were shining, and the leaves rustled in the woods ever so mournful; an I heard an owl, away off, who-whooing about somebody that was dead, and a whippoorwill and a dog crying about somebody that was going to die; and the wind was trying to whisper something to me, and I couldn't make out what it was, and so it made the cold shivers run over me. Then away out in the woods I heard that kind of a sound that a ghost makes when it wants to tell about something that's on its mind and can't make itself understood, and so can't rest easy in its grave, and has to go about that way every night grieving. I got so downhearted and scared that I did wish I had some company.

Pretty soon a spider went crawling up my shoulder, and I flipped it off and it lit in the candle; and before I could budge it was all shriveled up. I didn't need anybody to tell me that that was an awful bad sign and would fetch me some bad luck, so I was scared and most shook the clothes off of me. I got up and turned around in my tracks three times and crossed my breast every time; and then I tied up a little lock of my hair with a thread to keep witches away. But I hadn't no confidence. You do that when you've lost a horseshoe that you've found, instead of nailing it up over the door, but I hadn't ever heard anybody say it was any way to keep off bad luck when you'd killed a spider.

I set down again, a-shaking all over, and got out my pipe for a smoke; for the house was all as still as death now, and so the widow wouldn't know. Well, after a long time I heard the clock away off in the town go boom—boom—boom—twelve licks; and all still again—stiller than ever. Pretty soon I heard a twig snap down in the dark amongst the trees— something was a-stirring. I set still and listened. Directly I could just barely hear a *"Me-yow! Me-yow!"* down there. That was good! Says I, *"Me-yow! Me-yow!"* as soft as I could, and then I put out the light and scrambled out of the window on to the shed.

Then I slipped down to the ground and crawled in amongst the trees, and, sure enough, there was Tom Sawyer waiting for me.

CHAPTER II

The boys escape Jim–Tom Sawyer's gang–Deep-laid plans

WE WENT tiptoeing along a path amongst the trees back toward the end of the widow's garden, stooping down so as the branches wouldn't scrape our heads. When we was passing by the kitchen I fell over a root and made a noise. We scrouched down and laid still. Miss Watson's big nigger, named Jim, was setting in the kitchen door; we could see him pretty clear, because there was a light behind him. He got up and stretched his neck out about a minute, listening.

Then he says, "Who dah?"

He listened some more; then he came tiptoeing down and stood right between us. We could 'a' touched him, nearly. Well, likely it was minutes and minutes that there warn't a sound, and we all there so close together. There was a place on my ankle that got to itching, but I dasn't scratch it; and my left ear began to itch; and next my back, right between my shoulders. Seemed like I'd die if I couldn't scratch. Well, I've noticed that thing plenty times since. If you are with the quality or at a funeral or trying to go to sleep when you ain't sleepy—if you are anywheres where it won't do for you to scratch, why you will itch all over in upward of a thousand places.

Pretty soon Jim says, "Say, who is you? Whar is you? Dog my cats ef I didn' hear sumf'n. Well, I know what I's gwyne to do. I's gwyne to set down right here and listen tell I hears it ag'in."

So he set down on the ground betwixt me and Tom. He leaned his back up against a tree and stretched his legs out till one of them most touched one of mine. My nose begun to itch. It itched till the tears come into my eyes. But I dasn't scratch. Then it begun to itch on the inside. Next I got to itching underneath. I didn't know how I was going to set still. This miserableness went on as much as six or seven minutes, but it seemed a sight longer than that. I was itching in eleven different places now. I reckoned I couldn't stand it more'n a minute longer, but I set my teeth hard and got ready to try. Just then Jim begun to breathe heavy; next he begun to snore—and then I was pretty soon comfortable again.

Tom he made a sign to me—kind of a little noise with his mouth—and we went creeping away on our hands and knees. When we was ten foot off Tom whispered to me, and wanted to tie Jim to the tree for fun. But I said no. He might wake and make a disturbance, and then they'd find out I warn't in. Then Tom said he hadn't got candles enough, and he would slip in the kitchen and get some more. I didn't want him to try. I said Jim might wake up and come. But Tom wanted to resk it; so we slid in there and got three candles, and Tom laid five cents on the table for pay. Then we got out, and I was in a sweat to get away; but nothing would do Tom but he must crawl to where Jim was, on his hands and knees, and play something on him. I waited, and it seemed a good while.

As soon as Tom was back we cut along the path, around the garden fence, and by and by fetched up on the steep top of the hill the other side of the house. Tom said he slipped Jim's hat off his head and hung it on a limb right over him, and Jim stirred a little, but he didn't wake. Afterward Jim said the witches bewitched him and put him in a trance, and rode him all over the state, and then set him under the trees again, and hung his hat on a limb to show who done it.

Well, when Tom and me got to the edge of the hilltop we looked away down into the village and could see three or four lights twinkling, where there was sick folks, maybe; and the stars over us was sparkling ever so fine; and down by the village was the river, a whole mile broad, and awful still and grand. We went down the hill and found Joe Harper and Ben Rogers, and two or three more of the boys, hid in the old tanyard. So we unhitched a skiff and pulled down the river two mile and a half, and went ashore.

We went to a clump of bushes, and Tom made everybody swear to keep the secret, and then showed them a hole in the hill, right in the thickest part of the bushes. Then we lit the candles and crawled in on

12

our hands and knees. We went about two hundred yards, and then the cave opened up. Tom poked about amongst the passages and pretty soon ducked under a wall where you wouldn't 'a' noticed that there was a hole. We went along a narrow place and got into a kind of room, all damp and sweaty and cold, and there we stopped.

Tom says, "Now, we'll start this band of robbers and call it Tom Sawyer's Gang. Everybody that wants to join has got to take an oath and write his name in blood."

Everybody was willing. So Tom got out a sheet of paper that he had wrote the oath on, and read it. It swore every boy to stick to the band and never tell any of the secrets. And if anybody done anything to any boy in the band, whichever boy was ordered to kill that person and his family must do it, and he mustn't eat and he mustn't sleep till he had killed them and hacked a cross in their breasts, which was the sign of the band. And nobody that didn't belong to the band could use that mark, and if he did he must be sued; and if he done it again he must be killed. And if anybody that belonged to the band told the secrets, he must have his throat cut, and then have his carcass burnt up and the ashes scattered all around, and his name blotted off the list with blood and never mentioned again by the gang, but be forgot forever.

Everybody said it was a real beautiful oath and asked Tom if he got it out of his own head. He said some of it, but the rest was out of pirate books and robber books.

Some thought it would be good to kill the *families* of boys that told the secrets. Tom saying it was a good idea, took a pencil and wrote it in.

Then Ben Rogers says, "Here's Huck Finn, he hain't got no family. What you going to do 'bout him?"

"Well, hain't he got a father?" says Tom Sawyer.

"Yes, he's got a father, but you can't never find him these days. He used to lay drunk with the hogs in the tanyard, but he hain't been seen in these parts for a year or more."

They talked it over, and they was going to rule me out, because they said every boy must have a family or somebody to kill, or else it wouldn't be fair and square for the others. Well, nobody could think of anything to do—everybody was stumped, and set still. I was most ready to cry. But all at once I thought of a way, I offered them Miss Watson—they could kill her.

Everybody said, "Oh, she'll do. That's all right. Huck can come in."

Then they all stuck a pin in their fingers to get blood to sign with, and I made my mark on the paper.

Little Tommy Barnes was asleep now, and when they waked him up he was scared and cried and said he wanted to go home to his ma and didn't want to be a robber any more.

So they all made fun of him and called him cry-baby, and that made him mad, and he said he would go straight and tell all the secrets. But

Tom give him five cents to keep quiet and said we would all go home and meet next week.

Ben Rogers said he couldn't get out much, only Sundays, and so he wanted to begin next Sunday; but all the boys said it would be wicked to do it on Sunday, and that settled the thing. They agreed to get together and fix a day as soon as they could, and so started for home.

I clumb up the shed and crept into my window just before day was breaking. My clothes was all greased up and I was dog-tired all over.

CHAPTER III

Huck and the judge—Superstition

WELL, three or four months run along, and it was well into winter now. I had been to school most all the time and could spell and read and write just a little and could say the multiplication table up to six times seven is thirty-five, and I don't reckon I could ever get any further than that if I was to live forever. I don't take no stock in mathematics anyway.

At first I hated the school, but by and by I got so I could stand it. Whenever I got uncommon tired I played hooky, and the hiding I got next day done me good and cheered me up. So the longer I went to school the easier it got to be. I was getting sort of used to the widow's ways, too, and they warn't so raspy on me. Living in a house and sleeping in a bed pulled on me pretty tight mostly, but before the cold weather I used to slide out and sleep in the woods sometimes, and so that was a rest to me. I liked the old ways best, but I was getting so I liked the new ones, too, a little bit. The widow said I was coming along slow but sure, and doing very satisfactory. She said she warn't ashamed of me.

One morning I happened to turn over the saltcellar at breakfast. I reached for some of it as quick as I could to throw over my left shoulder and keep off the bad luck, but Miss Watson was in ahead of me and crossed me off.

She says, "Take your hands away, Huckleberry; what a mess you are always making!"

The widow put in a good word for me, but that warn't going to keep off the bad luck, I knowed that well enough. I started out after breakfast feeling worried and shaky, and wondering where it was going to fall on me and what it was going to be. There is ways to keep off some kinds of bad luck, but this wasn't one of them kind; so I never tried to do anything, but just poked along low-spirited and on the watchout.

I went down to the front garden and clumb over the stile, where you go through the high board fence. There was an inch of new snow on the ground, and I seen somebody's tracks. They had come up from the quarry and stood around the stile awhile and then went on around the garden fence. It was funny they hadn't come in, after standing around so. I couldn't make it out. I was very curious, somehow. I was going to follow around, but I stooped down to look at the tracks first. I didn't notice anything at first, but next I did. There was a cross in the left boot heel made with big nails, to keep off the devil.

I was up in a second and shinning down the hill. I looked over my shoulder every now and then, but I didn't see nobody. I was at Judge Thatcher's as quick as I could get there.

He said, "Why, my boy, you are all out of breath. Did you come for your interest?"

"No, sir," I says. "Is there some for me?"

"Oh, yes, a half-yearly is in last night–over a hundred and fifty dollars. Quite a fortune for you. You had better let me invest it along with your six thousand, because if you take it you'll spend it."

"No, sir," I says. "I don't want to spend it. I don't want it at all–nor the six thousand, nuther. I want you to take it; I want to give it to you– the six thousand and all."

He looked surprised. He couldn't seem to make it out. He says, "Why, what can you mean, my boy?"

I says, "Don't ask me no questions about it, please. You'll take it–won't you?"

He says, "Well, I'm puzzled. Is something the matter?"

"Please take it," says I, "and don't ask me nothing–then I won't have to tell no lies."

He studied awhile, and then he says, "Oho-o! I think I see. You want to *sell* all your property to me–not give it. That's the correct idea."

Then he wrote something on a paper and read it over, and says, "There; you see it says 'for a consideration.' That means I have bought it of you and paid you for it. Here's a dollar for you. Now you sign it."

So I signed it and left.

Miss Watson's nigger Jim had a hair-ball as big as your fist, which had been took out of the fourth stomach of an ox, and he used to do magic with it. He said there was a spirit inside of it, and it knowed everything. So I went to him that night and told him Pap was here again, for I found his tracks in the snow. What I wanted to know was, what he was going to do, and was he going to stay?

Jim got out his hair-ball and said something over it, and then he held it up and dropped it on the floor. It fell pretty solid, and only rolled about an inch. Jim tried it again and then another time, and it acted just the same. Jim got down on his knees and put his ear against it and listened. But it warn't no use; he said it wouldn't talk.

He said sometimes it wouldn't talk without money. I told him I had an old slick counterfeit quarter that warn't no good because the brass showed through the silver a little, and it wouldn't pass nohow, even if the brass didn't show, because it was so slick it felt greasy, and so that would tell

15

on it every time. (I reckoned I wouldn't say nothing about the dollar I got from the judge.) I said it was pretty bad money, but maybe the hair-ball would take it, because maybe it wouldn't know the difference. Jim smelt it and bit it and rubbed it and said he would manage so the hair-ball would think was good. He said he would split open a raw Irish potato and stick the quarter in between and keep it there all night, and next morning you couldn't see no brass, and it wouldn't feel greasy no more, and so anybody in town would take it in a minute, let alone a hair-ball. Well, I knowed a potato would do that before, but I had forgot it.

Jim put the quarter under the hair-ball and got down and listened again. This time he said the hair-ball was all right. He said it would tell my whole fortune if I wanted it to. I says, go on. So the hair-ball talked to Jim, and Jim told it to me.

He says, "Yo' ole father doan' know yit what he's a-gwyne to do. Sometimes he spec he'll go 'way, en den ag'in he spec he'll stay. De bes' way is to res' easy en let de ole man take his own way. Dey's two angels hoverin' roun' 'bout him. One uv 'em is white en shiny, en t'other one is black. De white one gits him to go right a little while, den de black one sail in en bust it all up. A body can't tell yit which one gwyne to fetch him at de las'.

"But you is all right. You gwyne to have considable trouble in yo' life, en considable joy. Sometimes you gwyne to git hurt, en sometimes you gwyne to git sick; but every time you's gwyne to git well ag'in. Dey's two gals flyin' 'bout you in yo' life. One uv 'em's light en t'other one is dark. One is rich en t'other is po'. You's gwyne to marry de po' one fust en de rich one by en by. You wants to keep 'way fum de water as much as you kin, en don't run no resk, 'kase it's down in de bills dat you's gwyne to git hung."

When I lit my candle and went up to my room that night there sat Pap—his own self!

CHAPTER IV

Huck's father—The fond parent—Reform

I HAD shut the door to. Then I turned around, and there he was. I used to be scared of him all the time, he tanned me so much. I reckoned I was scared now, too. But in a minute I see I was mistaken—that is, after the first jolt, as you may say, when my breath sort of hitched, he being so unexpected. But right away after, I see I warn't scared of him worth bothering about.

He was most fifty, and he looked it. His hair was long and tangled and greasy, and hung down, and you could see his eyes shining through like he was behind vines. It was all black, no gray; so was his long, mixed-up whiskers. There warn't no color in his face, where his face showed. It was white, not like another man's white, but a white to make a body sick, a white to make a body's flesh crawl—a tree-toad white, a fish-belly white.

As for the way his clothes looked—they was just rags, that was all. He had one ankle resting on t'other knee; the boot on that foot was busted, and two of his toes stuck through, and he worked them now and then. His hat was laying on the floor alongside of him—an old black slouch with the top caved in, like a lid.

I stood a-looking at him. He set there a-looking at me, with his chair tilted back a little. I set the candle down. I noticed the window was up; so he had clumb in by the shed. He kept a-looking me all over.

By and by he says, "Starchy clothes—very. You think you're a good deal of a big-bug, *don't* you?"

"Maybe I am, maybe I ain't," I says.

"Don't you give me none o' your lip," says he. "You've put on considerable many frills since I been away. I'll take you down a peg before I get done with you. You're educated, too, they say—can read and write. You think you're better'n your father, now, don't you, because he can't? *I'll* take it out of you. Who told you you might meddle with such hifalut'n foolishness, hey? Who told you you could?"

"The widow. She told me."

"The widow, hey? And who told the widow she could put in her shovel about a thing that ain't none of her business?"

"Nobody never told her."

"Well, I'll learn her how to meddle. And looky here—you drop that school, you hear? I'll learn people to bring up a boy to put on airs over his own father and let on to be better'n what *he* is. You lemme catch you fooling around that school again, you hear? Your mother couldn't read, and she couldn't write, nuther, before she died. None of the family couldn't before *they* died. *I* can't; and here you're a-swelling yourself up like this.

"I ain't the man to stand it—you hear? Say, lemme hear you read."

I took up a book and begun something about General Washington and the wars. When I'd read about a half a minute, he fetched the book a whack with his hand and knocked it across the house.

He says, "It's so. You can do it. I had my doubts when you told me. Now looky here; you stop that putting on frills. I won't have it. I'll lay for you, my smarty, and if I catch you about that school I'll tan you good. First you know you'll get religion, too. I never see such a son."

He took up a little blue and yaller picture of some cows and a boy and says, "What's this?"

"It's something they give me for learning my lessons good."

He tore it up and says, "I'll give you something better—I'll give you a cowhide."

He set there a-mumbling and a-growling a minute, and then he says,

"*Ain't* you a sweet-scented dandy, through? A bed, and bedclothes, and a look'n'-glass, and a piece of carpet on the floor–and your own father got to sleep with the hogs in the tanyard. I never see such a son. I bet I'll take some o' these frills out o' you before I'm done with you. Why, there ain't no end to your airs!

"They say you're rich. Hey? How's that?"

"They lie–that's how."

"Looky here–mind how you talk to me. I'm a-standing about all I can stand now–so don't gimme no sass. I've been in town two days, and I hain't heard nothing but about you bein' rich. I heard about it down the river, too. That's why I come. You git me that money tomorrow–I want it."

"I hain't got no money."

"It's a lie. Judge Thatcher's got it. You git it. I want it."

"I hain't got no money, I tell you. You ask Judge Thatcher; he'll tell you the same."

"All right. I'll ask him, and I'll make him pungle, too, or I'll know the reason why. Say, how much you got in your pocket? I want it."

"I hain't got only a dollar, and I want that to–"

"It don't make no difference what you want it for–you just shell it out."

He took it and bit it to see if it was good, and then said he was going downtown to get some whisky; said he hadn't had a drink all day. When he had got out on the shed he put his head in again and cussed me for putting on frills and trying to be better than him. And when I reckoned he was gone he come back and put his head in again and told me to mind about that school, because he was going to lay for me and lick me if I didn't drop that.

Next day he was drunk, and he went to Judge Thatcher's and bully-ragged him, and tried to make him give up the money. But he couldn't, and then he swore he'd make the law force him.

The judge and the widow went to law to get the court to take me away from him and let one of them be my guardian. But it was a new judge that had just come, and he didn't know the old man. So he said courts mustn't interfere and separate families if they could help it; said he'd druther not take a child away from its father. So Judge Thatcher and the widow had to quit on the business.

That pleased the old man till he couldn't rest. He said he'd cowhide me till I was black and blue if I didn't raise some money for him. I borrowed three dollars from Judge Thatcher, and Pap took it and got drunk and went a-blowing around and cussing and whooping and carrying on. He kept it up all over town with a tin pan till most midnight. Then they jailed him, and next day they had him before court and jailed him again for a week.

But he said *he* was satisfied; said he was boss of his son, and he'd make it warm for *him*.

When he got out, the new judge said he was a-going to make a man of him. So he took him to his own house, and dressed him up clean and nice, and had him to breakfast and dinner and supper with the family, and was just old pie to him, so to speak. And after supper he talked to him about temperance and such things till the old man cried and said he'd been a fool and fooled away his life, but now he was a-going to turn over a new leaf and be a man nobody wouldn't be ashamed of, and he hoped the judge would help him and not look down on him. The judge said he could hug him for them words, so *he* cried, and his wife cried again. Pap said he'd been a man that had always been misunderstood before, and the judge said he believed it. The old man said that what a man wanted that was down was sympathy, and the judge said it was so; so they cried again. And when it was bedtime the old man rose up and held out his hand and says, "Look at it, gentlemen and ladies all; take a-hold of it; shake it. There's a hand that was the hand of a hog; but it ain't so no more. It's the hand of a man that's started in on a new life, and'll die before he'll go back. You mark them words—don't forget I said them. It's a clean hand now. Shake it—don't be afeard."

So they shook it, one after the other, all around, and cried. The judge's wife, she kissed it. Then the old man, he signed a pledge—made his mark. The judge said it was the holiest time on record, or something like that. Then they tucked the old man into a beautiful room, which was the spare room, and in the night sometime he got powerful thirsty and clumb out on to the porch roof and slid down a stanchion and traded his new coat for a jug of forty-rod, and clumb back again and had a good old time. Toward daylight he crawled out again, drunks as a fiddler, and rolled off the porch and broke his left arm in two places and was most froze to death when somebody found him after sun-up. And when they come to look at the spare room they had to take soundings before they could navigate it.

The judge, he felt kind of sore. He said he reckoned a body could reform the old man with a shotgun, maybe, but he didn't know no other way.

CHAPTER V

He went for Judge Thatcher—Huck decides to leave—Thrashing around

WELL, pretty soon the old man was up and around again, and then he went for Judge Thatcher in the courts to make him give up that money, and he went for me, too, for not stopping school. He catched me a couple of times and thrashed me, but I went to school just the same and dodged him or outrun him most of the time. I didn't want go to school much before, but I reckoned I'd go now to spite Pap.

That law trial was a slow business—appeared like they warn't ever going to get started on it; so every now and then I'd borrow two or three dollars off the judge for him, to keep from getting a cowhiding. Every time he got money he got drunk; and every time he got drunk he raised Cain around town; and every time he raised Cain he got jailed. He was just suited—this kind of thing was right in his line.

He got to hanging around the widow's too much, and so she told him at last that if he didn't quit using around there she would make trouble for him. Well, *wasn't* he mad? He said he would show who was Huck Finn's boss. So he watched out for me one day in the spring, and catched me, and took me up the river about three mile in a skiff, and crossed over to the Illinois shore where it was woody and there warn't no houses but an old log hut in a place where the timber was so thick you couldn't find it if you didn't know where it was.

He kept me with him all the time, and I never got a chance to run off. We lived in that old cabin, and he always locked the door and put the key under his head nights. He had a gun which he had stole, I reckon, and we fished and hunted, and that was what we lived on. Every little while he locked me in and went down to the store, three miles, to the ferry and traded fish and game for whisky and fetched it home and got drunk and had a good time and licked me. The widow, she found out where I was by and by, and she sent a man over to try to get hold of me. But Pap drove him off with the gun, and it warn't long after that till I was used to being where I was and liked it—all but the cowhide part.

It was kind of lazy and jolly, laying off comfortable all day, smoking and fishing, and no books nor study. Two months or more run along, and my clothes got to be all rags and dirt, and I didn't see how I'd ever got to like it so well at the widow's, where you had to wash, and eat on a plate, and comb up, and go to bed and get up regular, and be forever bothering over a book, and have old Miss Watson pecking at you all the time. I didn't want to go back no more. I had stopped cussing, because the widow didn't like it; but now I took to it again because Pap hadn't no objections. It was pretty good times up in the woods there, take it all around.

But by and by Pap got too handy with his hick'ry, and I couldn't stand it. I was all over welts. He got to going away so much, too, and locking me in. Once he locked me in and was gone three days. It was dreadful lonesome. I judged he had got drownded, and I wasn't ever going to get out any more. I was scared. I made up my mind I would fix up some way to leave there.

I had tried to get out out of that cabin many a time, but I couldn't find no way. There warn't a window to it big enough for a dog to get through. I couldn't get up the chimbly; it was too narrow. The door was thick, solid oak slabs. Pap was pretty careful not to leave a knife or anything in the cabin when he was away; I reckon I had hunted the place over as much as a hundred times. Well, I was most all the time at it, because it was about the only way to put in the time. But this time I found something at last; I found an old rusty woodsaw without any handle; it was laid in between a rafter and the clapboards of the roof.

I greased it up and went to work. There was an old horse blanket nailed against the logs at the far end of the cabin behind the table to keep the wind from blowing through the chinks and putting the candle out. I got under the table and raised the blanket and went to work to saw a section of the big bottom log out–big enough to let me through. Well, it was a good long job, but I was getting toward the end of it when I heard Pap's gun in the woods. I got rid of the signs of my work, and dropped the blanket and hid my saw, and pretty soon Pap come in.

Pap warn't in a good humor–so he was his natural self. He said he was down to town and everything was going wrong. His lawyer said he reckoned he would win his lawsuit and get the money if they ever got started on the trial; but then there was ways to put it off a long time, and Judge Thatcher knowed how to do it. And he said people allowed there'd be another trial to get me away from him and give me to the widow for my guardian, and they guessed it would win.

This shook me up considerable, because I didn't want to go back to the widow's any more and be so cramped up and sivilized, as they called it. Then the old man got to cussing, and cussed everything and everybody he could think of and then cussed them all over again to make sure he hadn't skipped any, and after that he polished off with a kind of a general cuss all round, including a considerable parcel of people which he didn't know the names of, and so called them what's-his-name when he got to them, and kept going right along with his cussing.

He said he would like to see the widow get me. He said he would watch out, and if they tried to come any such game on him he knowed a place six or seven mile off to stow me in, where they might hunt till they dropped and they couldn't find me. That made me pretty uneasy again, but only for a minute. I reckoned I wouldn't stay on hand till he got that chance.

The old man made me go to the skiff and fetch the things he had got. There was a fifty-pound sack of cornmeal, and a side of bacon, ammunition, and a four-gallon jug of whisky, and an old book and two newspapers for wadding, besides some tow. I toted up a load and went back and set down on the bow of the skiff to rest. I thought it all over, and I reckoned I would walk off with the gun and some lines and take to the woods when I run away. I guessed I wouldn't stay in one place, but just tramp right across the country, mostly nighttimes, and hunt and fish to keep alive, and so get so far away that the old man nor the widow couldn't ever find me any more. I judged I would saw out and leave that night if Pap got drunk enough, and I reckoned he would. I got so full of it I didn't notice how long I was staying till the old man hollered and asked me whether I was asleep or drownded or what had happened to me.

I got the things up to the cabin, and then it was about dark. While I was cooking supper the old man took a swig or two and got sort of warmed up and went to ripping again. He had been drunk over in town and laid in the gutter all night, and he was a sight to look at.

After supper Pap took the jug again, and said he had enough whisky there for two drunks and one delirium tremens. That was always his word. I judged he would be blind drunk in about an hour, and then I would steal the key, or saw myself out, one or t'other. He drank and drank and tumbled down on his blankets by and by; but luck didn't run my way. He didn't go sound asleep, but was uneasy. He groaned and moaned and thrashed around this way and that for a long time. At last I got so sleepy I couldn't keep my eyes open all I could do. And so before I knowed what I was about, I was sound asleep, and the candle burning.

I don't know how long I was asleep, but all of a sudden there was an awful scream and I was up. There was Pap looking wild and skipping around every which way and yelling about snakes. He said they was crawling up his legs; and then he would give a jump and scream and say one had bit him on the cheek—but I couldn't see no snakes. He started and run round and round the cabin, hollering. "Take him off! Take him off! He's biting me on the neck!" I never see a man look so wild in the eyes. Pretty soon he was all fagged out and fell down panting. Then he rolled over and over wonderful fast, kicking things every which way, and striking and grabbing at the air with his hands and screaming and saying there was devils a-hold of him. He wore out by and by and laid still awhile, moaning. Then he laid stiller and didn't make a sound. I could hear the owls and the wolves away off in the woods, and it seemed terrible still. He was laying over by the corner. By and by he raised up part way and listened, with his head to one side.

He says, very low, "Tramp—tramp—tramp; that's the dead. Tramp—tramp—tramp, they're coming after me; but I won't go. Oh, they're here! Don't touch me—don't! Hands off—they're cold. Let go. Oh, let a poor devil alone!"

Then he went down on all fours and crawled off, begging them to let him alone, and he rolled himself up in his blanket and wallowed in under the old pine table, still a-begging; and then he went to crying. I could hear him through the blanket.

By and by he rolled out and jumped upon to his feet looking wild, and he see me and went for me. He chased me round and round the place with a clasp knife, calling me the Angel of Death, and saying he would kill me, and then I couldn't come for him no more. I begged and told him I was only Huck; but he laughed *such* a screechy laugh and roared and cussed and kept on chasing me up. Once when I turned short and dodged under his arm he made a grab and got me by the jacket between my shoulders, and I thought I was gone; but I slid out of the jacket quick as lightning and saved myself. Pretty soon he was all tired out, and dropped down with his back against the door and said he would rest a minute and then kill me. He put his knife under him and said he would sleep and get strong, and then he would see who was who.

So he dozed off pretty soon. By and by I got the old split-bottom chair and clumb up as easy as I could, not to make any noise, and got down the gun. I slipped the ramrod down it to make sure it was loaded, and then I laid it across the turnip-barrel, pointing toward Pap, and set down behind it to wait for him to stir.

CHAPTER VI

Laying for him—Locked in the cabin—Sinking the body—Resting

GIT up! What you 'bout?"

I opened my eyes and looked around, trying to make out where I was. It was after sunup, and I had been sound asleep. Pap was standing over me looking sour—and sick, too.

He says, "What you doin' with this gun?"

I judged he didn't know nothing about what he had been doing, so I says, "Somebody tried to get in, so I was laying for him."

"Why didn't you rouse me out?"

"Well, I tried to, but I couldn't. I couldn't budge you."

"Well, all right. Don't stand there palavering all day, but out with you and see if there's a fish on the lines for breakfast. I'll be along in a minute."

He unlocked the door, and I cleared out up the river bank. I noticed some pieces of limbs and such things floating down, and a sprinkling of bark; so I knowed the river had begun to rise. I reckoned I would have great times now if I was over at the town. The June rise used to be always luck for me, because as soon as that rise begins here comes cordwood floating down, and pieces of log rafts—sometimes a dozen logs together. All you have to do is to catch them and sell them to the woodyards and the sawmill.

I went along up the bank with one eye out for Pap and t'other one out for what the rise might fetch along. Well, all at once here comes a canoe; just a beauty, too, about thirteen or fourteen foot long, riding high like a duck. I shot head-first off of the bank like a frog, clothes and all on, and struck out for the canoe. I just expected there'd be somebody laying down in it, because people often done that to fool folks, and when a chap had pulled a skiff out most to it they'd raise up and laugh at him. But it warn't so this time. It was a drift-canoe sure enough, and I clumb in and paddled her ashore. Thinks I, the old man will be glad when he sees this—she's worth ten dollars. But when I got to shore Pap wasn't in sight yet, and as I was running her into a little creek like a gully, all hung over with vines and willows, I struck another idea: I judged I'd hide her good, and then, 'stead of taking to the woods when I run off, I'd go down the river about fifty mile and camp in one place for good and not have such a rough time tramping on foot.

It was pretty close to the shanty, and I thought I heard the old man coming all the time, but I got her hid. Then I out and looked around a bunch of willows, and there was the old man down the path a piece just drawing a bead on a bird with his gun. So he hadn't seen anything.

When he got along I was hard at it taking up a "trot" line. He abused me a little for being so slow; but I told him I fell in the river, and that was what made me so long. I knowed he would see I was wet, and then he would be asking questions. We got five cat-fish off the lines and went home.

While we laid off after breakfast to sleep up, both of us being about wore out, I got to thinking that if I could fix up some way to keep Pap and the widow from trying to follow me, it would be a certainer thing than trusting to luck to get far enough off before they missed me. You see, all kinds of things might happen.

Well, I didn't see no way for a while, but by and by Pap raised up a minute to drink another barrel of water, and he says, "Another time a man comes a-prowling round here you roust me out, you hear? That man warn't here for no good. I'd 'a' shot him. Next time you roust me out, you hear?" Then he dropped down and went to sleep again.

What he had been saying give me the very idea I wanted. I says to myself, I can fix it now so nobody won't think of following me.

About twelve o'clock we turned out and went along up the bank. The river was coming up pretty fast, and lots of driftwood going by on the rise. By and by along comes part of a log raft—nine logs fast together. We went out with the skiff and towed it ashore. Then we had dinner. Anybody but Pap would 'a' waited and seen the day through, so as to catch more stuff, but that warn't Pap's style. Nine logs was enough for one time; he must shove right over to town and sell.

So he locked me in and took the skiff and started off towing the raft about half past three. I judged he wouldn't come back that night. I waited till I reckoned he had got a good start. Then I out with my saw and went to work on that log again. Before he was t'other side of the river I was out of the hole; him and his raft was just a speck on the water away off yonder.

I took the sack of cornmeal and took it to where the canoe was hid, and shoved the vines and branches apart and put it in; then I done the same with the side of bacon; then the whisky jug. I took all the coffee and sugar there was, and all the ammunition; I took the wadding; I took the bucket and gourd; took a dipper and a tin cup and my old saw and two blankets and the skillet and the coffee-pot. I took fish-lines and matches and other things—everything that was worth a cent. I cleaned out the place. I wanted an ax, but there wasn't any, only the one out at the woodpile, and I

24

knowed why I was going to leave that. I fetched out the gun, and now I was done.

I had wore the ground a good deal crawling out of the hole and dragging out so many things. So I fixed that as good as I could, from the outside by scattering dust on the place, which covered up the smoothness and the sawdust. Then I fixed the piece of log back into place and put two rocks under it and one against it to hold it there, for it was bent up at that place and didn't quite touch ground. If you stood four or five foot away and didn't know it was sawed, you wouldn't never notice it; and besides, this was the back of the cabin, and it warn't likely anybody would go fooling around there.

It was all grass clear to the canoe, so I hadn't left a track. I followed around to see. I stood on the bank and looked out over the river. All safe. So I took the gun and went up a piece into the woods and was hunting around for some birds when I see a wild pig; hogs soon went wild in them bottoms after they had got away from the prairie-farms. I shot this fellow and took him into camp.

I took the ax and smashed in the door. I beat it and hacked it considerable a-doing it. I fetched the pig in, and took him back nearly to the table and hacked into his throat with the ax, and laid him down on the ground to bleed; I say ground because it *was* ground—hard packed and no boards. Well, next I took an old sack and put a lot of big rocks in it—all I could drag—and I started it from the pig and dragged it to the door and through the woods down to the river and dumped it in, and down it sunk, out of sight. You could easy see that something had been dragged over the ground.

I did wish Tom Sawyer was there; I knowed he would take an interest in this kind of business and throw in the fancy touches. Nobody could spread himself like Tom Sawyer in such a thing as that.

Well, last I pulled out some of my hair and blooded the ax good and stuck it on the back side and slung the ax in the corner. Then I took up the pig and held him to my breast with my jacket (so he couldn't drip) till I got a good piece below the house and then dumped him into the river.

Now I thought of something else. So I went and got the bag of meal and my old saw out of the canoe, and fetched them to the house. I took the bag to where it used to stand, and ripped a hole in the bottom of it with the saw, for there warn't no knives and forks on the place—Pap done everything with his clasp knife about the cooking. Then I carried the sack about a hundred yards across the grass and through the willows east of the house to a shallow lake that was five mile wide and full of rushes—and ducks, too, you might say, in the season. There was a slough or a creek leading out of it on the other side that went miles away, I don't know where, but it didn't go to the river. The meal sifted out and made a little track all the way to the lake. I dropped Pap's whetstone there, too, so as to look like it had been done by accident. Then I tied up the rip in the meal sack with a string, so it wouldn't leak no more, and took it and my saw to the canoe again.

It was about dark now, so I dropped the canoe down the river under some willows that hung over the bank, and waited for the moon to rise. I made fast to a willow. Then I took a bite to eat and by and by laid down in the canoe to smoke a pipe and lay out a plan. I says to myself, they'll follow the track of that sackful of rocks to the shore and then drag the river for me. And they'll follow that meal track to the lake and go browsing down the creek that leads out of it to find the robbers that killed me and took the things. They won't ever hunt the river for anything but my dead carcass. They'll soon get tired of that and won't bother no more about me.

All right, I can stop anywhere I want to. Jackson's Island is good enough for me; I know that island pretty well, and nobody ever comes there. And then I can paddle over to town nights and slink around and pick up things I want. Jackson's Island's the place.

I was pretty tired, and the first thing I knowed I was asleep. When I woke up I didn't know where I was for a minute. I set up and looked around, a little scared. Then I remembered. The river looked miles and miles across. The moon was so bright I could 'a' counted the drift-logs that went a-slipping along, black and still, hundreds of yards out from shore. Everything was dead quiet, and it looked late and *smelt* late. You know what I mean—I don't know the words to put it in.

I took a good gap and a stretch and was just going to unhitch and start when I heard a sound away over the water. I listened. Pretty soon I made it out. It was that dull kind of a regular sound that comes from oars working in rowlocks when it's a still night. I peeped out through the willow branches, and there it was—a skiff, away across the water. I couldn't tell how many was in it. It kept a-coming, and when it was abreast of me, I see there warn't but one man in it. Thinks I, maybe it's Pap, though I warn't expecting him. He dropped below me with the current, and by and by he came a-swinging up shore in the easy water, and he went by so close I could 'a' reached out the gun and touched him. Well, it *was* Pap, sure enough—and sober, too, by the way he laid his oars.

I didn't lose no time. The next minute I was a-spinning downstream soft, but quick, in the shade of the bank. I made two mile and a half and then struck out a quarter of a mile or more toward the middle of the river, because pretty soon I would be passing the ferry-landing, and people might see me and hail me. I got out amongst the driftwood, and then laid down in the bottom of the canoe and let her float. I laid there, and had a good rest and a smoke out of my pipe, looking away into the sky; not a cloud in it. The sky looks ever so deep when you lay down on your back in the moonshine; I never knowed it before.

And how far a body can hear on the water such nights! I heard people talking at the ferry-landing. I heard what they said, too—every word of it.

One man said it was getting toward the long days and the short nights now. T'other one said *this* warn't one of the short ones, he reckoned—and then they laughed, and he said it over again, and they laughed again; then they waked up another fellow and told him, and laughed, and he didn't laugh; he ripped out something brisk and said let him alone. The first fellow said he 'lowed to tell it to his old woman—she would think it was pretty good; but he said that warn't nothing to some things he had said in his time. I heard one man say it was nearly three o'clock, and he hoped daylight wouldn't wait more than about a week longer. After that the talk got further and further away, and I couldn't make out the words anymore; but I could hear the mumble, and now and then a laugh, too, but it seemed a long ways off.

I was away below the ferry now. I rose up, and there was Jackson's Island, about two mile and a half downstream, heavy-timbered and standing up out of the middle of the river, big and dark and solid, like a steamboat without any lights. There warn't any signs of the bar at the head—it was all under water now.

It didn't take me long to get there. I shot past the head at a ripping rate, the current was so swift, and then I got into the dead water and landed on the side toward the Illinois shore. I run the canoe into a deep dent in the bank that I knowed about. I had to part the willow branches to get in, and when I made fast nobody could 'a' seen the canoe from the outside.

I went up and set down on a log at the head of the island, and looked out on the big river and the black driftwood and away over to the town, three mile away, where there was three or four lights twinkling. A monstrous big lumber raft was about a mile upstream, coming along down, with a lantern in the middle of it. I watched it come creeping down, and when it was 'most abreast of where I stood I heard an man say, "Stern oars, there! Heave her head to stabboard!" I heard that just as plain as if the man was by my side.

There was a little gray in the sky now. So I stepped into the woods and laid down for a nap before breakfast.

CHAPTER VII

Sleeping in the woods—Raising the dead—Exploring the island—
Finding Jim—Jim's escape—Signs—The cave—The floating house

THE sun was up so high when I waked that I judged it was after eight o'clock. I laid there in the grass and the cool shade thinking about things and feeling rested and ruther comfortable and satisfied. I could see the sun out at one or two holes, but mostly it was big trees all about, and gloomy in there amongst them. There was freckled places on the ground where the light sifted through the leaves, and the freckled places swapped about a little, showing there was a little breeze up there. Then a couple of squirrels set on a limb and jabbered at me very friendly.

I was powerful lazy and comfortable–didn't want to get up and cook breakfast. Well, I was dozing off again when I thinks I hears a deep sound of "Boom!" away up the river. I rouses up and rests on my elbow and listens. Pretty soon I hears it again. I hopped up and went and looked out at a hole in the leaves, and I see a bunch of smoke laying on the water a long ways up–about abreast the ferry. And there was the ferryboat full of people floating along down.

"Boom!" I see the white smoke squirt out of the ferryboat's side. You see, they was firing cannon over the water, trying to make my carcass come to the top.

I was pretty hungry, but it warn't going to do for me to start a fire, because they might see the smoke. So I set there and watched the cannon-smoke and listened to the boom. The river was a mile wide there, and it always looks pretty on a summer morning–so I was having a good enough time seeing them hunt for my remainders if I only had a bite to eat.

Well, then I happened to think how they always put quicksilver in loaves of bread and float them off, because they always go right to the drownded carcass and stop there. So, says, I, I'll keep a lookout, and if any of them's floating around after me I'll give them a show. I changed to the Illinois edge of the island to see what luck I could have, and I warn't disappointed. A big double loaf come along, and I most got it with a long stick, but my foot slipped and she floated out further. Of course I was where the current set in the closest to the shore–I knowed enough for that. But by and by along comes another one, and this time I won. I took out the plug and shook out the litttle dab of quicksilver, and set my teeth in. It was "baker's bread"–what the quality eat; none of your lowdown corn pone.

I got a good place amongst the leaves, and set there on a log, munching the bread and watching the ferryboat and very well satisfied. And then something struck me. I says, I reckon the widow or the parson or some-body prayed that this bread would find me, and here it has gone and done it. So there ain't no doubt but there is something in that thing–that is, there's something in it when a body like the widow or the parson pray, but it don't work for me, and I reckon it don't work for only just the right kind.

I lit a pipe and had a good long smoke and went on watching. The ferryboat was floating with the current, and I allowed I'd have a chance to see who was aboard when she come along, because she would come in close, where the bread did. When she'd got pretty well along down toward me, I put out my pipe and went to where I fished out the bread, and laid down behind a log on the bank in a little open place. Where the log forked I could peep through.

By and by she come along, and she drifted in so close that they could 'a' run out a plank and walked ashore. Most everybody was on the boat. Pap and Judge Thatcher and Becky Thatcher and Joe Harper and Tom Sawyer and his old Aunt Polly, and Sid and Marry and plenty more.

Everybody was talking about the murder, but the captain broke in and says, "Look sharp, now. The current sets in the closest here, and maybe he's washed ashore and got tangled amongst the brush at the water's edge. I hope so, anyway."

I didn't hope so. They all crowded up and leaned over the rails, nearly in my face, and kept still, watching with all their might. I could see them first-rate, but they couldn't see me.

Then the captain sung out, "Stand away!" And the cannon let off such a blast right before me that it made me deef with the noise and pretty near blind with the smoke, and I judged I was gone. If they'd 'a' had some bullets in it, I reckon they'd 'a' got the corpse they was after. Well, I see I warn't hurt, thanks to goodness. The boat floated on and went out of sight around the shoulder of the island. I could hear the booming now and then, further and further off, and by and by, after an hour, I didn't hear it no more.

The island was three mile long. I judged they had got to the foot and was giving it up. But they didn't yet awhile. They turned around the foot of the island and started up the channel on the Missouri side, under steam, and booming once in a while as they went. I crossed over to that side and watched them. When they got abreast the head of the island they quit shooting and dropped over to the Missouri shore and went home to the town.

I knowed I was all right now. Nobody else would come a-hunting after me. I got my traps out of the canoe and made me a nice camp in the thick woods. I made a kind of a tent out of my blankets to put my things under so the rain couldn't get at them. I catched a catfish and haggled him open with my saw, and toward sundown I started my campfire and had supper. Then I set out a line to catch some fish for breakfast.

When it was dark I set by my campfire smoking and feeling pretty well satisfied. But by and by it got sort of lonesome, and so I went and set on the bank and listened to the current swashing along, and counted the stars and drift-logs and rafts that come down, and then went to bed. There ain't no better way to put in time when you are lonesome; you can't stay so, you soon get over it.

And so for three days and nights. No difference–just the same thing. But the next day I went exploring around down through the island. I was boss of it. It all belonged to me, so to say, and I wanted to know all about it, but mainly I wanted to put in the time. I found plenty strawberries, ripe and prime, and green summer grapes and green razberries; and green blackberries was just beginning to show. They would all come handy by and by, I judged.

Well, I went fooling along in the deep woods till I judged I warn't far from the foot of the island. I had my gun along, but I hadn't shot nothing. It was for protection; thought I would kill some game nigh home. About this time I mighty near stepped on a good-sized snake, and it went sliding off through the grass and flowers, and I after it, trying to get a shot at it. I clipped along, and all of a sudden I bounded right on to the ashes of a campfire that was still smoking.

My heart jumbed up amongst my lungs. I never waited for to look further, but uncocked my gun and went sneaking back on my tiptoes as fast as ever I could. Every now and then I stopped a second amongst the thick leaves and listened, but my breath come so hard I couldn't hear nothing else. I slunk along another piece further, then listened again; and so on, and so on. If I see a stump, I took it for a man; if I trod on a stick and broke it, it made me feel like a person had cut one of my breaths in two and I only got half, and the short half, at that.

When I got to camp I warn't feeling very brash, there warn't much sand in my craw; but I says, this ain't no time to be fooling around. So I got all my traps into my canoe again so as to have them out of sight, and I I put out the fire and scattered the ashes around to look like an old last-year's camp, and then clumb a tree.

I reckon I was up in the tree two hours; but I didn't see nothing, I didn't hear nothing—I only *thought* I heard and seen as much as a thousand things. Well, I couldn't stay up there forever; so at last I got down, but I kept in the thick woods and on the lookout all the time. All I could get to eat was berries and what was left over from breakfast.

By the time it was night I was pretty hungry. So when it was good and dark I slid out from shore before moonrise and paddled over to the Illinois bank—about a quarter of a mile. I went out in the woods and cooked a supper, and I had about made up my mind I would stay there all night when I heard a *plunkety-plunk, plunkety-plunk,* and says to myself, horses coming; and next I hear people's voices. I got everything into the canoe as quick as I could and then went creeping through the woods to see what I could find out.

I hadn't got far when I hear a man say, "We better camp here if we can find a good place; the horses is about beat out. Let's look around."

I didn't wait, but shoved out and paddled away easy. I tied up in the old place and reckoned I would sleep right there in the canoe.

I didn't sleep much. I couldn't, somehow, for thinking. And every time I waked up. I thought somebody had me by the neck. So the sleep didn't do me no good. By and by I says to myself, I can't live this way. I'm a-going to find out who it is that's here on the island with me. I'll find out or bust! Well, I felt better right off.

So I took my paddle and slid out from shore just a step or two, and then let the canoe drop along down amongst the shadows. The moon was shining, and outside of the shadows it made it most as light as day. I poked along well on to an hour, everything still as rocks and sound asleep.

Well, by this time I was most down to the foot of the island. A little ripply, cool breeze begun to blow, and that was as good as saying the night was about done.

I give her a turn with the paddle and brung her nose to shore; then I got my gun and slipped out and into the edge of the woods. I sat down there on a log and looked out through the leaves. I see the moon go off watch, and the darkness begin to blanket the river. But in a little while I see a pale streak over the treetops and knowed the day was coming. So I took my gun and slipped off toward where I had run across that campfire, stopping every minute or two to listen. But I hadn't no luck somehow; I couldn't seem to find the place.

But by and by, sure enough, I catched a glimpse of fire away through the trees. I went for it, cautious and slow. By and by I was close enough to have a look, and there laid a man on the ground. It most give me the fantods. He had a blanket around his head, and his head was nearly in the fire. I set there behind a clump of bushes in about six foot of him and kept my eyes on him steady. It was getting gray daylight now. Pretty soon he gapped and stretched himself and hove off the blanket, and it was Miss Watson's Jim! I bet I was glad to see him.

I says, "Hello, Jim!" and skipped out.

He bounced up and stared at me wild. Then he drops down on his knees and puts his hands together and says, "Doan' hurt me–don't! I hain't ever done no harm to a ghos'. I alwuz liked dead people, en done all I could for 'em. You go en git in de river ag'in, whah you b'longs, en doan' do nuffn to Ole Jim 'at 'uz alwuz yo' fren'."

Well, I warn't long making him understand I warn't dead. I was ever so glad to see Jim. I warn't lonesome now. I told him I warn't afraid of *him* telling the people where I was. I talked along, but he only set there and looked at me; never said nothing. Then I says, "It's good daylight. Le's get breakfast. Make up your campfire good."

"What's de use er makin' up de campfire to cook strawbries en sich truck? But you got a gun, hain't you? Den we kin git sumfn better den strawbries."

"Strawberries and such truck." I says. "Is that what you live on?"

"I couldn't git nuffn else," he says.

"Why, how long you been on the island, Jim?"

"I come heah de night arter you's killed."

"What, all that time?"

"Yes-indeedy."

"And ain't you had nothing but that kind of rubbage to eat, Jim?"

"No, sah–nuffn else."

"Well, you must be most starved, ain't you?"

"I reck'n I could eat a hoss. I think I could. How long you ben on de island'?"

"Since the night I got killed."

"No! W'y, what has you lived on? But you got a gun? Oh, yes, you got a gun. Dat's good. Now you kill sumfn en I'll make up de fire."

So we went over to where the canoe was, and while he built a fire in a grassy place amongst the trees, I fetched meal and bacon and coffee and coffeepot and frying pan and sugar and tin cups, and the nigger was set back considerable, because he reckoned it was all done with witchcraft. I catched a good big catfish, too, and Jim cleaned him with his knife and fried him.

When breakfast was ready we lolled on the grass and eat it smoking hot. Jim laid it in with all his might, for he was most about starved. Then when we had got pretty well stuffed, we laid off and lazied.

By and by Jim says, "But looky here, Huck, who wuz it dat 'uz killed in dat shanty ef it warn't you?"

Then I told him the whole thing, and he said it was smart. He said Tom Sawyer couldn't get up no better plan than what I had. Then I says, "How do you come to be here, Jim, and how'd you get here?"

He looked pretty uneasy and didn't say nothing for a minute. Then he says, "Maybe I better not tell."

"Why, Jim?"

"Well dey's reasons. But you wouldn't tell on me ef I 'uz to tell you, would you, Huck?"

"Blamed if I would, Jim."

"Well, I b'lieve you, Huck. I–I *run off*."

"Jim!"

"But mind, you said you wouldn't tell–you know you said you wouldn't tell, Huck."

"Well, I did. I said I wouldn't, and I'll stick to it. Honest *injun*, I will. People would call me a low-down Abolitionist and despise me for keeping mum–but that don't make no difference, I ain't a-going to tell, and I ain't a-going back there, anyways. So, now, le's know all about it."

"Well, you see, it 'uz dis way. Ole missus–dat's Miss Watson–she pecks on me all de time en treats me pooty rough, but she alwuz said she wouldn't sell me down to Orleans. But I noticed dey wuz a nigger trader roun' de place considable lately, en I begin to git oneasy. Well, one night I creeps to de do' pooty late, en de do' warn't quite shet, en I hear old missus tell de widder she gwyne to sell me down to Orleans, but she didn' want to, but she could git eight hund'd dollars for me, an it 'uz sich a big stack o' money she couldn' resis'. De widder she try to git her to say she wouldn't do it, but I never waited to hear de res'. I lit out mighty quick, I tell you.

"I tuck out en shin down de hill en 'spec to steal a skift 'long de sho' som'ers 'bove de town, but dey wuz people a-stirring yit, so I hid in de ole tumbledown cooper shop on de bank to wait for everybody to go 'way. Well, I wuz dah all night. Dey wuz somebody roun' all de time. 'Long 'bout six in de mawnin' skifts begin to go by, en 'bout eight er nine every skift dat went 'long wuz talkin' 'bout how yo' pap come over to de town en say you's killed. Dese las' skifts wuz full o' ladies en genlmen a-goin' over for to see de place. Sometimes dey'd pull up at de sho' en take a res' b'fo' dey started acrost, so by de talk I got to know all 'bout de killin'. I 'uz powerful sorry you's killed, Huck, but I ain't no mo' now.

"I laid dah under de shavin's all day. I 'uz hungry, but I warn't afeard; bekase I knowed ole missus en de widder wuz goin' to start to de camp meet'n' right arter breakfas' en be gone all day, en dey knows I goes off wid de cattle 'bout daylight, so dey wouldn' 'spec to see me roun' de place, en so dey wouldn' miss me tell arter dark in de evenin'. De yuther servants wouldn' miss me, kase dey'd shin out en take holiday soon as de ole folks 'uz out'n de way.

"Well, when it come dark I tuck out up de river road en went 'bout two miles or more to whah dey warn't no houses. I'd made up my mine 'bout what I's a-gwyne to do. You see, ef I kep' on tryin' to git away afoot, de dogs 'ud track me; ef I stole a skift to cross over, dey'd miss dat skift, you see, en dey'd know 'bout whah I'd lan' on de yuther side, an whah to pick up my track. So I says, a raff is what I's arter; it doan' *make* no track.

"I see a light a-comin' roun' de p'int bymeby, so I wade' in en shove' a log ahead o' me en swum more'n halfway acrost de river, en got in 'mongst de driftwood, en kep' my head down low, en kinder swum agin de current tell de raff come along. Den I swum to de stern uv it en tuck a-holt, It clouded up en 'uz potty dark for a little while. So I clumb up en laid down on de planks. De men 'uz all 'way yonder in de middle, whah de lantern wuz. De river wuz a'risin', en dey wuz a good current; so I reck'n d 'at by fo' in de mawnin' I'd be twenty-five mile down de river, en den I'd slip in jis b'fo' daylight en swim asho' en take to de woods on de Illinois side.

"But I didn' have no luck. When we 'uz mos' down to de head er de islan' a man begin to come aft wid de lantern. I see it warn't no use fer to wait, so I slid overboard en struck out fer de islan'. Well, I had a notion I could lan' mos' anywhers, but I couldn't—bank too bluff. I 'uz mos' to de foot er de islan' b' fo' I foun' a good place. I went into de woods en jedged I wouldn' fool wid raffs no mo', long as dey move de lantern roun' so. I had my pipe en a plug er dogleg en some matches in my cap, en dey warn't wet, so I 'uz all right."

I wanted to go and look at a place right about the middle of the island that I'd found when I was exploring. So we started and soon got to it, because the island was only three miles long and a quarter of a mile wide.

This place was a tolerable long, steep hill or ridge about forty foot high. We tramped and clumb around all over it, and by and by found a good big cavern in the rock. The cavern was as big as two or three rooms bunched together, and Jim could stand up straight in it.

So we went back and got the canoe and paddled up abreast the cavern and lugged all the traps up there. Then we hunted up a place close by to hide the canoe in, amongst the thick willows. We took some fish off of the lines and set them again and begun to get ready for dinner.

The door of the cavern was big enough to roll a hogshead in, and on one side of the door the floor stuck out a little bit and was flat and a good place to build a fire on. So we built it there and cooked dinner.

We spread the blankets inside for a carpet and eat our dinner in there. We put all the other things handy at the back of the cavern. Pretty soon it darkened up and begun to thunder and lighten. Directly it begun to rain, and it rained like all fury, too, and I never see the wind blow so.

"Jim, this is nice," I says. "I wouldn't want to be nowhere else but here. Pass me along another hunk of fish and some hot corn bread."

The river went on raising and raising for ten or twelve days, till at last it was over the banks. The water was three or four foot deep on the island in the low places and on the Illinois bottom.

One night we catched a little section of a lumber raft—nice pine planks. It was twelve foot wide and about fifteen or sixteen foot long, and the top stood above water six or seven inches, a solid level floor. We could see saw-logs go by in the daylight, sometimes, but we let them go; we didn't show ourselves in daylight.

Another night, just before daylight, here comes a frame house down on the west side of the island. She was a two-story and tilted over considerable. We paddled out and got aboard—clumb in at an upstairs window. But it was too dark to see yet, so we made the canoe fast and set in her to wait for daylight.

The light begun to come before we got to the foot of the island. Then we looked in at the window. We could make out a bed and a table and two old chairs and lots of things around about on the floor; and there was clothes hanging against the wall. There was something laying on the floor in the far corner that looked like a man.

So Jim says, "Hallo, you!"

But it didn't budge. So I hollered again, and then Jim says, "De man ain't asleep—he's dead. You hold still—I'll go en see."

He went and bent down and looked and says, "It's a dead man. Yes, indeedy; naked, too. He's ben shot in de back. I reck'n he's ben dead two er three days. Come in, Huck, but doan' look at his face—it's too gashly."

I didn't look at him at all. Jim throwed some old rags over him, but he needn't done it; I didn't want to see him. There was two old dirty calico dresses and a sunbonnet and some women's underclothes hanging against the wall, and some men's clothing, too. We put the lot into the canoe; it might come good. There was a boy's old speckled straw hat on the floor; I took that, too. And there was a bottle that had had milk in it; and it had a rag stopper for a baby to suck. We would 'a' took the bottle, but it was broke. There was a seedy old chest and an old hair trunk with the hinges broke. They stood open, but there warn't nothing left in them that was any account. The way things was scattered about, we reckoned the people left in a hurry and warn't fixed so as to carry off most of their stuff.

We got an old tin lantern, and a butcher knife without any handle, and a brand-new Barlow knife worth two bits in any store, and a lot of tallow candles, and a tin candlestick, and a gourd, and a tin cup, and a ratty old bed quilt off the bed, and a reticule with needles and pins and beeswax and buttons and thread and all such truck in it, and a hatchet, and some nails. and a fish-line as thick as my little finger, with some monstrous hooks on it, and a roll of buckskin, and a leather dog collar, and a horseshoe, and some vials of medicine that didn't have no label on them; and just as we was leaving I found a tolerable good currycomb, and Jim, he found a ratty old fiddle-bow, and a wooden leg. The straps was broke off of it, but barring that, it was a good enough leg, though it was too long for me and not long enough for Jim, and we couldn't find the other one, though we hunted all around.

And so, take it all around, we made a good haul. When we was ready to shove off, we was a quarter of a mile below the island, and it was pretty broad day. So I made Jim lay down in the canoe and cover up with the quilt, because if he set up, people could tell he was a nigger a good ways off. I paddled over to the Illinois shore, and drifted down most a half a mile doing it. I crept up the dead water under the bank and hadn't no accidents and didn't see nobody.

We got home all safe.

CHAPTER VIII

In disguise–Huck and the woman–The search–Prevarication
Going to Goshen

WELL, the days went along and the river went down between its banks again. One morning I said it was getting slow and dull, and I wanted to get a stirring-up some way. I said I reckoned I would slip over the river and find out what was going on. Jim liked that notion; but he said I must go in the dark and look sharp. Then he studied it over and said, couldn't I put on some of them old things and dress up like a girl?

That was a good notion, too. So we shortened up one of the calico gowns, and I turned up my trouser legs to my knees and got into it. Jim hitched it behind with the hooks, and it was a fair fit. I put on the sun-bonnet and tied it under my chin, and then for a body to look in and see my face was like looking down a joint of stovepipe. Jim said nobody would know me, even in the daytime, hardly. I practiced around all day to get the hang of the things, and by and by I could do pretty well in them, only Jim said I didn't walk like a girl. And he said I must quit pulling up my gown to get at my britches pocket. I took notice and done better.

I started up the Illinois shore in the canoe just after dark.

I headed across to the town from a little below the ferry-landing, and the drift of the current fetched me in at the bottom of the town. I tied up and started along the bank. There was a light burning in a little shanty that hadn't been lived in for a long time, and I wondered who had took up quarters there. I slipped up and peeped in at the window. There was a woman about forty years old in there knitting by a candle that was on a pine table. I didn't know her face; she was a stranger, for you couldn't start a face in that town that I didn't know. Now this was lucky, because I was weakening. I was getting afraid I shouldn't 'a' come; people might know my voice and find me out. But if this woman had been in such a little town two days she could tell me all I wanted to know. So I knocked at the door and made up my mind I wouldn't forget I was a girl.

"Come in," says the woman, and I did. She says, "Take a cheer." I done it. She looked me all over with her little shiny eyes and says, "What might your name be?"

"Sarah Williams."

"Where'bouts do you live? In this neighborhood?"

"No'm. In Hookerville, seven mile below. I've walked all the way and I'm all tired out."

"Hungry, too, I reckon. I'll find you something."

"No'm, I ain't hungry. I was so hungry I had to stop two miles below here at a farm; so I ain't hungry no more. It's what makes me so late. My mother's down sick and out of money and everything, and I come to tell my uncle, Abner Moore. He lives at the upper end of the town, she says. I hain't ever been here before. Do you know him?"

"No, but I don't know everybody yet. I haven't lived here quite two weeks. It's a considerable ways to the upper end of the town. You better stay here all night. Take off your bonnet."

"No," I says. "I'll rest awhile, I reckon, and go on. I ain't afeard of the dark."

She said she wouldn't let me go by myself, but her husband would be in by and by, maybe in a hour and a half, and she'd send him along with me. Then she got to talking about her husband, and about her relations up the river, and her relations down the river, and about how much better off they used to was, and how they didn't know but they'd made a mistake coming to our town instead of letting well alone—and so on and so on, till I was afeard I had made a mistake coming to her to find out what was going on in the town.

But by and by she dropped on to Pap and the murder, and then I was pretty willing to let her clatter right along. She told about me and Tom Sawyer finding the twelve thousand dollars (only she got it twenty) and all about Pap and what a hard lot he was, and what a hard lot I was, and at last she got down to where I was murdered.

I says, "Who done it? We've heard considerable about these goings-on down in Hookerville, but we don't know who 'twas that killed Huck Finn."

"Well, I reckon there's a right smart chance of people *here* that'd like to know who killed him. Some think old Finn done it himself."

"No—is that so?"

"Most everybody thought it at first. He'll never know how nigh he come to getting lynched. But before night they changed around and judged it was done by a runaway nigger named Jim."

"Why *he*—"

I stopped. I reckoned I better keep still. She run on and never noticed I had put in at all.

"The nigger run off the very night Huck Finn was killed. So there's a reward out for him—three hundred dollars. And there's a reward out for old Finn, too—two hundred dollars. You see, he come to town the morning after the murder, and told about it, and was out with 'em on the ferryboat hunt, and right away after he up and left. Before night they wanted to lynch him, but he was gone, you see.

"Well, next day they found out the nigger was gone; they found out he hadn't ben seen sence ten o'clock the night the murder was done. So then they put it on him, you see; and while they was full of it, next day, back comes old Finn and went boo-hooing to Judge Thatcher to get money to hunt for the nigger all over Illinois with. The judge gave him some, and that evening he got drunk and was around till after midnight with a couple of mighty hard-looking strangers, and then went off with them. Well, he hain't come back sence, and they ain't looking for him back till this thing blows over a little, for people thinks now that he killed his boy and fixed things so folks would think robbers done it, and then he'd get Huck's money without having to bother a long time with a lawsuit. People do say he warn't any too good to do it. Oh, he's sly, I reckon. If he don't come back for a year he'll be all right. You can't prove anything on him, you know. Everything will be quieted down then, and he'll walk into Huck's money as easy as nothing."

"Yes, I reckon so, 'm. I don't see nothing in the way of it. Has everybody quit thinking the nigger done it?"

"Oh, no, not everybody. A good many thinks he done it. But they'll get the nigger pretty soon now, and maybe they can scare it out of him."

"Why, are they after him yet?"

"Well, you're innocent, ain't you! Does three hundred dollars lay around every day for people to pick up? Some folks think the nigger ain't far from here. I'm one of them—but I hain't talked it around. A few days ago I was talking with an old couple that lives next door in the long shanty, and they happened to say hardly anybody ever goes to that island over yonder that they call Jackson's Island. Don't anybody live there? says I. No, nobody, says they. I didn't say any more, but I done some thinking. I was pretty near certain I'd seen smoke over there, about the head of the island, a day or two before that, so I says to myself, like as not that nigger's hiding over there. Anyway, says I, it's worth the trouble to give the place a hunt. I hain't see any smoke sence, so I reckon maybe he's gone, if it was him; but husband's going over to see–him and another man. He was gone up the river, but he got back today, and I told him as soon as he got here two hours ago."

I had got so uneasy I couldn't set still. I had to do something with my hands; so I took up a needle off the table and went to threading it. My hands shook, and I was making a bad job of it. When the woman stopped talking I looked up, and she was looking at me pretty curious and smiling a little.

I put down the needle and thread and let on to be interested–and I was, too–and says, "Three hundred dollars is a power of money. I wish my mother could get it. Is your husband going over there tonight?"

"Oh, yes. He went uptown with the man I was telling you of, to get a boat and see if they could borrow another gun. They'll go over after midnight."

"Couldn't they see better if they was to wait till daytime?"

"Yes. And couldn't the nigger see better, too? After midnight he'll likely be asleep, and they can slip around through the woods and hunt up his campfire all the better for the dark, if he's got one."

"I didn't think of that."

The woman kept looking at me pretty curious, and I didn't feel a bit comfortable. Pretty soon she says. "What did you say your name was, honey?"

"M-Mary Williams."

Somehow it didn't seem to me that I said it was Mary before, so I didn't look up–seemed to me I said it was Sarah. So I felt sort of cornered and was afeard maybe I was lokking it, too. I wished the woman would say something more. The longer she set still the uneasier I was.

But now she says, "Honey, I thought you said it was Sarah when you first come in?"

"Oh, yes'm, I did. Sarah Mary Williams. Sarah's my first name. Some calls me Sarah, some calls me Mary."

"Oh, that's the way of it?"

"Yes'm."

I was feeling better then, but I wished I was out of there, anyway. I couldn't look up yet.

Well, the woman fell to talking about how hard times was, and how poor they had to live, and how the rats was as free as if they owned the place, and so forth and so on, and then I got easy again. She was right about the rats. You'd see one stick his nose out of a hole in the corner every little while. She said she had to have things handy to throw at them when she was alone, or they wouldn't give her no peace. She showed me a bar of lead twisted up into a knot, and said she was a good shot with it generly, but she'd wrenched her arm a day or two ago and didn't know whether she could throw true now. But she watched for a chance and directly banged away at a rat; but she missed him wide and said, "Ouch!" it hurt her arm so.

Then she told me to try for the next one. I wanted to be getting away before the old man got back, but of course I didn't let on. I got the thing, and the first rat that showed his nose I let drive, and if he'd 'a' stayed where he was he'd 'a' been a tolerable sick rat. She said that was first-rate, and she reckoned I would hive the next one. She went and got the lump of lead and fetched it back, and brought along a hank of yarn which she wanted me to help her with. I held up my two hands and she put the hank over them and went on talking about her and her husband's matters.

But she broke off to say, "Keep your eye on the rats. You better have the lead in your lap, handy."

So she dropped the lump into my lap just at that moment, and I clapped my legs together on it, and she went on talking. But only about a minute. Then she took off the hank and looked me straight in the face, but very pleasant, and says, "Come, now, what's your real name?"

"Wh-what, mum?"

"What's your real name? Is it Bill or Tom or Bob?"

I reckon I shook like a leaf, and I didn't know hardly what to do. But I says, "Please to don't poke fun at a poor girl like me, mum. If I'm in the way here, I'll—"

"No, you won't. Set down and stay where you are. I ain't going to hurt you, and I ain't going to tell on you, nuther. You just tell me your secret and trust me. I'll keep it; and what's more, I'll help you. So'll my old man if you want him to. You see, you're a runaway 'prentice, that's all. It ain't anything. There ain't no harm in it. You've been treated bad, and you made up your mind to cut. Bless you, child, I wouldn't tell on you. Tell me all about it now, that's a good boy."

So I said it wouldn't be no use to try to play it any longer, and I would just make a clean breast and tell her everything, but she mustn't go back on her promise. Then I told her my father and mother was dead, and the law had bound me out to a mean old farmer in the country thirty mile back from the river, and he treated me so bad I couldn't stand it no longer; he went away to be gone a couple of days, and so I took my chance and stole some of his daughter's old clothes and cleared out, and I had been three nights coming the thirty miles. I traveled nights and hid daytimes and slept, and the bag of bread and meat I carried from home lasted me all the way, and I had a-plenty. I said I believed my uncle

Abner Moore would take care of me, and so that was why I struck out for this town of Goshen.

"Goshen, child? This ain't Goshen. This is St. Petersburg. Goshen's ten mile further up the river. Who told you this was Goshen?"

"Why, a man I met at daybreak this morning, just as I was going to turn into the woods for my regular sleep. He told me when the roads forked I must take the right hand, and five mile would fetch me to Goshen."

"He was drunk, I reckon. He told you just exactly wrong."

"Well, he did act like he was drunk, but it ain't no matter now. I got to be moving along. I'll fetch Goshen before daylight."

"Hold on a minute. I'll put you up a snack to eat."

So she put me up a snack and says, "Say, when a cow's laying down, which end of her gets up first? Answer up prompt now—don't stop to study over it. Which end gets up first?"

"The hind end, mum."

"Well, then, a horse."

"The for'ard end, mum."

"Which side of a tree does the moss grow on?"

"North side."

"If fifteen cows is browsing on a hillside, how many of them eats with their heads pointed the same direction?"

"The whole fifteen, mum."

"Well, I reckon you *have* lived in the country. I thought maybe you was trying to hocus me again. What's your real name, now?"

"George Peters, mum."

"Well, try to remember it, George. Don't forget and tell me it's Elexander before you go, and then get out by saying it's George Elexander when I catch you. And don't go about women in that old calico. You do a girl tolerable poor, but you might fool men, maybe. Bless you, child, when you set out to thread a needle don't hold the thread still and fetch the needle up to it. Hold the needle still and poke the thread at it; that's the way a woman most always does, but a man always does t'other way. And when you throw at a rat or anything, hitch yourself up a-tiptoe and fetch your hand up over your head as awkward as you can, and miss your rat about six or seven foot. Throw stiff-armed from the shoulder, like there was a pivot there for it to turn on, like a girl; not from the wrist and elbow, with your arm out to one side, like a boy. And, mind you, when a girl tries to catch anything in her lap she throws her knees apart; she don't clap them together, the way you did when you catched the lump of lead. Why, I spotted you for a boy when you was threading the needle; and I contrived the other things just to make certain.

"Now, trot along to your uncle, Sarah Mary Williams George Elexander Peters, and if you get into trouble send word to Mrs. Judith Loftus, which is me, and I'll do what I can to get you out of it. Keep the river road all the way, and next time you tramp take shoes and socks with you. The river road's a rocky one, and your feet'll be in a condition when you get to Goshen, I reckon."

I went up the bank about fifty yards, and then I doubled on my tracks and slipped back to where my canoe was, a good piece below the house. I jumped in and was off in a hurry. I went upstream far enough to make the head of the island and then started across. I took of the sunbonnet, for I didn't want no blinders on then. When I was about the middle I heard the clock begin to strike, so I stops and listens; the sound came faint over the water but clear—eleven. When I struck the head of the island I never waited to blow, though I was most winded, but I shoved right into the timber where my old camp used to be and started a good fire there on a high and dry spot.

Then I jumped in the canoe and dug out for our place, a mile and a half below, as hard as I could go. I landed and slopped through the timber and up the ridge and into the cavern. There Jim laid, sound asleep on the ground.

I roused him out and says, "Git up and hump yourself, Jim. There ain't a minute to lose. They're after us!"

Jim never asked no questions, he never said a word; but the way he worked for the next half an hour showed about how he was scared. By that time everything we had in the world was on our raft, and she was ready to be shoved out from the willow cove where she was hid. We put out the campfire at the cavern the first thing and didn't show a candle outside after that.

I took the canoe out from the shore a little piece and took a look; but if there was a boat around I couldn't see it, for stars and shadows ain't good to see by. Then we got out the raft and slipped along down in the shade, past the foot of the island dead still—never saying a word.

CHAPTER IX

Tying up daytimes—An astronomical theory—Running a temperance revival—The Duke of Bridgewater—The troubles of royalty

It must 'a' been close on to one o'clock when we got below the island at last, and the raft did seem to go mighty slow. If a boat was to come along we was going to take to the canoe and break for the Illinois shore. And it was well a boat didn't come, for we hadn't ever thought to put the gun in the canoe, or a fishing-line, or anything to eat. We was in ruther too much of a sweat to think of so many things. It warn't good judgment to put *everything* on the raft.

If the men went to the island, I just expect they found the campfire I built, and watched it all night for Jim to come. Anyways, they stayed away from us, and if my building the fire never fooled them it warn't no fault of mine. I played it as low down on them as I could.

When the first streak of day began to show, we tied up to a towhead in a big bend on the Illinois side, and hacked off cottonwood branches with the hatchet, and covered up the raft with them so she looked like there had been a cave-in in the bank there. A towhead is a sandbar that has cottonwoods on it as thick as harrow-teeth.

When it was beginning to come on dark we poked our heads out of the cottonwood thicket and looked up and down and across. Nothing in sight. So Jim took up some of the top planks of the raft and built a snug wigwam to get under in blazing weather and rainy, and to keep the things dry. Jim made a floor for the wigwam and raised it a foot or more above the level of the raft, so now the blankets and all the traps was out of reach of steamboat waves. Right in the middle of the wigwam we made a layer of dirt about five or six inches deep with a frame around it to hold it to its place; this was to build a fire on in sloppy weather or chilly; the wigwam would keep it from being seen. We made an extra steering-oar, too, because one of the others might get broke on a snag or something.

Every night now I used to slip ashore toward ten o'clock at some little village and buy ten or fifteen cents' worth of meal or bacon or other stuff to eat; and sometimes I lifted a chicken that warn't roosting comfortable and took him along.

Mornings before daylight I slipped into cornfields and borrowed a watermelon or a mushmelon or a punkin or some corn or things of that kind. Pap always said it warn't no harm to borrow things if you was meaning to pay them back sometime; but the widow said it warn't anything but a soft name for stealing, and no decent body would do it. Jim said he reckoned the widow was partly right and Pap was partly right; so the best way would be for us to pick out two or three things from the list and say we wouldn't borrow them anymore–then he reckoned it wouldn't be no harm to borrow the others.

We shot a waterfowl now and then that got up too early in the morning or didn't go to bed early enough in the evening. Take it all round, we lived pretty high.

Two or three more days and nights went by. I reckon I might say they swum by, they slid along so quiet and smooth and lovely.

Sometimes we'd have that whole river all to ourselves for the longest time. Yonder was the banks and the islands, across the water; and maybe a spark–which was a candle in a cabin window; and sometimes on the water you could see a spark or two–on a raft or a scow, you know; and maybe you could hear a fiddle or a song coming over from one of the crafts.

One morning about daybreak I took the canoe and crossed over a chute to the main shore–it was only two hundred yards–and paddled about a mile up a crick amongst the cypress woods, to see if I couldn't get some berries. Just as I was passing a place where a kind of cowpath crossed the crick, here comes a couple of men tearing up the path as tight as they could foot it. I thought I was a goner, for whenever anybody was after anybody I judged it was *me*–or maybe Jim. I was about to dig out from there in a hurry, but they was pretty close to me then, and sung out and begged me to save their lives–said they hadn't been doing nothing, and was being chased for it–said there was men and dogs a-coming.

They wanted to jump right in, but I says, "Don't you do it. I don't hear the dogs and horses yet. You've got time to crowd through the brush and get up the crick a little ways. Then you take to the water and wade down to me and get in–that'll throw the dogs off the scent."

They done it, and soon as they was aboard I lit out for our towhead, and in about five or ten minutes we heard the dogs and the men away off, shouting. We heard them come along toward the crick, but couldn't see them; they seemed to stop and fool around awhile. Then, as we got further and further away all the time, we couldn't hardly hear them at all. By the time we had left a mile of woods behind us and struck the river, everything was quiet, and we paddled over to the towhead and hid in the cottonwoods and was safe.

One of these fellows was about seventy or upwards and had a bald head and very gray whiskers. He had an old battered-up slouch hat on and a greasy blue woolen shirt and ragged old blue jeans britches stuffed into his boot-tops and home-knit galluses–no, he only had one. He had an old long-tailed blue jeans coat with slick brass buttons flung over his arm, and both of them had big, fat, ratty-looking carpetbags.

The other fellow was about thirty and dressed about as ornery. After breakfast we all laid off and talked, and the first thing that come out was that these chaps didn't know one another.

"What got you into trouble?" says the baldhead to the other chap.

"Well, I'd been selling an article to take the tartar off the teeth–and it does take it off, too, and generly the enamel along with it–but I stayed about one night longer than I ought to, and was just in the act of sliding out when I ran across you on the trail this side of town, and you told me they were coming, and begged me to help you to get off. So I told you I was expecting trouble myself and would scatter out *with* you. That's the whole yarn–what's yourn?"

"Well, I'd ben a-runnin' a little temperance revival thar 'bout a week and was the pet of the womenfolks, big and little, for I was makin' it mighty warm for the rummies, I *tell* you, and takin' as much as five or six dollars a night–ten cents a head, children and niggers free–and business a-growin' all the time, when somehow or another a little report got around last night that I had a way of puttin' in my time with a private jug on the sly. A nigger rousted me out this mornin' and told me the people was getherin' on the quiet with their dogs and horses, and they'd be along pretty soon and give me 'bout half an hour's start, and then run me down if they could; and if they got me they'd tar and feather me and ride me on a rail, sure. I didn't wait for no breakfast–I warn't hungry."

"Old man," said the young one, "I reckon we might double-team it together; what do you think?"

"I ain't undisposed. What's your line–mainly?"

"Jour printer by trade; do a little in patent medicines; theater-actor –tragedy, you know; take a turn to mesmerism and phrenology when there's a chance; teach singing-geography school for a change; sling a lecture sometimes–oh, I do lots of things–most anything that comes handy, so it ain't work. What's your lay?"

"I've done considerable in the doctoring way in my time. Layin' on o' hands is my best holt–for cancer and paralysis and sich things; and I k'n tell a fortune pretty good when I've got somebody along to find out the facts for me. Preachin's my line, too, and workin' camp meetin's, and missionaryin' around."

Nobody never said anything for a while. Then the young man hove a sigh and says, "Alas!"

"What're you alassin' about?" said the baldhead.

"To think I should have lived to be leading such a life and be degraded down into such company." And he begun to wipe the corner of his eye with a rag.

"Dern your skin, ain't the company good enough for you?" says the baldhead, pretty pert and uppish.

"Yes, it is good enough for me; it's as good as I deserve; for who fetched me so low when I was so high? I did myself. I don't blame you gentlemen–far from it; I don't blame anybody. I deserve it all. Let the cold world do its worst. One thing I know–there's a grave somewhere for me. The world may go on just as it's always done and take everything from me–loved ones, property, everything; but it can't take that. Some day I'll lie down in it and forget it all, and my poor broken heart will be at rest." He went on a-wiping.

"Drot your pore broken heart," says the baldhead. "What are you heaving your broken heart at us f'r? We hain't done nothing."

"No, I know you haven't. I ain't blaming you, gentlemen. I brought myself down–yes, I did it myself. It's right I should suffer–perfectly right– I don't make any moan."

"Brought you down from what? Whar was you brought down from?"

"Ah, you would not believe me. The world never believes–let it pass– tis no matter. The secret of my birth–"

"The secret of your birth! Do you mean to say–"

"Gentlemen," says the young man, very solemn, "I will reveal it to you, for I feel I may have confidence in you. By rights I am a duke!"

Jim's eyes bugged out when he heard that, and I reckon mine did, too. Then the baldhead says, "No! you can't mean it! A real duke?"

"Yes. My great-grandfather, eldest son of the Duke of Bridgewater, fled to this country about the end of the last century, to breathe the pure air of freedom; married here and died, leaving a son, his own father dying about the same time. The second son of the late duke seized the titles and estates—the infant real duke was ignored. I am the lineal descendant of that infant—I am the rightful Duke of Bridgewater. And here am I, forlorn, torn from my high estate, hunted of men, despised by the cold world, ragged, worn, heartbroken, and degraded to the companionship of felons on a raft!"

Jim pitied him ever so much, and so did I. We tried to comfort him, but he said it warn't much use, he couldn't be much comforted; said if we was a mind to acknowledge him, that would do him more good than most anything else. So we said we would, if he would tell us how. He said we ought to bow when we spoke to him, and say "your grace" or "my lord" or "your lordship"—and he wouldn't mind if we called him plain "Bridgewater," which, he said, was a title anyway and not a name. And one of us ought to wait on him at dinner, and do any little thing for him he wanted done.

Well, that was all easy, so we done it. All through dinner Jim stood around and waited on him and says, "Will yo' grace have some o' dis or some o' dat?" and so on, and a body could see it was mighty pleasing to him.

But the old man got pretty silent by and by—didn't have much to say, and didn't look pretty comfortable over all that petting that was going on around that duke. He seemed to have something on his mind.

So, along in the afternoon, he says, "Looky here, Bilgewater," he says, "I'm nation sorry for you, but you ain't the only person that's had troubles like that."

"No?"

"No, you ain't. You ain't the only person that's ben snaked down wrongfully out'n a high place."

"Alas!"

"No, you ain't the only person that's had a secret of his birth." And, by jings, *he* begins to cry.

"Hold! What do you mean?"

"Bilgewater, kin I trust you?" says the old man, still sort of snuffling and sobbing.

"To the bitter death!" He took the old man by the hand and squeezed it and says, "That secret of your being: speak!"

"Bilgewater, I am the late Dauphin!"

You bet you, Jim and me stared this time. Then the duke says, "You are what?"

"Yes, my friend, it is too true—your eyes is lookin' at this very moment on the pore disappeared Dauphin, Looy the Seventeen, son of Looy the Sixteen and Marry Antonette."

"You! At your age! No! You mean you're the late Charlemagne; you must be six or seven hundred years old, at the very least."

"Trouble has done it, Bilgewater, trouble has done it; trouble has brung these gray hairs and this premature balditude. Yes, gentlemen, you see before you, in blue jeans and misery, the wanderin' exiled, trampled-on, and sufferin' rightful King of France."

Well, he cried and took on so that me an Jim didn't know hardly what to do, we was so sorry—and so glad and proud we'd got him with us, too. So we set in, like we done before with the duke, and tried to comfort *him*. But he said it warn't no use, nothing but to be dead and done with it all could do him any good; though he said it often made him feel easier and better for a while if people treated him according to his rights, and got down on one knee to speak to him, and always called him "your majesty", and waited on him first at meals, and didn't set down in his presence till he asked them. So Jim and me set to majestying him, and doing this and that and t'other for him, and standing up till he told us we might set down. This done him heaps of good, and so he got cheerful and comfortable. But the duke kind of soured on him and didn't look a bit satisfied with the way things was going. Still, the king acted real friendly towards him, and said the duke's great-grandfather and all the other Dukes of Bilgewater was a good deal thought of by *his* father and was allowed to come to the palace considerable.

But the duke stayed huffy a good while, till by and by the king says, "Like as not we got to be together a blamed long time on this h'yer raft, Bilgewater, and so what's the use o' your bein' sour? It'll only make things oncomfortable. It ain't my fault I warn't born a duke, it ain't your fault you warn't born a king—so what's the use to worry? Make the best o' things the way you find 'em, says I—that's my motto. This ain't no bad thing that we've struck here—plenty grub and an easy life—come, give us your hand, duke, and le's all be friends."

The duke done it, and Jim and me was pretty glad to see it. It took away all the uncomfortableness and we felt mighty good over it, because it would 'a' been a miserable business to have any unfriendliness on the raft. What you want above all things on a raft is for everybody to be satisfied and feel right and kind towards the others.

It didn't take me long to make up my mind that these liars warn't no kings nor dukes at all, but just low-down humbugs and frauds. But I never said nothing, never let on; kept it to myself; it's the best way; then you don't have no quarrels and don't get into no trouble. If they wanted us to call them kings and dukes, I hadn't no objections, 'long as it would keep peace in the family. And it warn't no use to tell Jim, so I didn't tell him. If I never learnt nothing else out of Pap, I learnt that the best way to get along with his kind of people is to let them have their own way.

CHAPTER X

Huck explains—Laying out a campaign—Working the camp meeting—
A pirate at the camp meeting—The Duke is a printer

THEY asked us considerable many questions; wanted to know what we covered up the raft that way for, and laid by in the daytime instead of running—was Jim a runaway nigger?

Says I, "Goodness sakes! Would a runaway nigger run *south?*"

No, they allowed he wouldn't. I had to account for things some way, so I says, "My folks was living in Pike County, in Missouri, where I was born, and they all died off but me and Pa and my brother Ike. Pa, he 'lowed he'd break up and go down and live with Uncle Ben, who's got a little one-horse place on the river forty-five mile below Orleans. Pa was pretty poor and had some debts; so when he'd squared up there warn't nothing left but sixteen dollars and our nigger, Jim. That warn't enough to take us fourteen hundred mile, deck passage nor no other way. Well, when the river rose Pa had an streak of luck one day; he ketched this piece of a raft. So we reckoned we'd go down to Orleans on it. Pa's luck didn't hold out; a steamboat run over the forrard corner of the raft one night, and we all went overboard and dove under the wheel. Jim and me come up all right, but Pa was drunk, and Ike was only four years old, so they never come up no more.

"Well, for the next day or two we had considerable trouble, because people was always coming out in skiffs and trying to take Jim away from me, saying they believed he was a runaway nigger. We don't run daytimes no more now; nights they don't bother us when they can't see us."

The duke says, "Leave me alone to cipher out a way so we can run in the daytime if we want to. I'll think the thing over—I'll invent a plan that'll fix it. We'll let it alone for today, because of course we don't want to go by that town yonder in daylight—it mightn't be healthy."

Towards night it begun to darken up and look like rain. The heat lightning was squirting around low down in the sky, and the leaves was beginning to shiver—it was going to be pretty ugly, it was easy to see that. So the duke and the king went to overhauling our wigwam, to see what the beds was like. My bed was a straw tick—better than Jim's, which was a corn-shuck tick. There's always cobs around about in a shuck tick, and they poke into you and hurt, and when you roll over the dry shucks sound like you was rolling over in a pile of dead leaves; it makes such a rustling that you wake up. Well, the duke allowed he would take my bed; but the king allowed he wouldn't.

He says, "I should 'a' reckoned the difference in rank would 'a' sejested to you that a corn-shuck bed warn't just fitten for me to sleep on. Your grace'll take the shuck bed yourself."

Jim and me was in a sweat again for a minute, being afraid there was going to be some more trouble amongst them. So we was pretty glad when the duke says, " 'Tis my fate to be always ground into the mire under the iron heel of oppression. Misfortune has broken my once haughty spirit. I yield, I submit; 'tis my fate. I am alone in the world-let me suffer; I can bear it."

We got away as soon as it was good and dark. The king told us to stand well out toward the middle of the river and not show a light till we got a long ways below the town.

The king got out an old ratty deck of cards after breakfast, and him and the duke played seven-up awhile, five cents a game. Then they got tired of it and allowed they would "lay out a campaign," as they called it. The duke went down into his carpetbag and fetched up a lot of little printed bills and read them out loud. One bill said, "The celebrated Dr. Armand de Montalban of Paris," would "lecture on the Science of Phrenology" at such and such a place, on the blank day of blank, at ten cents admission, and "furnish charts of character at twenty-five cents apiece." The duke said that was *him*. In another bill he was the "world-renowned Shakespearian tragedian, Garrick the Younger, of Drury Lane, London." In other bills he had a lot of other names and done other wonderful things, like finding water and gold with "a divining rod," "dissipating witch spells," and so on.

By and by he says, "But the histrionic muse in the darling. Have you ever trod the boards, Royalty?"

"No," says the king.

"You shall, then, before you're three days older, Fallen Grandeur," says the duke. "The first good town we come to we'll hire a hall and do the sword fight in 'Richard III' and the balcony scene in 'Romeo and Juliet.' How does that strike you, now?"

"I'm in, up to the hub, for anything that will pay, Bilgewater; but, you see, I don't know nothing about play-actin', and hain't ever seen much of it. I was too small when Pap used to have 'em at the palace. Do you reckon you can learn me?"

"Easy!"

"All right. I'm jist a-freezin' for something fresh, anyway. Le's commence right away."

So the duke he told him all about who Romeo was and who Juliet was, and said he was used to being Romeo, so the king could be Juliet.

"But if Juliet's such a young gal, duke, my peeled head and my white whiskers is goin' to look oncommon odd on her, maybe."

"No, don't you worry; these country jakes won't ever think of that. Besides, you know, you'll be in costume, and that makes all the difference in the world. Juliet's in a balcony, enjoying the moonlight before she goes to bed, and she's got on her nightgown and her ruffled nightcap. Here are all the costumes for the parts."

He got out two or three curtain-calico suits, which he said was meedyevil armor for Richard III and t'other chap, and a long white cotton nightshirt and a ruffled nightcap to match. The king was satisfied. So the duke got out his book and read the parts over in the most splendid spread-eagle way, prancing around and acting at the same time, to show how it had got to be done. Then he give the book to the king and told him to get his part by heart.

There was a little one-horse town about three miles down the bend, and after dinner the duke said he had ciphered out his idea about how to run in daylight without it being dangerous for Jim. So he allowed he would go down to the town and fix that thing. The king allowed he would go, too, and see if he couldn't strike something. We was out of coffee, so Jim said I better go along with them in the canoe and get some.

When we got there, there warn't nobody stirring; streets empty and perfectly dead and still, like Sunday. We found a sick nigger sunning himself in a back yard, and he said everybody that warn't too young or too sick or too old was gone to camp meeting, about two mile back in the woods. The king got the directions, and allowed he'd go and work that camp meeting for all it was worth.

The duke said what he was after was a printing office. We found it, a little bit of a concern up over a carpenter shop—carpenters and printers all gone to the meeting and no doors locked. It was a dirty, littered-up place and had ink marks and handbills with pictures of horses and runaway niggers on them, all over the walls. The duke shed his coat and said he was all right now. So me and the king lit out for the camp meeting.

We got there in about a half an hour fairly dripping, for it was a most awful hot day. There was as much as a thousand people there from twenty mile around. The woods was full of teams and wagons, hitched everywheres, feeding out of the wagon-troughs and stomping to keep off the flies. There was sheds made out of poles and roofed over with branches where they had lemonade and gingerbread to sell.

The preaching was going on under the same kind of sheds, only they was bigger and held crowds of people. The benches was made out of outside slabs of logs, with holes bored in the round side to drive sticks into for legs. They didn't have no backs. The preachers had high platforms to stand on at one end of the sheds.

The first shed we come to, the preacher was lining out a hymn. He lined out two lines, everybody sung it, and it was kind of grand to hear, there was so many of them and they done it in such a rousing way. Then he lined out two more for them to sing—and so on. The people woke up more and more and sung louder and louder; and toward the end some begun to groan, and some begun to shout. Then the preacher begun to preach, and begun in earnest, too; and went weaving first to one side of the platform and then the other, and then a-leaning down over the front of it, with his arms and his body going all the time, and shouting his words out with all his might. And every now and then he would hold up his Bible and spread it open, and kind of pass it around this way and that, shouting, "It's the brazen serpent in the wilderness! Look upon it and live!" And people would shout, "Glory!–A-a-*men!*" And so he went on, and the people groaning and crying and saying amen.

Well, the first I knowed the king got a-going, and you could hear him over everybody. And next he went a-charging up onto the platform, and the preacher, he begged him to speak to the people, and he done it. He told them he was a pirate–been a pirate for thirty years out in the Indian Ocean–and his crew thinned out considerable last spring in a fight, and he was home now to take out some fresh men, and thanks to goodness he'd been robbed last night and put ashore off a steamboat without a cent, and he was glad of it. It was the blessedest thing that ever happened to him, because he was a changed man now, and happy for the first time in his life. And, poor as he was, he was going to start right off to work his way back to the Indian Ocean and put in the rest of his life trying to turn the pirates into the true path; for he could do it better than anybody else, being acquainted with all pirate crews in that ocean; and though it would take him a long time to get there without money, he would get there any-way, and every time he convinced a pirate he would say to him, "Don't you thank me, don't you thank me, don't you give me no credit. It belongs to them dear people in Pokeville camp meeting, natural brothers and bene-factors of the race, and that dear preacher there, the truest friend a poor pirate ever had!"

And then he busted into tears, and so did everybody. Then somebody sings out, "Take up a collection for him, take up a collection!" Well, a half a dozen made a jump to do it, but somebody sings out, "Let *him* pass the hat around!" Then everybody said it, the preacher, too.

So the king went all through the crowd with his hat, swabbing his eyes and blessing the people and praising them and thanking them for being so good to the poor pirates away off there. And every little while the prettiest kind of girls, with tears running down their cheeks, would up and ask him would he let them kiss him for to remember him by, and he always done it. Some of them hugged and kissed as many as five or six times–and he was invited to stay a week. Everybody wanted him to live in their houses, and said they'd think it was an honor; but he said as this was the last day of the camp meeting he couldn't do no good, and besides he was in a sweat to get to the Indian Ocean right off and go to work.

When we got back to the raft and he come to count up he found he had collected eighty-seven dollars and seventy-five cents. And then he had fetched away a three-gallon jug of whisky, too, that he found under a wagon when he was starting home through the woods. The king said, take it all around, it laid over any day he'd ever put in in the missionarying line. He said it warn't no use talking, heathens don't amount to shucks along-side of pirates to work a camp meeting with.

The duke was thinking *he'd* been doing pretty well until the king come to show up, but after that he didn't think so much. He had set up and

printed off two little jobs for farmers in that printing office–horse bills–
and took the money, four dollars. And he had got in ten dollars' worth of
advertisements for the paper, which he said he would put in for four
dollars if they would pay in advance–so they done it. The price of the
paper was two dollars a year, but he took in three subscriptions for a half
dollar apiece on condition of them paying him in advance; they were
going to pay in cordwood and onions as usual, but he said he had just
bought the concern and knocked down the price as low as he could afford
it, and was going to run it for cash. He set up a little piece of poetry, which
he made, himself, out of his own head–three verses–kind of sweet and
saddish–the name of it was, "Yes, crush, cold world, this breaking heart"–
and he left that all set up and ready to print in the paper, and didn't
charge nothing for it. Well, he took in nine dollars and a half, and said
he'd done a pretty square day's work for it.

Then he showed us another little job he'd printed and hadn't charged
for, because it was for us. It had a picture of a runaway nigger with a
bundle on a stick on his shoulder, and "$ 200 reward" under it. The
reading was all about Jim and just described him to a dot. It said he run
away from St. Jacques's plantation, forty mile below New Orleans, last
winter, and likely went north, and whoever would catch him and send him
back he could have the reward.

"Now," says the duke, "after tonight we can run in the daytime if we
want to. Whenever we see anybody coming we can tie Jim hand and foot
with a rope, and lay him in the wigwam and show this handbill and say
we captured him up the river, and were too poor to travel on a steamboat,
so we got this little raft on credit from our friends and we are going to get
the reward."

We all said the duke was pretty smart, and there couldn't be no trouble
about running daytimes. We judged we could make miles enough that
night to get out of the reach of the powwow we reckoned the duke's work
in the printing office was going to make in that little town. Then we could
boom right along if we wanted to.

We laid low and kept still and never shoved out till nearly ten o'clock;
then we slid by, pretty wide away from the town, and didn't hoist our
lantern till we was clear out of sight.

When Jim called me to take the watch at four in the morning, he says,
"Huck, does you reck'n we gwyne to run acrost any mo' kings on dis
trip?"

"No," I says, "I reckon not."

"Well," says he, "dat's all right, den. I doan' mine one er two kings,
but dat's enough. Dis one's powerful drunk, en de duke ain' much better."

I found Jim had been trying to get him to talk French, so he could hear
what it was like; but he said he had been in this country so long, and had
so much trouble, he'd forgot it.

CHAPTER XI

*Sword exercise–Hamlet's soliloquy–They loafed around town–
A lazy town–Attending the circus–Intoxication in the ring–
The thrilling tragedy*

IT WAS after sunup now, but we went right on and didn't tie up. The king and the duke turned out by and by looking pretty rusty; but after they'd jumped overboard and took a swim it chippered them up a good deal.

After breakfast the king, he took a seat on the corner of the raft, and pulled off his boots and rolled up his britches and let his legs dangle in the water, so as to be comfortable, and lit his pipe; and went to getting his "Romeo and Juliet" by heart. When he had got it pretty good him and the duke begun to practice it together. The duke had to learn him over and over again how to say every speech, and he made him sigh and put his hand on his heart, and after a while he said he done it pretty well.

"Only," he says, "you mustn't bellow out *Romeo!* that way, like a bull–you must say it soft and sick and languishy, so–*R-o-o-meo!* That is the idea, for Juliet's a dear sweet mere child of a girl, you know, and she doesn't bray like a jackass."

Well, next they got out a couple of long swords that the duke made out of oak laths, and begun to practice the sword fight–the duke called himself Richard III; and the way they laid on and pranced around the raft was grand to see. But by and by the king tripped and fell overboard, and after that they took a rest and had a talk about all kinds of adventures they'd had in other times along the river.

The first chance we got, the duke, he had some show bills printed. And after that, for two or three days as we floated along, the raft was a most uncommon lively place, for there warn't nothing but sword fighting and rehearsing–as the duke called it–going on all the time. One morning, when we was pretty well down the state of Arkansaw, we come in sight of a little one-horse town in a big bend. So we tied up about three-quarters of a mile above it, in the mouth of a crick which was shut in like a tunnel by the cypress trees, and all of us but Jim took the canoe and went down there to see if there was any chance in that place for our show.

We struck it mighty lucky; there was going to be a circus there that afternoon, and the country people was already beginning to come in, in all kinds of shackly wagons and on horses. The circus would leave before night, so our show would have a pretty good chance. The duke, he hired the courthouse, and we went around and stuck up our bills.

Then we went loafing around town. The stores and houses was most all old, shackly, dried-up frame concerns that hadn't ever been painted. They was set up three or four foot above ground on stilts, so as to be out of reach of the water when the river was overflowed. The houses had little gardens around them, but they didn't seem to raise hardly anything in them but jimpsonweeds and sunflowers and ash piles and old curled-up boots and shoes and pieces of bottles and rags and played-out tinware. The fences was made of different kinds of boards, nailed on at different times; and they leaned every which way and had gates that didn't generly have but one hinge–a leather one. Some of the fences had been white-washed some time or another, but the duke said it was in Columbus's time, like enough. There was generly hogs in the garden, and people driving them out.

Well, that night we had *our* show; but there warn't only about twelve people there–just enough to pay expenses. And they laughed all the time, and that made the duke mad; and everybody left, anyway, before the show was over, but one boy which was asleep. So the duke said these Arkansaw lunkheads couldn't come up to Shakespeare; what they wanted was low comedy–and maybe something ruther worse than low comedy, he reckoned. He said he could size their style. So next morning he got some big sheets of wrapping paper and some black paint, and drawed off some handbills and stuck them up all over the village. The bills said:

AT THE COURT HOUSE!
FOR 3 NIGHTS ONLY!
The World-Renowned Tragedians
DAVID GARRICK THE YOUNGER!
and EDMUND KEAN THE ELDER!
Of the London and Continental Theatres,
In their Thrilling Tragedy of
THE KING'S CAMELOPARD,
OR
THE ROYAL NONESUCH ! ! !
Admission 50 cents.

Then at the bottom was the biggest line of all, which said:

LADIES AND CHILDREN NOT ADMITTED

"There," says he, "if that line don't fetch them, I don't know Arkansaw!"

CHAPTER XII

Sold–Royal comparisons–Jim gets homesick

WELL, all day him and the king was hard at it, rigging up a stage and a curtain and a row of candles for footlights; and that night the house was jam full of men in no time. When the place couldn't hold no more, the duke, he quit tending door and went around the back way and come onto the stage and stood up before the curtain and made a little speech, and praised up this tragedy, and said it was the most thrillingest one that ever was; and so he went on a-bragging about the tragedy, and about Edmund Kean the Elder, which was to play the main principal part in it. At last when he'd got everybody's expectations up high enough, he rolled up the curtain, and the next minute the king come a-prancing out on all fours, naked; and he was painted all over, ring-streaked-and-striped, all sorts of colors, as splendid as a rainbow. And—but never mind the rest of his outfit, it was just wild, but it was awful funny. The people most killed themselves laughing; and when the king got done capering and capered off behind the scenes, they roared and clapped and stormed and hawhawed till he come back and done it over again, and after that they made him do it another time. Well, it would make a cow laugh to see the shines that old idiot cut.

Then the duke he lets the curtain down, and bows to the people, and says the great tragedy will be performed only two nights more, on account of pressing London engagements. Then he makes them another bow, and says if he has succeeded in pleasing them and instructing them, he will be deeply obleeged if they will mention it to their friends and get them to come and see it.

Twenty people sings out, "What, is it over! Is that *all?*"

The duke says yes. Than there was a fine time. Everybody sings out, "Sold!" and rose up mad, and was a-going for that stage and them trage- dians.

But a big, fine-looking man jumps up on a bench and shouts, "Hold on! Just a word, gentlemen." They stopped to listen. "We are sold—mighty badly sold. But we don't want to be the laughingstock of this whole town, I reckon, and never hear the last of this thing as long as we live. *No.* What we want is to go out of here quiet, and talk this show up, and sell the *rest* of the town! Then we'll all be in the same boat. Ain't that sen- sible?"

"You bet it is! The jedge is right!" everybody sings out.

"All right, then—not a word about any sell. Go along home and advise everybody to come and see the tragedy."

Next day you couldn't hear nothing around that town but how splendid that show was. House was jammed again that night, and we sold this crowd the same way. When me and the king and the duke got home to the raft we all had a supper. And by and by, about midnight, they made Jim and me back her out and float her down the middle of the river, and fetch her in and hide her about two mile below town.

The third night the house was crammed again—and they warn't new- comers this time, but people that was at the show the other two nights. I stood by the duke at the door, and I see that every man that went in had his pockets bulging, or something muffled up under his coat—and I see it warn't no perfumery, neither, not by a long sight. I smelt sickly eggs by the barrel, and rotten cabbages, and such things. And if I know the signs of a dead cat being around, and I bet I do, there was sixty-four of them went in. I shoved in there for a minute, but it was too various for me; I couldn't stand it. Well, when the place couldn't hold no more people the duke, he give a fellow a quarter and told him to tend door for him a minute, and then he started around for the stage door, I after him.

But the minute we turned the corner and was in the dark he says, "Walk fast now till you get away from the houses, and then shin for the raft like the dickens was after you!"

I done it, and he done the same. We struck the raft at the same time, and in less than two seconds we was gliding downstream, all dark and still, and edging toward the middle of the river, nobody saying a word.

I reckoned the poor king was in for a gaudy time of it with the audience, but nothing of the sort. Pretty soon he crawls out from under the wigwam and says, "Well, how'd the old thing pan out this time?" He hadn't been uptown at all.

We never showed a light till we was about ten mile below the village. Then we lit up and had a supper, and the king and the duke fairly laughed their bones loose over the way they'd served them people.

The duke says, "Greenhorns, flatheads! *I* knew the first house would keep mum and let the rest of the town get roped in. And *I* knew they'd lay for us the third night and consider it was *their* turn now. Well, it *is* their turn, and I'd give something to know how much they'd take for it. I *would* just like to know how they're putting in their opportunity. They can turn it into a picnic if they want to—they brought plenty provisions."

Them rapscallions took in four hundred and sixty-five dollars in that three nights. I never see money hauled in by the wagonload like that before.

CHAPTER XIII

Jim in royal robes—They take a passenger
Getting information—Family grief

NEXT day, toward night, we laid up under a little willow towhead out in the middle, where there was a village on each side of the river, and the duke and the king begun to lay out a plan for working them towns. Jim, he spoke to the duke and said he hoped it wouldn't take but a few hours, because it got mighty heavy and tiresome to him when he had to lay all day in the wigwam tied with the rope. You see, when we left him alone we had to tie him, because if anybody happened on to him all by himself and not tied, it wouldn't look much like was a runaway nigger, you know. So the duke said it *was* kind of hard to lay roped all day, and he'd cipher out some way to get around it.

He was uncommon bright, the duke was, and he soon struck it. He dressed Jim up in King Lear's outfit—it was a long curtain-calico gown, and a white horsehair wig and whiskers; and then he took his theater paint and painted Jim's face and hands and ears and neck all over a dead, solid blue, like a man that's been drownded nine days. Blamed if he warn't the horriblest-looking outrage I ever see. Then the duke took and wrote out a sign on a shingle so:

Sick Arab—but harmless when not out of his head.

And he nailed that single to a lath and stood the lath up four or five foot in front of the wigwam. Jim was satisfied. He said it was a sight better than lying tied a couple of years every day, and trembling all over every time there was a sound. The duke told him to make himself free and easy, and if anybody ever come meddling around, he must hop out of the wigwam and carry on a little and fetch a howl or two like a wild beast, and he reckoned they would light out and leave him alone. Which was sound enough judgement; but you take the average man, and he wouldn't wait for him to howl. Why, he didn't only look dead, he looked considerable more than that.

These rapscallions wanted to try the Nonesuch again, because there was so much money in it, but they judged it wouldn't be safe because maybe the news might 'a' worked along down by this time. They couldn't hit no project that suited exactly; so at last the duke said he reckoned he'd lay off and work his brains an hour or two and see if he couldn't put up something on the Arkansaw village; and the king he allowed he would drop over to t'other village without any plan, but just trust in Providence to lead him the profitable way—meaning the devil, I reckon.

We had all bought store clothes where we stopped last; and now the king put his'n on, and he told me to put mine on. I done it, of course. The king's duds was all black, and he did look real swell and starchy. I never knowed how clothes could change a body before. Why, before, he looked like the orneriest old rip that ever was; but now, when he'd take off his new white beaver and make a bow and do a smile, he looked that grand and good and pious that you'd say he had walked right out of the ark, and maybe was old Leviticus himself. Jim cleaned up the canoe, and I got my paddle ready. There was a big steamboat laying at the shore away up under the point, about three mile above the town—been there a couple of hours, taking on freight.

Says the king, "Seein' how I'm dressed, I reckon maybe I better arrive down from St. Louis or Cincinnatti, or some other big place. Go for the steamboat, Huckleberry. We'll come down to the village on her."

I didn't have to be ordered twice to go and take a steamboat ride. I fetched the shore a half a mile above the village and then went scooting along the bluff in the easy water. Pretty soon we come to a nice innocent-looking young country jake setting on a log swabbing the sweat off his face; he had a couple of big carpetbags by him.

"Run her nose inshore", says the king. I done it. "Wher' you bound for, young man?"

"For the steamboat; going to Orleans."

"Git aboard," says the king. "Hold on a minute, my servant'll he'p you with them bags." Meaning me, I see.

I done so, and then we three started on again. The young chap was mighty thankful; said it was tough work toting his baggage such weather. He asked the king where he was going, and the king told him he'd come down the river and landed at the other village this morning, and now he was going up a few mile to see an old friend on a farm up there.

The young fellow says, "When I first see you I says to myself, 'It's Mr. Wilks, sure, and he come mighty near getting here in time.' But then I says again. 'No, I reckon it ain't him, or else he wouldn't be paddling up the river.' You *ain't* him, are you?"

"No, my name's Blodgett–Alexander Blodgett–*Reverend* Alexander Blodgett, I s'pose I must say, as I'm one o' the Lord's poor servants. But still I'm jist as able to be sorry for Mr. Wilks for not arriving in time, all the same, if he's missed anything by it–which I hope he hasn't."

"Well, he don't miss any property by it, because he'll get that all right. But he's missed seeing his brother Peter die–which he mayn't mind, nobody can tell as to that–but his brother would 'a' give anything in this world to see *him* before he died. Never talked about nothing else all these three weeks. Hadn't seen him since they was boys together–and hadn't ever see his brother William at all–that's the deef and dumb one–William ain't more than thirty or thirty-five. Peter and George were the only ones that come out here. George was the married brother; him and his wife both died last year. Harvey and William's the only ones left."

"Din anybody send 'em word?"

"Oh, yes; a month or two ago, when Peter was first took, because Peter said then that he sorter felt like he warn't going to get well this time. You see, he was pretty old, and George's g'yirls was too young to be much company for him, except Mary Jane, the redheaded one. And so he was kinder lonesome after George and his wife died, and didn't seem to care much to live. He most desperately wanted to see Harvey–and William, too, for that matter–because he was one of them kind that can't bear to make a will. He left a letter behind for Harvey, and said he'd told in it where his money was hid and how he wanted the rest of the property divided up so George's g'yirls would be all right–for George didn't leave nothing. And that letter was all they could get him to put a pen to."

"Why do you reckon Harvey don't come? Wher' does he live?"

"Oh, he lives in England–Sheffield–preaches there–hasn't ever been in this country. He hasn't had any too much time–and he mightn't 'a' got the letter at all, you know."

"Too bad, too bad he couldn't 'a' lived to see his brothers, poor soul. You going to Orleans, you say?"

"Yes, but that ain't only a part of it. I'm going in a ship, next Wednesday, for Ryo Janeero, where my uncle lives."

"It's a pretty long journey. But it'll be lovely. I wisht I was a-going. Is Mary Jane the oldest? How old is the others?"

"Mary Jane's nineteen, Susan's fifteen, and Joanna's about fourteen —that's the one that gives herself to good works and has a harelip."

"Poor things! To be left alone in the cold world so."

"Well, they could be worse off. Old Peter had friends, and they ain't going to let them come to no harm. There's Hobson, the Babtis' preacher; and Deacon Lot Hovey, and Ben Rucker, and Abner Shackleford, and Levi Bell, the lawyer, and Dr. Robinson, and their wives, and the widow Bartley, and—well, there's a lot of them; but these are the ones that Peter was thickest with and used to write about sometimes; so Harvey'll know where to look for friends when he gets here."

Well, the old man went on asking questions till he just fairly emptied that young fellow. Blamed if he didn't inquire about everybody and everything in that blessed town, and all about the Wilkses; and about Peter's business—which was a tanner; and about George's—which was a carpenter; and about Harvey's—which was a dissentering minister; and so on, and so on. Then he says, "What did you want to walk all the way up to the steamboat for?"

"Because she's a big Orleans boat, and I was afeared she mightn't stop there. When they're deep they won't stop for a hail. A Cincinnati boat will, but this is a St. Louis one."

"Was Peter Wilks well off?"

"Oh, yes, pretty well off. He had houses and land, and it's reckoned he left three or four thousand in cash hid up som'ers."

"When did you say he died?"

"I didn't say, but it was last night."

"Funeral tomorrow, likely?"

"Yes, 'bout the middle of the day."

"Well, it's all terrible sad; but we've all got to go, one time or another. So what we want to do is to be prepared."

When we struck the boat she was about done loading and pretty soon she got off. The king never said nothing about going aboard, so I lost my ride, after all. When the boat was gone the king made me paddle up a mile to a lonesome place.

Then he got ashore and says, "Now hustle back, right off, and fetch the duke up here, and the new carpetbags. And if he's gone to t'other side, go over there and git him. And tell him to git himself up regardless. Shove along, now."

I see what *he* was up to; but I never said nothing, of course. When I got back with the duke we hid the canoe, and then they set down on a log, and the king told him everything, just like the young fellow had said it—every last word of it. And all the time he was a-doing it he tried to talk like an Englishman; and he done it pretty well, too, for a slouch. I can't imitate him, and so I ain't a-going to try to; but he really done it pretty good. Then he says, "How are you on the deef and dumb, Bilgewater?"

The duke said, leave him alone for that; said he had played a deef and dumb person on the histrionic boards. So then they waited for a steamboat.

About the middle of the afternoon a couple of little boats come along, but they didn't come from high enough up the river. But at last there was a big one, and they hailed her. She sent out her yawl, and we went aboard, and she was from Cincinnati; and when they found we only wanted to go four or five miles they was booming mad, and gave us a cussing, and said they wouldn't land us. But the king was ca'm.

He says, "If gentlemen kin afford to pay a dollar a mile apiece to be took on and put off in a yawl, a steamboat kin afford to carry 'em, can't it?"

So they softened down and said it was all right, and when we got to the village they yawled us ashore. About two dozen men flocked down when they see the yawl a-coming, and when the king says, "Kin any of you gentlemen tell me wher' Mr. Peter Wilks lives?" they give a glance at one another and nodded their heads, as much as to say, "What'd I tell you?"

Then one of them says, kind of soft and gentle, "I'm sorry, sir, but the best we can do is to tell you where he *did* live."

Sudden as winking, the ornery old cretur went all to smash, and fell up against the man, and put his chin on his shoulder, and cried down his back, and says, "Alas, alas, our poor brother—gone, and we never got to see him! Oh, it's too, *too* hard!" And he sobs and moans.

Then he turns around, blubbering, and makes a lot of idiotic signs to the duke on his hands, and blamed if *he* didn't drop a carpet bag and bust out a-crying. If they warn't the beatenest lot, them two frauds, that ever I struck!

Well, the men gathered around and sympathized with them, and said all sorts of kind things to them, and carried their carpetbags up the hill for them, and let them lean on them and cry, and told the king all about his brother's last moments, and the king, he told it all over again on his hands to the duke, and both of them took on about that dead tanner like they'd lost the twelve disciples. It was enough to make a body ashamed of the human race.

CHAPTER XIV

*Is it them?-Singing the "Doxologer"-Awful square-Funeral orgies-
A bad investment*

THE news was all over town in two minutes, and you could see the people tearing down on the run from every which way, some of them putting on their coats as they come. Pretty soon we was in the middle of a crowd, and the noise of the tramping was like a soldier march. The windows and dooryards was full, and every minute somebody would say, over a fence, "Is it *them?*"

And somebody trotting along with the gang would answer back and say, "You bet it is."

When we got to the house the street in front of it was packed, and the three girls was standing in the door. Mary Jane *was* redheaded, but that don't make no difference. She was most awful beautiful, and her face and her eyes was all lit up like glory, she was so glad her uncles was come. The king he spread his arms, and Mary Jane she jumped for them, and the harelip jumped for the duke, and there they *had* it! Everybody, most, leastways women, cried for joy to see them meet again at last and have such good times.

Then the king he hunched the duke private-I see him do it-and then he looked around and see the coffin, over in the corner on two chairs. So then him and the duke, with a hand across each other's shoulder and t'other hand to their eyes, walked slow and solemn over there, everybody dropping back to give them room, and all the talk and noise stopping, people saying "Sh!" and all the men taking their hats off and drooping their heads, so you could 'a' heard a pin fall. And when they got there they bent over and looked in the coffin, and took one sight, and then they bust out a-crying so you could 'a' heard them to Orleans, most. And then they put their arms around each other's necks, and hung their chins over each other's shoulders, and then for three minutes, or maybe four, I never see two men leak the way they done. And, mind you, everybody was doing the same, and the place was that damp I never see anything like it. Then one of them got on one side of the coffin, and t'other on t'other side, and they kneeled down and rested their foreheads on the coffin and let on to pray all to themselves. Well, when it come to that, it worked the crowd like you never see anything like it, and everybody broke down and went to sobbing right out loud-the poor girls, too. And every woman, nearly, went up to the girls without saying a word, and kissed them, solemn, on the forehead, and then put their hand on their head and looked up toward the sky, with the tears running down, and then busted out and went off sobbing and swabbing, and give the next woman a show. I never see anything so disgusting.

Well, by and by the king he gets up and comes forward a little, and works himself up and slobbers out a speech, all full of tears and flapdoodle, about its being a sore trial for him and his poor brother to lose the diseased, and to miss seeing diseased alive after the long journey of four thousand mile, but it's a trial that's sweetened and sanctified to us by this dear sympathy and these holy tears, and so he thanks them out of his heart and out of his brother's heart, because out of their mouths they can't, words being too weak and cold, and all that kind of rot and slush, till it was just sickening; and then he blubbers out a pious goody-goody Amen, and turns himself loose and goes to crying fit to bust.

And the minute the words were out of his mouth somebody over in the crowd struck up the doxolojer, and everybody joined in with all their might, and it just warmed you up and made you feel as good as church letting out. Music *is* a good thing; and after all that soul-butter and hogwash I never see it freshen up things so, and sound so honest and bully.

Then the king begins to work his jaw again, and says how him and his nieces would be glad if a few of the main principal friends of the family would take supper here with them this evening and set up with the ashes of the diseased; and says if his poor brother laying yonder could speak he knows who he would name, for they was names that was very dear to him, and mentioned often in his letters; and so he will name the same, to wit, as follows; viz:–Rev. Mr. Hobson, and Deacon Lot Hovey, and Mr. Ben Rucker, and Abner Shackleford, and Levi Bell, and Dr. Robinson, and their wives, and the widow Bartley.

Rev. Hobson and Dr. Robinson was down to the end of the town a-hunting together– that is, I mean the doctor was shipping a sick man to t'other world and the preacher was pinting him right. Lawyer Bell was away up to Louisville on business. But the rest was on hand, and so they all come and shook hands with the king and thanked him and talked to him. And then they shook hands with the duke and didn't say nothing, but just kept a-smiling and bobbing their heads like a passel of sapheads whilst he made all sorts of signs with his hands and said "Goo-goo–goo-goo-goo" all the time, like a baby that can't talk.

So the king he blattered along, and managed to inquire about pretty much everybody and dog in town, by his name, and mentioned all sorts of little things that happened one time or another in the town, or to George's family, or to Peter. And he always let on that Peter wrote him the things. But that was a lie. He got every blessed one of them out of that young flathead that we canoed up to the steamboat.

Then Mary Jane, she fetched the letter her father left behind, and the king he read it out loud and cried over it. It give the dwellinghouse and three thousand dollars, gold, to the girls. And it give the tanyard (which was doing a good business), along with some other houses and land (worth about seven thousand), and three thousand dollars in gold to Harvey and William, and told where the six thousand cash was hid down cellar. So these two frauds said they'd go and fetch it up, and have everything square and above-board, and told me to come with a candle. We shut the cellar door behind us, and when they found the bag they spilt it out on the floor, and it was a lovely sight, all them yaller-boys. My, the way the king's eyes did shine!

He slaps the duke on the shoulder and says, "Oh, *this* ain't bully nor noth'n! Why, Bilgy, it beats the Nonesuch!"

The duke allowed it did. They pawed the yaller-boys, and sifted them through their fingers and let them jingle down on the floor. The king says, "It ain't no use talkin'; bein' brothers to a rich dead man and representatives of furrin heirs that's got left is the line for you and me, Bilge. This h'yer comes of trust'n to Providence. It's the best way, in the long run. I've tried 'em all, and ther' ain't no better way."

Most everybody would 'a' been satisfied with the pile, and took it on trust; but no, they must count it. So they counts it, and it comes out four hundred and fifteen dollars short. Says the king, "Dern him, I wonder what he done with that four hundred and fifteen dollars?"

They worried over that awhile, and ransacked all around for it. Then the duke says, "Well, he was a pretty sick man, and likely he made a mistake–I reckon that's the way of it. The best way's to let it go, and keep still about it. We can spare it."

"Oh, shucks, yes, we can *spare* it. I don't k'yer nothing 'bout that–it's the *count* I'm thinkin' about. We want to be awful square and open and aboveboard here, you know. We want to lug this h'yer money upstairs and count it before everybody–then ther' ain't noth'n suspicious. But when the dead man says ther's six thous'n dollars, you know, we don't want to–"

"Hold on," says the duke. "Let's make up the deffisit," and he begun to haul out yaller-boys out of his pocket.

"It's a most amaz'n good idea, duke–you *have* go a rattlin' clever head on you," says the king. "Blest if the old Nonesuch ain't a heppin' us out ag'in." And *he* begun to haul out yaller-jackets and stack them up.

It almost busted them but they made up the six thousand clean and clear.

"Say," says the duke, "I got another idea. Le's go upstairs and count this money, and then take and *give it to the girls.*"

"Good land, duke, lemme hug you! It's the most dazzling idea 'at ever a man struck. You have cert'nly got the most astonishin' head I ever see. Oh, this is the boss dodge, ther' ain't no mistake 'bout it. Let 'em fetch along their suspicions now if they want to–this'll lay 'em out."

When we got upstairs everybody gethered around the table, and the king, he counted it and stacked it up, three hundred dollars in a pile–twenty elegant little piles. Everybody looked hungry at it and licked their chops. Then they raked it into the bag again, and I see the king begin to swell himself for another speech.

He says, "Friends all, my poor brother that lays yonder has done generous by them that's left behind in the vale of sorres. He has done generous by these yer poor little lambs that he loved and sheltered, and that's left fatherless and motherless. Yes, and we that knowed him knows that he would 'a' done *more* generous by 'em if he hadn't been afeared o' woundin' his dear William and me. Now, *wouldn't* he? Ther' ain't no question 'bout it in *my* mind. Well, then, what kind o' brothers would it be that'd stand in his way at sech a time? And what kind o' uncles would it be that'd rob —yes, *rob*—sech poor sweet lambs as these 'at he loved so at sech a time? If I know William—and I *think* I do—he—well, I'll jest ask him." He turns around and begins to make a lot of signs to the duke with his hands, and the duke he looks at him stupid and leatherheaded awhile. Then all of a sudden he seems to catch his meaning, and jumps for the king, goo-gooing with all his might for joy, and hugs him about fifteen times before he lets up.

Then the king says, "I knowed it; I reckon *that*'ll convince anybody the way *he* feels about it. Here, Mary Jane, Susan, Joanner, take the money— take it *all*. It's the gift of him that lays yonder, cold but joyful."

Mary Jane she went for him, Susan and the harelip went for the duke, and then such another hugging and kissing I never see yet. And everybody crowded up with the tears in their eyes, and most shook the hands off of them frauds, saying all the time, "You *dear* good souls! How *lovely!* How *could* you!"

Well, then, pretty soon all hands got to talking about the diseased again, and how good he was, and what a loss he was, and all that; and before long a big iron-jawed man worked himself in there from outside and stood a-listening and looking and not saying anything; and nobody saying anything to him either, because the king was talking and they was all busy listening. The king was saying—in the middle of something he'd started in on—

"—they bein' partickler friends o' the diseased. That's why they're in- vited here this evenin'. But tomorrow we want *all* to come—everybody; for he respected everybody, he liked everybody, and so it's fitten that his funeral orgies sh'd be public."

And so he went a-mooning on and on, liking to hear himself talk, and every little while he fetched in his funeral orgies again, till the duke, he couldn't stand it no more. So he writes on a little scrap of paper, "*Ob-sequies*, you old fool," and folds it up, and goes to goo-gooing and reaching it over people's heads to him.

The king, he reads it and puts it in his pocket and says, "Poor William, afflicted as he is, his *heart's* aluz right. Asks me to invite everybody to come to the funeral—wants me to make 'em all welcome. But he needn't 'a' worried—it was jest what I was at."

Then he weaves along again, perfectly ca'm, and goes to dropping in his funeral orgies again every now and then, just like he done before. And when he done it the third time he says, "I say orgies, not because it's the common term, because it ain't—obsequies bein' the common term—but because orgies in the right term. Obsequies ain't used in England no more now—it's gone out. We say orgies now in England. Orgies is better, because it means the thing you're after more exact. It's a word that's made up out'n the Greek *orgo*, outside, open, abroad; and the Hebrew *jeesum*, to plant, cover up; hence in*ter*. So, you see, funeral orgies is an open er public funeral."

He was the *worst* I ever struck. Well, the iron-jawed man he laughed right in his face. Everybody was shocked. Everybody says, "Why, *doctor!*"

And Abner Shackleford says, "Why, Robinson, hain't you heard the news? This is Harvey Wilks."

The king, he smiled eager, and shoved out his flapper, and says, "*Is* it my poor brother's dear good friend and physician? I am—"

"Keep your hands off me!" says the doctor. "*You* talk like an Englishman, *don't* you? It's the worst imitation I ever heard. *You* Peter Wilks's brother! You're a fraud, that's what you are!"

Well, how they all took on! They crowded around the doctor and tried to quiet him down, and tried to explain to him and tell him how Harvey's showed in forty ways that he *was* Harvey, and knowed everybody by name, and the names of the very dogs, and begged and *begged* him not to hurt Harvey's feelings and the poor girls' feelings, and all that. But it warn't no use; he stormed right along, and said any man that pretended to be an Englishman and couldn't imitate the lingo no better than what he did was a fraud and a liar. The poor girls was hanging to the king and crying; and all of a sudden the doctor ups and turns on *them*.

He says, "I was your father's friend, and I'm your friend, and I warn you *as* a friend, and an honest one that wants to protect you and keep you out of harm and trouble, to turn your backs on that scoundrel and have nothing to do with him, the ignorant tramp, with his idiotic Greek and Hebrew, as he calls it. He is the thinnest kind of an impostor—has come here with a lot of empty names and facts which he picked up somewheres; and you take them for *proofs*, and are helped to fool yourselves by these foolish friends here, who ought to know better. Mary Jane Wilks, you know me for your friend, and for your unselfish friend, too. Now listen to me; turn this pitiful rascal out—I *beg* you to do it. Will you?"

Mary Jane straightened herself up, and my, but she was handsome! She says, "*Here* is my answer." She hove up the bag of money and put it in the king's hands, and says, "Take this six thousand dollars and invest for me and my sisters any way you want to and don't give us no receipt for it."

Then she put her arm around the king on one side, and Susan and the harelip done the same on the other. Everybody clapped their hands and stomped on the floor like a perfect storm, whilst the king held up his head and smiled proud.

The doctor says, "All right; I wash *my* hands of the matter. But I warn you all that a time's coming when you're going to feel sick whenever you think of this day."

And away he went.

"All right, doctor," says the king, kinder mocking him. "We'll try and get 'em to send for you." Which made them all laugh, and they said it was a prime good hit.

CHAPTER XV

A pious King–The King's clergy–She asked his pardon–
Hiding in the room–Huck takes the money

WELL, when they was all gone, the king, he asks Mary Jane how they was off for spare rooms, and she said she had one spare room, which would do for Uncle William, and she'd give her own room to Uncle Harvey, which was a little bigger, and she would turn into the room with her sisters and sleep on a cot. And up garret was a little cubby, with a pallet in it. The king said the cubby would do for his valley—meaning me.

So Mary Jane took us up, and she showed them their rooms, which was plain but nice. She said she'd have her frocks and a lot of other traps took out of her room if they was in Uncle Harvey's way, but he said they warn't. The frocks was hung along the wall, and before them was a curtain made out of calico that hung down to the floor. There was an old hair trunk in one corner, and a guitarbox in another, and all sorts of little knickknacks and jim-cracks around, like girls brisken up a room with. The king said it was all the more homely and more pleasanter for these fixings, and so don't disturb them. The duke's room was pretty small, but plenty good enough; so was my cubby.

That night they had a big supper, and all them men and women was there, and I stood behind the king and the duke's chairs and waited on them, and the niggers waited on the rest. Mary Jane she set at the head of the table, with Susan alongside of her, and said how bad the biscuits was, and how mean the preserves was, and how ornery and tough the fried chicken was—and all that kind of rot, the way women always do for to force out compliments. And the people all knowed everything was tiptop, and said so—said "How *do* you get biscuits to brown so nice?" and "Where, for the land's sake, *did* you get these amaz'n pickles?" and all that kind of humbug talky-talk, just the way people always does at a supper, you know.

And when it was all done, me and the harelip had supper in the kitchen off of the leavings, whilst the others was helping the niggers clean up the things. The harelip, she got to pumping me about England, and blest if I didn't think the ice was getting mighty thin sometimes. She says, "Did you ever see the king?"

"Who? William Fourth? Well, I bet I have—he goes to our church."

I knowed he was dead years ago, but I never let on. So when I says he goes to our church, she says, "What—regular?"

"Yes—regular. His pew's right over opposite ourn—on t'other side the pulpit."

"I thought he lived in London?"

"Well, he does. Where *would* he live?"

"But I thought *you* lived in Sheffield?"

I see I was up a stump. I had to let on to get choked with a chicken bone, so as to get time to think how to get down again. Then I says, "I mean he goes to our church regular when he's in Sheffield. That's only in the summertime, when he comes there to take the sea baths."

"Why, how you talk—Sheffield ain't on the sea."

"Well, who said it was?"

"Why, you did."

"I *didn't* nuther."

"You did!"

"I didn't."

"You did."

"I never said nothing of the kind."

"Well, what *did* you say, then?"

"Said he come to take the sea *baths*—that's what I said."

"Well, then, how's he going to take the sea baths if it ain't on the sea?"

"Looky here," I says. "Did you ever see any Congress-water?"

"Yes."

"Well, did you have to go to Congress to get it?"

"Why, no."

"Well, neither does William Fourth have to go to the sea to get a sea bath."

"How does he get it, then?"

"Gets it the way people down here gets Congress-water—in barrels. There in the palace at Sheffield they've got furnaces, and he wants his water hot. They can't bile that amount of water off there at the sea. They haven't got no conveniences for it."

"Oh, I see, now. You might 'a' said that in the first place and saved time."

When she said that, I see I was out of the woods again, and so I was comfortable and glad.

Next she says, "Do you go to church, too?"

"Yes—regular."

"Where do you set?"

"Why, in our pew."

"*Whose* pew?"

"Why, *ourn*—your Uncle Harvey's."

"His'n? What does *he* want with a pew?"

"Wants it to set in. What'd you *reckon* he wanted with it?"

"Why, I thought he'd be in the pulpit."

Rot him, I forgot he was a preacher. I see I was a stump again, so I played another chicken bone and got another think. Then I says, "Blame it, do you suppose there ain't but one preacher to a church?"

"Why, what do they want with more?"

"What! To preach before a king? I never did see such a girl as you. They don't have no less than seventeen."

"Seventeen! My land! Why, I wouldn't set out such a string as that, not if I *never* got to glory. It must take 'em a week."

"Shucks, they don't *all* of 'em preach the same day—only *one* of 'em."

"Well, then, what does the rest of 'em do?"

"Oh, nothing much. Loll around, pass the plate—and one thing or another. But mainly they don't do nothing."

"Well, then, what are they *for?*"

"Why, they're for *style*. Don't you know nothing?"

"Well, I don't *want* to know such foolishness as that. How is servants treated in England? Do they treat 'em better 'n we treat our niggers?"

"No! A servant ain't nobody there. They treat them worse than dogs."

"Don't they give 'em holidays, the way we do, Christmas and New Year's week, and Fourth of July?"

"Oh, just listen! A body could tell *you* hain't ever been to England by that. Why, Hare-l—why, Joanna, they never see a holiday from year's end to year's end; never go to the circus, nor theater, nor nigger shows, nor nowheres."

"Nor church?"

"Nor church."

"But *you* always went to church."

Well, I was gone up again. I forgot I was the old man's servant. But next minute I whirled in on a kind of an explanation how a valley was different from a common servant, and *had* to go to church whether he wanted to or not, and set with the family, on account of its being the law. But I didn't do it good, and when I got done I see she warn't satisfied.

She says, "Honest injun, now, hain't you been telling me a lot of lies?"

"Honest injun," says I.

"None of it at all?"

"None of it at all. Not a lie in it," says I.

"Lay your hand on this book and say it."

I see it warn't nothing but a dictionary, so I laid my hand on it and said it. So then she looked a little better satisfied, and says, "Well, then, I believe some of it; but I hope to gracious if I'll believe the rest."

"What is it you won't believe, Jo?" says Mary Jane, stepping in with Susan behind her. „It ain't right nor kind for you to talk so to him, and him a stranger and so far from his people. How would you like to be treated so?"

"That's always your way, Maim—always sailing in to help somebody before they're hurt. I hain't done nothing to him. He's told some stretchers,

I reckon, and I said I wouldn't swallow it all; and that's every bit and grain I *did* say. I reckon he can stand a little thing like that, can't he?"

"I don't care whether 'twas little or whether 'twas big; he's here in our house and a stranger, and it wasn't good of you to say it. If you was in his place it would make you feel ashamed; and so you oughtn't to say a thing to another person that will make *them* feel ashamed."

"Why, Maim, he said—"

"It don't make no difference what he *said*—that ain't the thing. The thing is for you to treat him *kind*, and not be saying things to make him remember he ain't in his own country and amongst his own folks."

I says to myself, *this* is a girl that I'm letting that old reptile rob her of her money!

Then Susan *she* waltzed in; and if you'll believe me, she did give Harelip hark from the tomb!

Says I to myself, an this is *another* one that I'm letting him rob her of her money!

Then Mary Jane she took another inning, and went in sweet and lovely again—which was her way; but when she got done there warn't hardly anything left o' poor Harelip. So she hollered.

"All right, then," says the other girls. "You just ask his pardon."

She done it, too, and she done it beautiful. She done it so beautiful it was good to hear, and I wished I could tell her a thousand lies, so she could do it again.

I says to myself, this is *another* one that I'm letting him rob her of her money. And when she got through they all jest laid theirselves out to make me feel at home and know I was amongst friends. I felt so ornery and low down and mean that I says to myself, my mind's made up. I'll hive that money for them or bust.

So then I lit out—for bed, I said, meaning some time or another. When I got by myself I went to thinking the thing over. I says to myself, shall I go to that doctor, private, and blow on these frauds? No—that won't do. He might tell who told him; then the king and the duke would make it warm for me. Shall I go, private, and tell Mary Jane? No—I dasn't do it. Her face would give them a hint, sure; they've got the money, and they'd slide right out and get away with it. If she was to fetch help I'd get mixed up in the business before it was done with, I judge.

No, there ain't no good way but one. I got to steal that money, some-how, and I got to steal it some way that they won't suspicion that I done it. They've got a good thing here, and they ain't a-going to leave till they've played this family and this town for all they're worth, so I'll find a chance time enough. I'll steal it and hide it, and by and by, when I'm away down the river, I'll write a letter and tell Mary Jane where it's hid. But I better hive it tonight if I can, because the doctor maybe hasn't let up as much as he lets on he has. He might scare them out of here yet.

So, thinks I, I'll go and search them rooms. Upstairs the hall was dark, but I found the duke's room and started to paw around it with my hands. But I recollected it wouldn't be much like the king to let anybody else take care of that money but his own self. So then I went to his room and begun to paw around there. But I see I couldn't do nothing without a candle, and I dasn't light one, of course. So I judged I'd got to do the other thing-lay for them and eavesdrop.

About that time I hears their footsteps coming, and was going to skip under the bed. I reached for it, but it wasn't where I thought it would be. But I touched the curtain that hid Mary Jane's frocks, so I jumped in behind that and snuggled amongst the gowns and stood perfectly still.

They come in and shut the door, and the first thing the duke done was to get down and look under the bed. Then I was glad I hadn't found the bed when I wanted it. And yet, you know, it's kind of natural to hide under the bed when you are up to anything private.

They sets down then, and the king says, "Well, what is it? And cut it middlin' short, because it's better for us to be down there a-whoopin' up the mournin' than up here givin' 'em a chance to talk us over."

"Well, this is it, Capet. I ain't easy. I ain't comfortable. That doctor lays on my mind. I wanted to know your plans. I've got a notion, and I think it's a sound one."

"What is it, duke?"

"That we better glide out of this before three in the morning, and clip it down the river with what we've got. Specially, seeing we got it so easy—*given* back to us, flung at our heads, as you may say, when of course we allowed to have to steal it back. I'm for knocking off and lighting out."

That made me feel pretty bad. About an hour or two ago it would 'a' been a little different, but now it made me feel bad and disappointed.

The king rips out and says, "What! And not sell out the rest o' the property? March off like a passel of fools and leave eight or nine thous'n dollar's worth o' property layin' around jest sufferin' to be scooped in? And all good, salable stuff, too."

The duke, he grumbled; said the bag of gold was enough, and he didn't want to go no deeper—didn't want to rob a lot of orphans of *everything* they had.

"Why, how you talk!" says the king. "We sha'n't rob 'em of nothing at all but jest this money. The people that *buys* the property in the suff'rers; because as soon 's it's found out 'at we didn't own it—which won't be long after we've slid—the sale won't be valid, and it'll all go back to the estate. These yer orphans'll git their house back ag'in, and that's enough for *them*. They're young and spry and k'n easy earn a livin'. *They* ain't a-goin' to suffer. Why, jest think—there's thous'n's an' thous'n's that ain't so well off. Bless you, *they* ain't got noth'n' to complain of."

Well, the king, he talked him blind. So at last he give in and said all right, but said he believed it was blamed foolishness to stay and that doctor hanging over them.

69

But the king says, "Cuss the doctor! What do we k'yer for *him?* Hain't we got all the fools in town on our side? And ain't that a big enough majority in any town?"

So they got ready to go downstairs again. The duke says, "I don't think we put that money in a good place."

That cheered me up. I'd begun to think I warn't going to get a hint of no kind to help me.

The king says, "Why?"

"Because Mary Jane'll be in mourning from this out, and first you know the nigger that does up the rooms will get an order to box these duds up and put 'em away. And do you reckon a nigger can run across money and not borrow some of it?"

"Your head's level ag'in, duke," says the king. And he comes a-fumbling under the curtain two or three foot from where I was. I stuck to the wall and kept mighty still, though quivery, and I wondered what them fellows would say to me if they catched me. I tried to think what I'd better do if they did catch me. But the king, he got that old bag before I could think more than about a half a thought, and he never suspicioned I was around. They took and shoved the bag through a rip in the straw tick that was under the featherbed, and crammed it in a foot or two amongst the straw and said it was all right now, because a nigger only makes up the featherbed and don't turn over the straw tick only about twice a year, and so it warn't in no danger of getting stole now.

But I knowed better. I had it out of there before they was halfway downstairs. I groped along up to my cubby, and hid it there till I could get a chance to do better. I judged I better hide it outside of the house somewheres, because if they missed it they would give the house a good ransacking; I knowed that very well. Then I turned in, with my clothes all on. But I couldn't 'a' gone to sleep if I'd 'a' wanted to, I was in such a sweat to get through with the business.

By and by I heard the king and the duke come up; so I rolled off my pallet and laid with my chin at the top of my ladder, and waited to see if anything was going to happen. But nothing did.

So I held on till all the late sounds had quit and the early ones hadn't begun yet. And then I slipped down the ladder.

CHAPTER XVI

The funeral–Satisfying curiosity–Suspicious of Huck–
Quick sales and small profits

I CREPT to their doors and listened; they was snoring. So I tiptoed along and got downstairs all right. There warn't a sound anywheres. I peeped through a crack of the dining-room door and see the men that was wat-

70

ching the corpse all sound asleep on their chairs. The door was open into the parlor, where the corpse was laying, and there was a candle in both rooms. I passed along, and the parlor door was open, but I see there warn't nobody in there but the remainders of Peter. So I shoved on by. But the front door was locked, and the key wasn't there.

Just then I heard somebody coming down the stairs behind me. I run in the parlor and took a swift look around, and the only place I see to hide the bag was in the coffin. The lid was shoved along about a foot, showing the dead man's face down in there, with a wet cloth over it, and his shroud on. I tucked the money-bag in under the lid, just down beyond where his hands was crossed, which made me creep, they was so cold, and then I run back across the room and in behind the door.

The person coming was Mary Jane. She went to the coffin, very soft, and kneeled down and looked in. Then she put up her handkerchief, and I see she begun to cry though I couldn't hear her, and her back was to me. I slid out, and as I passed the dining room I thought I'd make sure them watchers hadn't seen me. So I looked through the crack, and everything was all right. They hadn't stirred.

I slipped up to bed, feeling ruther blue, on accounts of the thing playing out that way after I had took so much trouble and run so much resk about it. Says I, if it could stay where it is, all right, because when we got down the river a hundred mile or two I could write to Mary Jane, and she could dig him up again and get in. But that ain't the thing that's going to happen. The thing that's going to happen is, the money'll be found when they come to screw on the lid. Then the king'll get it again, and it'll be a long day before he gives anybody another chance to smouch it from him.

Of course I *wanted* to slide down and get it out of there, but I dasn't try it. Every minute it was getting earlier now, and pretty soon some of them watchers would begin to stir, and I might get catched—catched with six thousand dollars in my hands that nobody had'nt hired me to take care of. I don't wish to be mixed up in no such business as that, I says to myself.

When I got downstairs in the morning the parlor was shut up, and the watchers was gone. There warn't nobody around but the family and the widow Bartley and our tribe. I watched their faces to see if anything had been happening, but I couldn't tell.

Toward the middle of the day the undertaker come with his man, and they set the coffin in the middle of the room on a couple of chairs, and then set all our chairs in rows, and borrowed more from the neighbors till the hall and the parlor and the dining room was full. I see the coffin lid was the way it was before, but I dasn't go to look in under it, with so many folks around.

Then the people begun to flock in, and the beats and the girls took seats in the front row at the head of the coffin, and for a half an hour the people filed around slow, in single rank, and looked down at the dead man's face a minute, and some dropped in a tear, and it was all very still and solemn, only the girls and the beats holding handkerchiefs to their eyes and keeping their heads bent, and sobbing a little. There warn't no other sound but the scraping of the feet on the floor and blowing noses—because people always blows them more at a funeral than they do at other places except church.

When the place was packed full the undertaker, he slid around in his black gloves with his softy soothering ways, putting on the last touches, and getting people and things all shipshape and comfortable, and making no more sound than a cat. He never spoke; he moved people around, he squeezed in late ones, he opened up passageways, and done it with nods and signs with his hands. Then he took his place over against the wall. He was the softest, glidingest, stealthiest man I ever see, and there warn't no more smile to him than there is to a smoked ham.

They had borrowed a melodeum—a sick one; and when everything was ready a young woman set down and worked it, and it was pretty skreeky and colicky, and everybody joined in and sung, and Peter was the only one that had a good thing, according to my notion. Then the Reverend Hobson opened up, slow and solemn, and begun to talk.

Well, the funeral sermon was very good, but pison long and tiresome. And then the king, he shoved in and got off some of his usual rubbage, and at last the job was through, and the undertaker begun to sneak up on the coffin with his screwdriver in his hand.

I was in a sweat then, and watched him pretty keen. But he never meddled at all, just slid the lid along as soft as mush, and screwed it down tight and fast. So there I was! I didn't know whether the money was in there or not. So, says I, s'pose somebody has hogged that bag on the sly? Now how do *I* know whether to write Mary Jane or not? S'pose she dug him up and didn't find nothing, what would she think of me? Blame it, I says, I might get hunted up and jailed. I'd better lay low and keep dark and not write at all. The thing's awful mixed up now. Trying to better it, I've worsened it a hundred times, and I wish to goodness I'd just let it alone, dad fetch the whole business!

They buried him, and we come back home, and I went to watching faces again—I couldn't help it, and I couldn't rest easy. But nothing come of it. The faces didn't tell me nothing.

The king, he visited around in the evening and sweetened everybody up and made himself ever so friendly. And he give out the idea that his congregation over in England would be in a sweat about him, so he must hurry and settle up the estate right away and leave for home. He was very sorry he was so pushed, and so was everybody. They wished he could stay longer, but they said they could see it couldn't be done. And he said of course him and William would take the girls home with them, and that pleased everybody, too, because then the girls would be well fixed and amongst their own relations. It pleased the girls, too—tickled them so they clean forgot they ever had a trouble in the world, and told him to sell out as quick as he wanted to. They would be ready. Them poor things was that glad and happy it made my heart ache to see them getting fooled and lied to so, but I didn't see no safe way for me to chip in and change the general tune.

Well, blamed if the king didn't bill the house and the niggers and all the property for auction straight off—sale two days after the funeral. But anybody could buy private beforehand if they wanted to.

So the next day after the funeral, long about noontime, the girls' joy got the first jolt. A couple of nigger-traders come along, and the king sold them niggers reasonable, for three-days drafts as they called it, and away they went, the two sons up the river to Memphis, and their mother down the river to Orleans. I thought them poor girls and them niggers would break their hearts for grief. They cried around each other and took on so it most made me down sick to see it. The girls said they hadn't ever dreamed of seeing the family separated or sold away from the town. I can't ever get it out of my memory, the sight of them poor miserable girls and niggers hanging around each other's necks and crying. And I reckon I couldn't 'a' stood it all, but would 'a' had to bust out and tell on our gang if I hadn't knowed the sale warn't no account and the niggers would soon be back home.

The thing made a big stir in the town, too, and a good many come out flatfooted and said it was scandalous to separate the mother and the children that way. It injured the frauds some; but the old fool he bulled right along, spite of all the duke could say or do, and I tell you the duke was powerful uneasy.

Next day was auction day. About broad day in the morning the king and the duke come up in the garret and woke me up, and I see by their look that there was trouble.

The king says, "Was you in my room night before last?"

"No, your majesty"—which was the way I always called him when nobody but our gang warn't around.

"Was you in there yisterday er last night?"

"No, your majesty."

"Honor bright, now—no lies."

"Honor bright, your majesty, I'm telling you the truth. I hain't been a-near your room since Miss Mary Jane took you and the duke and showed it to you."

The duke says, "Have you seen anybody else go in there?"

"No, your grace, not as I remember, I believe."

"Stop and think."

I studied awhile and see my chance. Then I says, "Well, I see the niggers go in there several times."

Both of them gave a little jump, and looked like they hadn't ever expected it, and then like they *had*. Then the duke says, "What, *all* of them?"

"No—leastways, not all at once—that is, I don't think I ever see them all come *out* at once but just one time."

"Hello! When was that?"

"It was the day we had the funeral. In the morning. It warn't early, because I overslept. I was just starting down the ladder, and I see them."

"Well, go on, *go* on! What did they do? How'd they act?"

"They didn't do nothing. And they didn't act anyway much, as fur as I see. They tiptoed away; so I seen, easy enough, that they'd shoved in there to do up your majesty's room or something, s'posing you was up, and found you *warn't* up, and so they was hoping to slide out of the way of trouble without waking you up, if they hadn't already waked you up."

"Great guns, *this* is a go!" says the king. And both of them looked pretty sick and tolerable silly. They stood there a-thinking and scratching their heads a minute, and the duke he bust into a kind of a little raspy chuckle and says, "It does beat all how neat the niggers played their hand. They let on to be *sorry* they was going out of this region! And I believed they *was* sorry, and so did you, and so did everybody. Don't ever tell *me* any more that a nigger ain't got any histrionic talent. Why, the way they played that thing it would fool *anybody*. In my opinion, there's a fortune in 'em. If I had capital and a theater, I wouldn't want a better layout than that—and here we've gone and sold 'em for a song. Yes, and ain't privileged to sing the song yet. Say, where *is* that song—that draft?"

"In the bank for to be collected. Where *would* it be?"

"Well, *that's* all right then, thank goodness."

Says I, kind of timidlike, "Is something gone wrong?"

The king whirls on me and rips out, "None o' your business! You keep your head shet and mind y'r own affairs—ifyou got any. Long as you're in this town don't forgit *that*—you hear?" Then he says to the duke, "We got to jest swaller it and say noth'n: mum's the word for *us*."

As they was starting down the ladder the duke he chuckles again and says, "Quick sales *and* small profits!"

The king snarl around on him and says, "I was trying to do for the best in sellin' 'em out so quick. If the profits has turned out to be none, lackin' considerable, and none to carry, is it my fault any more'n it's yourn?"

"Well, *they'd* be in this house yet and we *wouldn't* if I could 'a' got my advice listened to."

The king sassed back as much as was safe for him, and then swapped around and lit into *me* again. He give me down the banks for not coming and *telling* him I see the niggers come out of his room acting that way—said any fool would 'a' *knowed* something was up. And then waltzed in and cussed *himself* awhile, and said it all come of him not laying late and taking his natural rest that morning, and he'd be blamed if he'd ever do it again. So they went off a-jawing; and I felt dreadful glad I'd worked it all off onto the niggers, and yet hadn't done the niggers no harm by it.

CHAPTER XVII

The trip to England—"The brute!"—Mary Jane decides to leave—
Huck parting with Mary Jane—Mumps—The opposition line

By AND BY it was getting-up time. So I come down the ladder and started for downstairs. But as I come to the girls' room the door was open, and I see Mary Jane setting by her old hair trunk, which was open and she'd been packing things in it—getting ready to go to England. But she had stopped now with a folded gown in her lap, and had her face in her hands, crying. I felt awful bad to see it.

I went in there and says, "Miss Mary Jane, you can't a-bear to see people in trouble, and *I* can't. Tell me about it."

So she did, and it was the niggers—I just expected it. She didn't know *how* she was ever going to be happy, knowing the mother and children warn't ever going to see each other no more.

"But they *will*—and inside of two weeks—and I *know* it!"

Laws, it was out before I could think! And before I could budge she throws her arms around my neck and told me to say it *again*, say it *again*, say it *again*!

I see I had spoken too sudden and said too much, and was in a close place. I asked her to let me think a minute; and she set there, very impatient and excited and handsome, but looking kind of happy and eased-up, like a person that's had a tooth pulled out.

So I went to studying it out. I says to myself, I reckon a body that ups and tells the truth when he is in a tight place is taking considerable many resks. But here's a case where I'm blest if it don't look to me like the truth is better an actuly *safer* than a lie. Well, I'm a-going to chance it, though it does seem most like setting down on a kag of powder and touching it off just to see where you'll go to.

Then I says, "Miss Mary Jane, is there any place out of town a little ways where you could go and stay for three or four days?"

"Yes; Mr. Lothrop's. Why?"

"Never mind why yet. If I tell you how I know the niggers will see each other again—inside of two weeks—here in this house—and *prove* how I know it—will you go to Mr. Lothrop's and stay four days?"

"Four days!" she says. "I'll stay a year!"

"All right", I says. "I don't want nothing more out of *you* than just your word—I druther have it than another man's kiss-the Bible." She smiled and reddened up very sweet, and I says, "If you don't mind it, I'll shut the door—and bolt it."

Then I come back and set down again and says, "Don't you holler. Just set still and take it like a man. I got to tell the truth, and it's going to be hard to take, but there ain't no help for it. These uncles of yourn ain't no uncles at all; they're a couple of frauds—regular deadbeats."

It jolted her up like everything, of course. But I was over the shoal water now, so I went right along, her eyes a-blazing higher and higher all the time, and told her every blame thing, from where we first struck that young fool going up to the steamboat, clear through to where she flung herself onto the king's breast at the front door and he kissed her sixteen or seventeen times.

Then up she jumps, with her face afire like sunset, and says, "The brute! Come, don't waste a minute—not a *second*—we'll have them tarred and feathered and flung in the river!"

Says I, "Cert'nly. But do you mean *before* you go to Mr. Lothrop's, or—"

"Oh", she says, "what am I *thinking* about!" she says, and set right down again. "Don't mind what I said—please don't—you *won't*, now, *will* you?" Laying her silky hand on mine in that kind of a way that I said I would die first. "I never thought, I was so stirred up," she says. "Now go on, and I won't do so any more. You tell me what to do, and whatever you say, I'll do it."

"Well,", I says, "it's a rough gang, them two frauds. I'm fixed so I got to travel with them a while longer, whether I want to or not—I druther not tell you why. And if you was to blow on them, this town would get me out of their claws, and *I'd* be all right. But there'd be another person that you don't know about who'd be in big trouble. Well, we got to save *him* hain't we? Of course. Well, then, we won't blow on them."

Saying them words put a good idea in my head. I see how maybe I could get me and Jim rid of the frauds; get them jailed here, and then leave. But I didn't want to run the raft in the daytime without anybody aboard to answer questions but me; so I didn't want the plan to begin working till pretty late tonight.

I says, "Miss Mary Jane, I'll tell you what we'll do, and you won't have to stay at Mr. Lothrop's so long. How fur is it?"

"A little short of four miles—right out in the country."

"Well, that'll answer. Now you go along out there and lay low till nine or half past tonight, and then get them to fetch you home—tell them you've thought of something. If you get here before eleven put a candle in this window, and if I don't turn up wait *till* eleven, and *then* if I don't turn up it means I'm gone and out of the way and safe. Then you come out and spread the news around and get these beats jailed."

"Good", she says. "I'll do it."

"And if it just happens so that I don't get away, but get took up along with them, you must up and say I told you the whole thing beforehand, and you must stand by me all you can then."

"Stand by you! Indeed I will. They sha'n't touch a hair of your head!" she says, and I see her nostrils spread and her eyes snap when she said it, too.

"If I get away I sha'n't be here," I says, "to prove these rapscallions ain't your uncles, and I couldn't do it if I *was* here. I could swear they

76

was beats and bummers, that's all, though that's worth something. Well, there's others can do that better than what I can, and they're people that ain't going to be doubted as quick as I'd be. I'll tell you how to find them. Gimme a pencil and a piece of paper. There–'*Royal Nonesuch, Bricksville.*' Put it away and don't lose it. When the court wants to find out something about these two, let them send up to Bricksville and say they've got the men that played the 'Royal Nonesuch', and ask for some witnesses–why, you'll have the entire town down here before you can hardly wink, Miss Mary. And they'll come a-biling, too, you can bet on that."

I judged we had got everything fixed about right now. So I says, "Just let the auction go right along, and don't worry. Nobody don't have to pay for the things they buy till a whole day after the auction on accounts of the short notice, and they ain't going out of this till they get that money; and the way we've fixed it the sale ain't going to count, and they ain't going to *get* no money. It's just like the way it was with the niggers –it warn't no sale, and the niggers will be back before long. Why, they can't collect the money for the *niggers* yet–they're in the worst kind of a fix, Miss Mary."

"Well," she says, "I'll run down to breakfast now, and then I'll start straight for Mr. Lothrop's."

" 'Deed, *that* ain't the ticket, Miss Mary Jane," I says, "by no manner of means. Go before breakfast."

"Why?"

"What did you reckon I wanted you to go all for, Miss Mary?"

"Well, I never thought–and come to think, I don't know. What was it?"

"Why, it's because you ain't one of the leatherface people. I don't want no better book than what your face is. A body can set down and read it off like coarse print. Do you reckon you can go and face your uncles when they come to kiss you good-morning, and never–"

"There, there, don't! Yes, I'll go before breakfast–I'll be glad to. And leave my sisters with them?"

"Yes; never mind about them. They've got to stand it yet awhile. They might suspicion something if all of you was to go. I don't want you to see them, nor your sisters, nor nobody in this town. If a neighbor was to ask how is your uncles this morning your face would tell something. No, you go right along, Miss Mary Jane, and I'll fix it with all of them. I'll tell Miss Susan to give your love to your uncles and say you've went away for a few hours for to get a little rest and change, or to see a friend, and you'll be back tonight or early tomorrow morning."

"Gone to see a friend is all right, but I won't have my love given to them."

"Well, then, it sha'n't be." It was well enough to tell *her* so–no harm in it. It was only a little thing to do, and no trouble; and it's the little things that smooths people's roads the most, down here below. It would make Mary Jane comfortable, and it wouldn't cost nothing.

Then I says, "There's one more thing–there's that bag of money."

"Well, they're got that, and it makes me feel pretty silly to think *how* they got it."

"No, you're out, there. They hain't got it."

"Why, who's got it?"

"I wished I knowed, but I don't. I *had* it, because I stole it from them, and I stole it to give to you. I know where I hid it, but I'm afraid it ain't there no more. I'm awful sorry, Miss Mary Jane, I'm just as sorry as I can be; but I done the best I could. I did, honest. I come nigh getting caught, and I had to shove it into the first place I come to and run–and it warn't a good place."

"Oh, stop blaming yourself–it's too bad to do it, and I won't allow it –you couldn't help it. It wasn't your fault. Where did you hide it?"

I didn't want to set her to thinking about her troubles again, and I couldn't seem to get my mouth to tell her what would make her see that corpse laying in the coffin with that bag of money on his stomach.

So for a minute I didn't say nothing; then I says, "I'd rather not *tell* you where I put it, Miss Mary Jane, if you don't mind letting me off. But I'll write it for you on a piece of paper, and you can read it along the road to Mr. Lothrop's, if you want to. Do you reckon that'll do?"

So I wrote, "I put it in the coffin. It was in there when you was crying there, away in the night. I was behind the door, and I was mighty sorry for you, Miss Mary Jane."

It made my eyes water a little to remember her crying there all by herself in the night, and them devils laying there right under her own roof, shaming her and robbing her. And when I folded it up and give it to her I see the water come into her eyes, too.

She shook me by the hand, and says, "*Good*-bye. I'm going to do everything just as you've told me; and if I don't ever see you again. I sha'n't ever forget you, and I'll think of you a many and a many a time, and I'll *pray* for you, too!" And she was gone.

Pray for me! I reckoned if she knowed me she'd take a job that was more nearer her size. But I bet she done it, just the same–she was just that kind. She had the grit to pray for Judus if she took the notion–there warn't no back-down to her, I judge. You may say what you want to, but in my opinion she had more sand in her than any girl I ever see; in my opinion she was just full of sand. It sounds like flattery, but it ain't no flattery. And when it comes to beauty–and goodness, too–she lays over them all. I hain't ever seen her since that time that I see her go out of the door. No, I hain't ever seen her since, but I reckon I've thought of her a many and many a million times, and of her saying she would pray for me. And if ever I'd 'a' thought it would do any good for me to pray for *her*, blamed if I wouldn't 'a' done it or busted tryin'.

78

Well, Mary Jane, she lit out the back way, I reckon, because nobody see her go. When I struck Susan and the harelip, I says, "What's the name of them people over on t'other side of the river that you all goes to see sometimes?"

They says, "There's several, but it's the Proctors, mainly."

"That's the name," I says. "I most forgot it. Well, Miss Mary Jane, she told me to tell you she's gone over there in a dreadful hurry—one of them's sick."

"Which one?"

"I don't know; leastways, I kinder forgot, but I think it's—"

"Sakes alive, I hope it ain't *Hanner*?"

"I'm sorry to say it," I says, "but Hanner's the very one."

"My goodness, and she so well only last week! Is she took very bad?"

"It ain't no name for it. They set up with her all night, Miss Mary Jane said, and they don't think she'll last many more hours."

"Only think of that, now! What's the matter with her?"

I couldn't think of anything reasonable, right off that way, so I says, "Mumps."

"Mumps your granny! They don't set up with people that's got the mumps."

"They don't, don't they? You better bet they do with *these* mumps. These mumps is different. It's a new kind, Miss Mary Jane said."

"How's it a new kind?"

"Because it's mixed up with other things."

"What other things?"

"Well, measles and whooping cough and erysiplas and consumption and yaller janders and brain fever and I don't know what all."

"My land! And they call it the *mumps*?"

"That's what Miss Mary Jane said."

"Well, what in the nation do they call it the *mumps* for?"

"Why, because it *is* the mumps. That's what it starts with."

"Well, ther' ain't no sense in it. A body might stump his toe and take pison and fall down the well and break his neck and bust his brains out, and somebody come along and ask what killed him, and some numskull up and say. 'Why, he stumped his *toe*.' Would ther' be any sense in that? *No*. And ther' ain't no sense in *this*, nuther. Is it ketching?"

"Is it *ketching*? Why, how you talk. Is a *harrow* catching—in the dark? If you don't hitch on to one tooth, you're bound to on another, ain't you? And you can't get away with that tooth without fetching the whole harrow along, can you? Well, these kind of mumps is a kind of a harrow, as you may say—and it ain't no slouch of a harrow, nuther, you come to get it hitched on good."

"Well, it's awful, *I* think', says the harelip. "I'll go to Uncle Harvey and—"

"Oh, yes", I says, "I *would*. Of *course* I would. I wouldn't lose no time."

"Well, why wouldn't you?"

"Just look at it a minute and maybe you can see. Hain't your uncles obleeged to get along home to England as fast as they can? And do you reckon they'd be mean enough to go off and leave you to go all that journey by yourselves? *You* know they'll wait for you. So fur, so good. Your Uncle Harvey's a preacher, ain't he? Very well, then; is a *preacher* going to deceive a steamboat clerk? Is he going to deceive a *ship clerk*? So as to get them to let Miss Mary Jane go aboard? Now *you* know he ain't. What *will* he do, then? Why, he'll say, It's a great pity, but my church matters has got to get along the best way they can; for my niece has been exposed to the dreadful pluribus-unum mumps, and so it's my bounden duty to set down here and wait the three months it takes to show on her if she's got it.' But never mind, if you think it's best to tell your uncle Harvey—"

"Shucks, and stay fooling around here when we could all be having good times in England whilst we was waiting to find out whether Mary Jane's got it or not? Why, you talk like a muggins."

"Well, maybe you'd better tell some of the neighbors."

"Listen at that, now. You do beat all for natural stupidity. Can't you *see* that *they'd* go and tell? Ther' ain't no way but just to not tell anybody at *all*."

"Well, maybe you're right—yes, I judge you *are* right."

"But I reckon we ought to tell Uncle Harvey she's gone out awhile, anyway, so he won't be uneasy about her?"

"Yes, Miss Mary Jane, she wanted you to do that. She says, 'Tell them to give Uncle Harvey and William my love and a kiss, and say I've run over the river to see Mr.'—Mr.—what *is* the name of that rich family your uncle Peter used to think so much of? I mean the one that—"

"Why, you must mean the Apthorps, ain't it?"

"Of course. Bother them kind of names, a body can't ever seem to remember them half the time, somehow. Yes, she said, she has run over for to ask the Apthorps to be sure and come to the auction and buy this house, because she allowed her uncle Peter would ruther they had it than anybody; and she's going to stick to them till they say they'll come, and then, if she ain't too tired, she's coming home; and if she is, she'll be home in the morning anyway. She said, don't say nothing about the Proctors, but only about the Apthorps—which'll be perfectly true, because she *is* going there to speak about their buying the house; I know it, because she told me so herself."

"All right", they said, and cleared out to lay for their uncles and give them love and the kisses and tell them the message.

Everything was all right now. The girls wouldn't say nothing because they wanted to go to England; and the king and the duke would ruther Mary Jane was off working for the auction than around in reach of Doctor Robinson. I felt very good; I judged I had done it pretty neat—I reckoned Tom Sawyer couldn't 'a' done it no neater himself. Of course he would 'a' throwed more style into it, but I can't do that very handy, not being brung up to it.

Well, they held the auction in the public square along toward the end of the afternoon, and it strung along and strung along, and the old man, he was on hand and looking his level pisonest, up there long-side of the auctioneer, and chipping in a little Scripture now and then, or a little goody-goody saying of some kind, and the duke he was around goo-gooing for sympathy all he knowed how and just spreading himself generly.

But by and by the thing dragged through, and everything was sold—everything but a little old trifling lot in the graveyard. So they'd got to work *that* off—I never see such a girafft as the king was for wanting to swallow *everything*. Well, whilst they was at it a steamboat landed, and in about two minutes up comes a crowd a-whooping and yelling and laughing and carrying on, and singing out:

"*Here's* your opposition line! Here's your two sets o' heirs to old Peter Wilks—and you pays your money and you takes your choice!"

CHAPTER XVIII

Contested relationship—The King explains the loss—
A question of handwriting—Digging up the corpse—Huck escapes

THEY was fetching a very nice-looking old gentleman along, and a nice-looking younger one, with his right arm in a sling. And, my souls, how the people yelled and laughed, and kept it up.

But I didn't see no joke about it, and I judged it would strain the duke and the king some to see any. I reckoned they'd turn pale. But no, nary a pale did *they* turn. The duke he never let on he suspicioned what was up, but just went a goo-gooing around, happy and satisfied, like a jug that's googling out buttermilk; and as for the king, he just gazed and gazed down sorrowful on them newcomers like it give him the stomach-ache in his very heart to think there could be such frauds and rascals in the world. Oh, he done it admirable.

Lots of the principal people gethered around the king to let him see they was on his side. That old gentleman that had just come looked all puzzled to death. Pretty soon he begun to speak, and I see straight off he pronounced *like* an Englishman—not the king's way, though the king's *was* pretty good for an imitation. I can't give the old gent's words, nor I can't imitate him; but he turned around to the crowd and says about like this, "This is a surprise to me which I wasn't looking for, and I'll acknowledge, candid and frank, I ain't very well fixed to meet it and answer it. For my brother and me has had misfortunes; he's broke his arm, and our baggage got put off at the town above here last night in the night by some mistake.

"I am Peter Wilk's brother Harvey, and this is his brother William, which can't hear nor speak—and can't even make signs to amount to much, now he's only got one hand to work them with. We are who we say we are, and in a day or two, when I get the baggage, I can prove it. But up till then I won't say nothing more, but go to the hotel and wait."

So him and the new dummy started off, and the king he laughs and blethers out, "Broke his arm—*very* likely, *ain't it?* And very convenient, too, for a fraud that's got to make signs, and ain't learnt how. Lost their baggage! That's *mighty* good! And mighty ingenious, under the *circumstances!*"

So he laughed again, and so did everybody else, except three or four, or maybe half a dozen. One of these was the doctor; another one was a sharp-looking gentleman with a carpetbag of the old-fashioned kind made out of carpet-stuff, that had just come off the steamboat and was talking to him in a low voice, and glancing toward the king now and then and nodding his head. It was Levi Bell, the lawyer that was gone up to Louisville. Another one was a big, rough husky that come along and listened to all the old gentleman said, and was listening to the king now. And when the king got done, this husky up and says, "Say, looky here, if you are Harvey Wilks, when'd you come to this town?"

"The day before the funeral, friend," said the king.

"But what time o' day?"

"In the evenin'—'bout an hour er two before sundown."

"How'd you come?"

"I come down on the *Susan Powell* from Cincinnati."

"Well, then, how'd you come to be up at the Pint in the *mornin'*—in a canoe?"

"I warn't up at the Pint in the mornin'."

"It's a lie."

Several of them jumped for him and begged him not to talk that way to an old man and a preacher.

"Preacher be hanged, he's a fraud and a liar. He was up at the Pint that mornin'. I live up there, don't I? Well, I was up there, and he was up there. I *see* him there. He come in a canoe, along with Tim Collins and a boy."

The doctor, he up and says, "Would you know the boy again if you was to see him, Hines?"

"I reckon I would, but I don't know. Why, yonder he is, now. I know him perfectly easy."

It was me he pointed at.

The doctor says, "Neighbors, I don't know whether the new couple is frauds or not; but if *these* two ain't frauds, I am an idiot, that's all. I think it's our duty to see that they don't get away from here till we've looked into this thing. Come along, Hines. Come along, the rest of you. We'll take these fellows to the tavern and affront them with t'other couple, and I reckon we'll find out *something* before we get through."

It was nuts for the crowd, though maybe not for the king's friends; so we all started. It was about sundown. The doctor, he led me along by the hand and was plenty kind enough, but he never let *go* my hand.

We all got in a big room in the hotel and lit up some candles and fetched in the new couple.

First, the doctor says, "I don't wish to be too hard on these two men, but *I* think they're frauds, and they may have complices that we don't know nothing about. If they have, won't the complices get away with that bag of gold Peter Wilks left? It ain't unlikely. If these men ain't frauds, they won't object to sending for that money and letting us keep it till they prove they're all right—ain't that so?"

Everybody agreed to that. So I judged they had our gang in a pretty tight place right at the outstart.

But the king he only looked sorrowful and says, "Gentlemen, I wish the money was there, for I ain't got no disposition to throw anything in the way of a fair, open, out-and-out investigation o' this misable business. But, alas, the money ain't there. You k'n send and see, if you want to."

"Where is it, then?"

"Well, when my niece give it to me to keep for her, I took and hid it inside o' the straw tick o' my bed, not wishin' to bank it for the few days we'd be here, and considerin' the bed a safe place, we not bein' used to niggers, and suppos'n' 'em honest, like servants in England. The niggers stole in the very next mornin' after I had went downstairs; and when I sold 'em I hadn't missed the money yit, so they got clean away with it. My servant k'n tell you 'bout it, gentlemen."

The doctor and several said "Shucks!" and I see nobody didn't altogether believe him. One man asked me if I see the niggers steal it. I said no, but I see them sneaking out of the room and hustling away, and I never thought nothing, only I reckoned they was afraid they had waked up my master and was trying to get away before he made trouble with them. That was all they asked me.

Then the doctor whirls on me and snaps out, "Are *you* English, too?"

I says yes, and him and some others laughed to each other and said, "Stuff!"

Well, then they sailed in on the general investigation, and there we had it, up and down, hour in, hour out, and nobody never said a word about supper, nor ever seemed to think about it—and so they kept it up and kept it up; and it *was* the worst mixed-up thing you ever see. They made the king tell his yarn, and they made the old gentleman tell his'n; and anybody but a lot of prejudiced chuckleheads would 'a' *seen* that the old gentleman was spinning truth and t'other one lies. By and by they had me up to tell what I knowed.

The king, he give me a left-handed look out of the corner of his eye, and so I knowed enough to talk on the right side. I begun to tell about Sheffield and how we lived there and all about the English Wilkses and so on, but I didn't get pretty fur till the doctor begun to laugh.

Levi Bell, the lawyer, says, "Set down, my boy. I wouldn't strain myself if I was you. I reckon you ain't used to lying, it don't seem to come handy. What you want is practice. You do it pretty awkward."

I didn't care nothing for the compliment, but I was glad to be let off, anyway.

The doctor, he started to say something, and turns and says, "If you'd been in town at first, Levi Bell—"

The king broke in and reached out his hand and says, "Why, is this my poor dead brother's old friend that he's wrote so often about?"

The lawyer and him shook hands, and the lawyer smiled and looked pleased, and they talked right along awhile, and then got to one side and talked low. At last the lawyer speaks up and says, "That'll fix it. I'll take the order and send it, along with your brother's, and then they'll know it's all right."

So they got some paper and a pen, and the king, he set down and twisted his head to one side, and chawed his tongue, and scrawled off something. Then they give the pen to the duke—and then for the first time the duke looked sick. But he took the pen and wrote. So then the lawyer turns to the new old gentleman and says, "You and your brother please write a line or two and sign your names."

The old gentleman wrote, but nobody couldn't read it.

The lawyer looked powerful astonished and says, "Well, it beats *me*"—and snaked a lot of old letters out of his pocket and examined them, and then examined the old man's writing carefully, and then *them* again.

Then he says, "These old letters is from Harvey Wilks, and here's *these* two handwritings, and anybody can see *they* didn't write them (the king and the duke looked sold and foolish, I tell you, to see how the lawyer took them in) "and here's *this* old gentleman's handwriting, and anybody can tell, easy enough, *he* didn't write them—fact is, the scratches he makes ain't properly *writing* at all. Now, here's some letters from—"

The new old gentleman says, "If you please, let me explain. Nobody can read my hand but my brother there—so he copies for me. It's *his* hand you've got there, not mine."

"*Well!*" says the lawyer. "This *is* a state of things. I've got some of William's letters, too. So if you'll get him to write a line or so we can com—"

"He *can't* write with his left hand," says the old gentleman. "If he could use his right hand, you would see that he wrote his own letters and mine, too. Look at both, please—they're by the same hand."

The lawyer done it and says, "I believe it's so—and if it ain't so, there's a heap stronger resemblance than I'd noticed before, anyway. Well, well,

well! I thought we was right on the track of a solution, but it's gone to grass, partly, But anyway, *one* thing is proved-*these* two ain't either of 'em Wilkses!" And he wagged his head toward the king and the duke.

Well, what do you think? That mule-headed old fool wouldn't give in *then!* Indeed he wouldn't. Said it warn't no fair test. Said his brother William was the cussedest joker in the world, and hadn't *tried* to write—he see William was going to play one of his jokes the minute he put the pen to paper. And so he warmed up and went warbling right along till he was actually beginning to believe what he was saying *himself.*

But pretty soon the new gentleman broke in and says, "I've thought of something. Is there anybody here that helped to lay out my br–helped to lay out the late Peter Wilks for burying?"

"Yes," says somebody. "Me and Ab Turner done it. We're both here."

Then the old man turns toward the king and says, "Perhaps this gentleman can tell me what was tattooed on his breast?"

Blamed if the king didn't have to brace up mighty quick, or he'd 'a' squshed down like a bluff bank that the river has cut under, it took him so sudden; and, mind you, it was a thing that was calculated to make most *anybody* sqush to get fetched such a solid one as that without any notice, because how was *he* to know what was tattooed on the man? He whitened a little; he couldn't help it. And it was mighty still in there, and everybody bending a little forwards and gazing at him. Says I to myself, *Now* he'll throw up the sponge—there ain't no more use. Well, did he? A body can't hardly believe it, but he didn't. I reckon he thought he'd keep the thing up till he tired them people out, so they'd thin out, and him and the duke could break loose and get away.

Anyway, he set there, and pretty soon he begun to smile, and says, "Mf! It's a *very* tough question, *ain't* it! Yes, sir, I k'n tell you what's tattooed on his breast. It's jest a small, thin, blue arrow–that's what it is; and if you don't look clost, you can't see it. *Now* what do you say–hey?"

Well, *I* never see anything like that old blister for clean out-and-out cheek.

The new old gentleman turns brisk toward Ab Turner and his pard, and his eye lights up like he judged he'd got the king *this* time, and he says, "There–you've heard what he said! Was there any such mark on Peter Wilks's breast?"

Both of them spoke up and says, "We didn't see no such mark on him."

"Good!" says the old gentleman. "Now, what you *did* see on his breast was a small dim P, and a B (which is an initial he dropped when he was young), and a W, and dashes between them, so: P–B–W"–and he marked them that way on a piece of paper. "Come, ain't that what you saw?"

Both of them spoke up again and says, "No- we *didn't*. We never seen any marks at all."

Well, everybody *was* in a state of mind now, and they sings out, "The whole *bilin'* of 'm 's frauds! Le's duck 'em! Le's drown 'em! Le's ride 'em

85

on a rail!" and everybody was whooping at once, and there was a rattling powwow.

But the lawyer he jumps on the table and yells and says, "Gentlemen—gentle*men!* Hear me just a word—just a *single* word—if you PLEASE! There's one way yet—let's dig up the corpse and look."

That took them.

"Hooray!" they all shouted, and was starting right off. But the lawyer and the doctor sung out, "Hold on, hold on! Collar all these four men and the boy and fetch *them* along, too!"

"We'll do it!" they all shouted. "And if we don't find them marks we'll lynch the whole gang!"

I *was* scared, now, I tell you. But there warn't no getting away, you know. They gripped us all and marched us right along, straight for the graveyard, which was a mile and a half down the river, and the whole town at our heels, for we made noise enough, and it was only nine in the evening.

As we went by our house I wished I hadn't sent Mary Jane out of town; because now if I could tip her the wink she'd light out and save me, and blow on our deadbeats.

Well, we swarmed along down the river road, just carrying on like wildcats; and to make it more scary the sky was darking up, and the lightning beginning to wink and flitter, and the wind to shiver amongst the leaves. This was the most awful trouble and most dangersome I ever was in, and I was kinder stunned; everything was going so different from what I had allowed for. Stead of being fixed so I could take my own time if I wanted to, and see all the fun, and have Mary Jane at my back to save me and set me free when the close-fit come, here was nothing in the world betwixt me and sudden death but just them tattoo-marks. If they didn't find them—

I couldn't bear to think about it, and yet, somehow, I couldn't think about nothing else. It got darker and darker, and it was a beautiful time to give the crowd the slip, but that big husky, had me by the wrist—Hines—and a body might as well try to give Goliar the slip. He dragged me right along, he was so excited, and I had to run to keep up.

When they got there they swarmed into the graveyard and washed over it like an overflow. And when they got to the grave they found they had about a hundred times as many shovels as they wanted, but nobody hadn't thought to fetch a lantern. But they sailed into digging anyway by the flicker of the lightning, and sent a man to the nearest house, a half a mile off, to borrow one.

So they dug and dug like everything; and it got awful dark, and the rain started, and the wind swished and swushed along, and the lightning come brisker and brisker, and the thunder boomed. But them people never took no notice of it, they was so full of this business. One minute you could see everything and every face in that big crowd and the shovelfuls of dirt sailing up out of the grave, and the next second the dark wiped it all out, and you couldn't see nothing at all.

At last they got out the coffin and begun to unscrew the lid, and then such another crowding and shouldering and shoving as there was, to scrouge in and get a sight, you never see; and in the dark, that way, it was awful. Hines, he hurt my wrist dreadful pulling and tugging so, and I reckon he clean forgot I was in the world, he was so excited and panting.

All of a sudden the lightning let go a perfect sluice of white glare and somebody sings out, "By the living jingo, here's the bag of gold on his breast!"

Hines let out a whoop, like everybody else, and dropped my wrist and gave a big surge to bust his way and get a look, and the way I lit out and shinned for the road in the dark there ain't nobody can tell.

I had the road all to myself, and fairly flew—leastways, I had it all to myself except the solid dark, and the now-and-then glares, and the buzzing of the rain, and the thrashing of the wind, and the splitting of the thunder; and sure as you are born I did clip it along!

When I struck the town, I see there warn't nobody out in the storm, so I never hunted for no back streets, but humped it straight through the main one; and when I begun to get toward our house I aimed my eye and set it. No light there; the house all dark—which made me feel sorry and disappointed, I didn't know why. But at last, just as I was sailing by, *flash* comes the light in Mary Jane's window! And my heart swelled up sudden, like to bust; and the same second the house and all was behind me in the dark, and wasn't ever going to be before me no more in this world. She *was* the best girl I ever see, and had the most sand.

The minute I was far enough above the town to see I could make the towhead, I begun to look sharp for a boat to borrow, and the first time the lightning showed me one that wasn't chained I snatched it and shoved. It was a canoe and warn't fastened with nothing but a rope. The towhead was a rattling big distance off, away out there in the middle of the river, but I didn't lose no time; and when I struck the raft at last I was so fagged I would 'a' just laid down to blow and gasp if I could afforded it. But I didn't.

As I sprung aboard I sung out, "Out with you, Jim, and set her loose! Glory be to goodness, we're shut of them!"

Jim lit out, and was a-coming for me with both arms spread, he was so full of joy. But when I glimpsed him in the lightning my heart shot up in my mouth and I went overboard backwards; for I forgot he was old King Lear and a drownded A-rab all in one, and it most scared the livers and lights out of me. But Jim fished me out and was going to hug me and bless me and so on, he was so glad I was back and we was shut of the king and the duke.

But I says, "Not now! Have it for breakfast, have it for breakfast! Cut loose and let her slide!"

So in two seconds away we went a-sliding down the river, and it *did* seem good to be free again and all by ourselves on the big river and nobody to bother us. I had to skip around a bit and jump up and crack my heels a few times—I couldn't help it. But about the third crack I noticed a sound that I knowed mighty well, and held my breath and listened and waited. And sure enough, when the next flash busted out over the water, here they come! And just a-laying to their oars and making their skiff hum! It was the king and the duke.

So I wilted right down onto the planks then and give up, and it was all I could do to keep from crying.

CHAPTER XIX

The King went for him—A royal row—Powerful mellow

WHEN they got aboard, the king went for me and shook me by the collar and says, "Tryin' to give us the slip, was ye, you pup! Tired of our company, hey?"

I says, "No, your majesty, we warn't—*please* don't, your majesty!"

"Quick, then, and tell us what *was* your idea, or I'll shake the insides out o' you!"

"Honest, I'll tell you everything just as it happened, your majesty. The man that had a-holt of me was very good to me, and kept saying he had a boy about as big as me that died last year, and he was sorry to see a boy in such a dangerous fix. And when they was all took by surprise by finding the gold, and made a rush for the coffin, he lets go of me and whispers, 'Heel it now, or they'll hang ye, sure!' And I lit out of there.

"It wasn't no good for *me* to stay—*I* couldn't do nothing, and I didn't want to be hung if I could get away. So I never stopped running till I found the canoe. And when I got here I told Jim to hurry, or they'd catch me and hang me yet, and said I was afeared you and the duke wasn't alive now, and I was awful sorry, and so was Jim, and we was both awful glad when we see you coming; you may ask Jim if I didn't tell him that."

Jim said it was so; and the king told him to shut up, and said, "Oh, yes, it's *mighty* likely!" And shook me up again and said he reckoned he'd drownd me. But the duke says, "Leggo the boy, you old idiot! Would *you* 'a' done any different? Did you inquire around for *him* when you got loose? *I* don't remember it."

So the king let go of me and begun to cuss that town and everybody in it. But the duke says:

"You better a blame' sight give *yourself* a good cussing, for you're the one that's entitled to it most. You hain't done a thing from the start that had any sense in it, except coming out so cool and cheeky with that imaginary blue-arrow mark tattooed on the corpse.

"That *was* bright—it was right-down bully, and was the thing that saved us. For if it hadn't been for that they'd 'a' jailed us till them Englishmen's baggage come—and then—the penitentiary, you bet! But that trick took 'em to the graveyard, and the gold done us a bigger kindness; for if the excited fools hadn't let go all holts and made that rush to get a look we'd 'a' slept in our cravats tonight—cravats warranted to *wear*, too—longer than *we'd* need 'em."

They was still a minute—thinking. Then the king says, kind of absent-minded like, "Mf! And we reckoned the *niggers* stole it!"

That made me squirm!

"Yes," says the duke, kinder slow and deliberate and sarcastic, *"we* did."

After about a half a minute the king drawls out, "Leastways, *I* did."

The duke says, the same way, "On the contrary, *I* did."

The king kind of ruffles up and says, "Looky here, Bilgewater, what'r you referrin' to?"

The duke says, pretty brisk, "When it comes to that, maybe you'll let me ask what was *you* referring to?"

"Shucks!" said the king, very sarcastic. "But *I* don't know—maybe you was asleep and didn't know what you was about."

The duke bristles up now and says, "Oh, let *up* on this cussed nonsense. Do you take me for a blame' fool? Don't you reckon *I* know who hid that money in that coffin?"

"*Yes*, sir! I know you *do* know, because you done it yourself!"

"It's a lie!" And the duke went for him.

The king sings out, "Take y'r hands off—leggo my throat! I take it all back!"

The duke says, "Well, you just own up, first, that you *did* hide that money there, intending to give me the slip one of these days and come back and dig it up and have it all to yourself."

"Wait jest a minute, duke—answer me this one question, honest and fair. If you didn't put the money there, say it, and I'll b'lieve you and take back everything I said."

"You old scoundrel, I didn't, and you just know I didn't. There now!"

"Well, then, I b'lieve you. But answer me only jest this one more—now *don't* git mad. Didn't you have it in your *mind* to hook the money and hide it?"

The duke never said nothing for a little bit. Then he says, "Well, I don't care if I *did*, I didn't *do* it, anyway. But you not only had it in mind to do it, but you *done* it."

"I wisht I never die if I done it, duke, and that's honest. I won't say I warn't *goin'* to do it, because I *was*. But you—I mean somebody—got in ahead o' me."

"It's a lie! You done it, and you got to *say* you done it, or—"

The king began to gurgle, and then gasps out, " 'Nough!—I *own up!*"

I was very glad to hear him say that; it made me feel much more easier than what I was feeling before.

So the duke took his hands off and says, "If you ever deny it again, I'll drown you. It's *well* for you to set there and blubber like a baby—it's fitten for you, after the way you've acted. I never see such an old ostrich for wanting to gobble everything—and I a-trusting you all the time, like you was my own father. You ought to be ashamed of yourself to stand by and hear it saddled on to a lot of poor niggers, and you never say a word for 'em. It makes me feel ridiculous to think I was soft enough to *believe* that rubbage. Cuss you, I can see now why you was so anxious to make up the deffersit—you wanted to get what money I'd got out of the 'Nonesuch' and one thing or another, and scoop it *all!*"

The king says, timid, and still a-snuffling, "Why, duke, it was you that said make up the deffersit. It warn't me."

"Dry up! I don't want to hear no more *out* of you!" said the duke. "And *now* you see what you *got* by it. They've got all their own money back, and all of *ourn* but a shekel or two *besides*.

"G'long to bed and don't you deffersit *me* no more deffersits, long's *you* live!"

So the king sneaked into the wigwam and took to his bottle for comfort, and before long the duke tackled *his* bottle; and so in about a half an hour they was as thick as thieves again, and the tighter they got the lovinger they got, and went off a-snoring in each other's arms. They both got powerful mellow, but I noticed the king didn't get mellow enough to forget to remember to not deny about hiding the money-bag again. That made me feel easy and satisfied.

Of course when they got to snoring we had a long gabble, and I told Jim everything.

CHAPTER XX

Ominous plans—News from Jim—Old recollections—
A sheep story—Valuable information

WE DASN'T stop again at any town for days and days; kept right along down the river. We was down south in the warm weather now, and a mighty long ways from home. We begun to come to trees with Spanish moss on them, hanging down from the limbs like long, gray beards. It was the first I ever see it growing, and it made the woods look solemn and dismal. So now the frauds reckoned they was out of danger, and they begun to work the villages again.

First they done a lecture on temperance, but they didn't make enough for them both to get drunk on. Then in another village they started a dancing school, but they didn't know no more how to dance than a kangaroo does; so the first prance they made the general public jumped in and pranced them out of town. Another time they tried to go at yellocution, but they didn't yellocute long till the audience got up and give them a solid good cussing and made them skip out. They tackled missionarying and mesmerizing and doctoring and telling fortunes and a little of everything; but they couldn't seem to have no luck. So at last they got just about dead broke and laid around the raft as she floated along, thinking and thinking, and never saying nothing, by the half a day a time, and dreadful blue and desperate.

And at last they took a change and begun to lay their heads together in the wigwam and talk low and confidential two or three hours at a time. Jim and me got uneasy. We didn't like the look of it. We judged they was studying up some kind of worse deviltry than ever. We turned it over and over and at last we made up our minds they was going to break into somebody's house or store, or was going into the counterfeiting business or something. So then we was pretty scared and made up an agreement that we wouldn't have nothing in the world to do with such actions, and if we ever got the least show we would give them the cold shake and clear out and leave them behind.

Well, early one morning we hid the raft in a good, safe place about two mile below a little bit of a shabby village named Pikesville, and the king, he went ashore and told us all to stay hid while he went up to town and smelt around to see whether anybody had got any wind of the "Royal Nonesuch" there yet.

"To find a house to rob, you *mean*," thinks I. "And when you get through robbing it, you'll come back here and wonder what has become of me and Jim and the raft—and you'll have to take it out in wondering."

And he said if he warn't back by midday the duke and me would know it was all right, and we was to come along.

So we stayed where we was. The duke, he fretted and sweated around and was in a mighty sour way. He scolded us for everything, and we couldn't seem to do nothing right; he found fault with every little thing. Something was a-brewing, sure. I was good and glad when midday come and no king. We could have an change, anyway—and maybe a chance for *the* change on top of it. So me and the duke went up to the village and hunted around there for the king, and by and by we found him in the back room of a little low doggery, very tight, and a lot of loafers bullyragging him for sport, and he a-cussing and a-threatening with all his might, and so tight he couldn't walk and couldn't do nothing to them.

The duke, he begun to abuse him for an old fool, and the king begun to sass back, and the minute they was fairly at it I lit out and shook the reefs out of my hind legs and spun down the river road like a deer, for I see our chance. And I made up my mind that it would be a long day before they ever see me and Jim again.

I got down there all out of breath but loaded up with joy, and sung out, "Set her loose, Jim! We're all right now!"

But there warn't no answer, and nobody come out of the wigwam.

Jim was gone! I set up a shout–and then another–and then another one; and run this way and that in the woods, whooping and screeching. But it warn't no use–old Jim was gone. Then I set down and cried; I couldn't help it. But I couldn't set still long. Pretty soon I went out on the road, trying to think what I better do, and I run across a boy walking and asked him if he'd seen a strange nigger dressed so and so, and he says, "Yes."

"Whereabouts?" says I.

"Down to Silas Phelps's place, two mile below here. He's a runaway nigger, and they've got him. Was you looking for him?"

"You bet I ain't! I run across him in the woods about an hour or two ago, and he said if I hollered he'd cut my livers out–and told me to lay down and stay where I was, and I done it. Been there ever since, afeared to come out."

"Well," he says, "you needn't be afeared no more, becuz they've got him. He run off f'm down South, som'ers."

"It's a good job they got him."

"Well, I *reckon!* There's two hundred dollars' reward on him. It's like picking up money out'n the road."

"Yes, it is–and *I* could 'a' had it if I'd been big enough. I see him first. Who nailed him?"

"It was an old fellow–a stranger–and he sold out his chance in him for forty dollars, becuz he's got to go up the river and can't wait. Think o' that, now! You bet *I'd* wait, if it was seven year."

"That's me, every time," says I. "But maybe his chance ain't worth no more than that, if he'll sell so cheap. Maybe there's something ain't straight about it."

"But it *is*, though–straight as a string. I see the handbill myself. It tells all about him to the dot–paints him like a picture and tells the plantation he's frum, below New*rleans*. No-sirree-*bob*, they ain't no trouble 'bout *that* speculation, you bet. Say, gimme a chaw tobacker, won't ye?"

I didn't have none, so he left. I went to the raft and set down in the wigwam to think. But I couldn't come to nothing. I thought till I wore my head sore, but I couldn't see no way out of the trouble. After all this journey, and after all we'd done for them scoundrels, here it was all come to nothing, everything all busted up and ruined, because they could have the heart to serve Jim such a trick as that, and make him a slave again all his life, and among strangers, too, for forty dirty dollars.

Once I said to myself it would be a thousand times better for Jim to be a slave at home where his family was, as long as he'd *got* to be a slave, and so I'd better write a letter to Tom Sawyer and tell him to tell Miss Watson where he was. But I soon give up that notion for two things; she'd be mad and disgusted at his rascality and ungratefulness for leaving her, and so she'd sell him straight down the river again. And if she didn't, everybody naturally despises an ungrateful nigger, and they'd make Jim feel it all the time, and so he'd feel ornery and disgraced.

And then think of *me!* It would get all around that Huck Finn helped a nigger to get his freedom, and if I was ever to see anybody from that town again I'd be ready to get down and lick his boots for shame.

So I was full of trouble, full as I could be; and didn't know what to do. At last I had an idea. And I says, I'll go and write the letter—and *then* see if I can pray. Why, it was astonishing, the way I felt as light as a feather right straight off, and my troubles all gone. So I got a piece of paper and pencil, all glad and excited, and set down and wrote:

> Miss Watson, your runaway nigger Jim is down here two mile below Pikesville, and Mr. Phelps has got him an he will give him up for the reward if you send.
>
> HUCK FINN

I laid the paper down and set there thinking—thinking how good it was all this happened so, and how near I come to being lost and going to hell. And went on thinking. And got to thinking over our trip down the river. And I see Jim before me all the time, in the day and in the night-time, sometimes moonlight, sometimes storms, and we a-floating along, talking and singing and laughing. I was the best friend old Jim ever had in the world, and the *only* one he's got now; and then I happened to look around and see that paper.

It was a close place. I took it up and held it in my hand. I was a-trembling, because I'd got to decide, forever, betwixt two things, and I knowed it.

I studied a minute, sort of holding my breath, and then says to myself, "All right, then, I'll *go* to hell!" And I tore it up.

And for a starter I would go to work and steal Jim out of slavery again. And if I could think up anything worse, I would do that, too, because as long as I was in, I might as well go the whole hog.

Then I set to thinking over how to get at it, and turned over some considerable many ways in my mind; and at last fixed up a plan that suited me. So then I took the bearing of a woody island that was down the river a piece, and as soon as it was fairly dark I crept out with my raft and went for it and hid it there and then turned in. I slept the night through, and got up before it was light, and had my breakfast, and put on my store clothes, and tied up some others and one thing or another in a bundle, and took the canoe and cleared for shore. I landed below where I judged was Phelps's place and hid my bundle in the woods, and then filled up the canoe with water and loaded rocks into ler and sunk her where I could find her again when I wanted her, about a quarter of a mile below a little steam sawmill.

Then I struck up the road, and when I passed the mill I see a sign on it. "Phelps's Sawmill," and when I come to the farmhouses, two or three hundred yards further along, I kept my eyes peeled, but didn't see nobody around, though it was good daylight now. But I didn't mind, because I didn't want to see nobody just yet—I only wanted to get the lay of the land. According to my plan, I was going to turn up there from the village, not from below. So I just took a look and shoved along, straight for town. Well, the very first man I see when I got there was the duke. He was sticking up a bill for the "Royal Nonesuch"—three-night performance—like that other time. *They* had the cheek, them frauds! I was right on him before I could shirk.

He looked astonished and says. "Hel-*lo!* Where'd *you* come from?" Then he says, kind of glad and eager, "Where's the raft? Got her in a good place?"

I says, "Why, that's just what I was going to ask your grace."

Then he didn't look so joyful and says, "What was your idea for asking *me?*" he says.

"Well," I says, "when I see the king in that doggery yesterday I says to myself, we can't get him home for hours, till he's soberer. So I went a-loafing around town to put in the time and wait. A man up and offered me ten cents to help him pull a skiff over the river and back to fetch a sheep, and so I went along; but when we was dragging him to the boat, and the man left me a-holt of the rope and went behind him to shove him along, he was too strong for me and jerked loose and run, and we after him. We didn't have no dog, and so we had to chase him all over the country till we tired him out. We never got him till dark; then we fetched him over, and I started down for the raft. When I got there and see it was gone, I says to myself. 'They've got into trouble and had to leave; and they've took my nigger, which is the only nigger I've got in the world, and now I'm in a strange country, and ain't got no property no more, nor nothing, and no way to make my living.' So I set down and cried. I slept in the woods all night. But what *did* become of the raft, then? And Jim—poor Jim! What happened to him?"

"Blamed if *I* know—that is, what's become of the raft. That old fool had made a trade and got forty dollars, and when we found him in the doggery the loafers had matched half dollars with him and got every cent but what he'd spent for whisky. When I got him home last night and found the raft gone, we said, 'That little rascal has stole our raft and shook us, and run off down the river.'"

"I wouldn't shake my *nigger*, would I? The only nigger I had in the world, and the only property."

"We never thought of that. Fact is, I reckon we'd come to consider him *our* nigger. Yes, we did consider him so—goodness knows we had trouble enough for him. So when we see the raft was gone and we flat broke, there warn't anything for it but to try the 'Royal Nonesuch' another shake.

And I've pegged along ever since, dry as a powderhorn. Where's that ten cents? Give it here."

I had considerable money, so I give him ten cents, but begged him to spend it for something to eat and give me some, because it was all the money I had, and I hadn't had nothing to eat since yesterday. He never said nothing.

The next minute he whirls on me and says, "Do you reckon that nigger would blow on us? We'd skin him if he done that!"

"How can he blow? Hain't he run off?"

"No! That old fool sold him and never divided with me and the money's gone."

"*Sold* him?" I says and begun to cry. "Why, he was *my* nigger, and that was my money. Where is he? Where is he? I want my nigger."

"Well, you can't *get* your nigger, that's all—so dry up your blubbering. Looky here—do you think *you'd* venture to blow on us? Blamed if I think I'd trust you. Why, if you *was* to blow on us—"

He stopped, but I never see the duke look so ugly out of his eyes before. I went on a-whimpering and says, "I don't want to blow on nobody, and I ain't got no time to blow, nohow. I got turn out and find my nigger."

He looked kinder bothered, and stood there with his bills fluttering on his arm, thinking, and wrinkling up his forehead. At last he says, "I'll tell you something. We got to be here three days. If you'll promise you won't blow, and won't let the nigger blow, I'll tell you where to find him."

So I promised, and he says, "A farmer by the name of Silas Ph—" and then he stopped. You see, he started to tell me the truth; but when he stopped that way, and begun to study and think again, I reckoned he was changing his mind. And so he was. He wouldn't trust me; he wanted to make sure of having me out of the way the whole three days.

So pretty soon he says, "The man that bought him is named Abram Foster—Abram G. Foster—and he lives forty mile back here in the country, on the road to Lafayette."

"All right," I says. "I can walk it in three days. And I'll start this very afternoon."

"No, you won't, you'll start *now*, and don't you lose any time about it, neither, nor do any gabbling by the way. Just keep a tight tongue in your head and move right along, and then you won't get into trouble with *us*, d'ye hear?"

That was the order I wanted, and that was the one I played for. I wanted to be left free to work my plans.

"So clear out," he says. "And you can tell Mr. Foster whatever you want to. Maybe you can get him to believe that Jim *is* your nigger—some idiots don't require documents—leastways I've heard there's such down South here. And when you tell him the handbill and reward's bogus, maybe he'll believe you when you explain to him what the idea was for getting 'em out. Go 'long now and tell him anything you want to. But mind you don't work your jaw any *between* here and there."

So I left and struck for the back country. I didn't look around, but I kinder felt like he was watching me. But I knowed I could tire him out at that. I went straight out in the country as much as a mile before I stopped; then I doubled back through the woods toward Phelps's. I reckoned I better start in on my plan straight off without fooling around, because I wanted to stop Jim's mouth till these fellows could get away. I didn't want no trouble with their kind. I'd seen all I wanted to and wanted to get entirely shut of them.

CHAPTER XXI

Still and Sundaylike–Mistaken identity–Up a stump–In a dilemma

WHEN I got there it was all still and Sundaylike, and hot and sunshiny. The hands was gone to the fields, and there was them kind of faint dronings of bugs and flies in the air that makes it seem so lonesome and like everybody's dead and gone.

Phelp's was one of these little one-horse cotton plantations, and they all look alike. A rail fence round a two-acre yard; a stile made out of logs sawed off and up-ended in steps, like barrels of a different length, to climb over the fence with, and for the women to stand on when they are going to jump onto a horse; some sickly grass-patches in the big yard, but mostly it was bare and smooth, big double log house for the white folks.

I went around and clumb over the back stile by the ash-hopper and started for the kitchen. When I got a little ways I heard the dim hum of a spinning wheel wailing along up and sinking along down again; and then I knowed for certain I wished I was dead-for that *is* the lonesomest sound in the whole world.

I went right along, not fixing up any particular plan, but just trusting to Providence to put the right words in my mouth when the time come; for I'd noticed that Providence always did put the right words in my mouth if I left it alone.

When I got halfway, first one hound and then another got up and went for me, and of course I stopped and faced them, and kept still. And such another powwow as they made! In a quarter of a minute I was a kind of hub of a wheel, as you may say–spokes made out of dogs–circle of fifteen of them packed together around me, with their necks and noses stretched up toward me, a-barking and howling; and more a-coming; you could see them sailing over fences and around corners from everywheres.

A nigger woman come tearing out of the kitchen with a rolling pin in her hand, singing out, "Begone! *You* Tige! You Spot! Begone sah!" And she fetched first one and then another of them a clip and sent them howling, and then the rest followed. And the next second, half of them come back wagging their tails around me and making friends with me. There ain't no harm in a hound, nohow.

And behind the woman comes a little nigger girl and two little nigger boys without anything on but tow-linen shirts, and they hung on to their mother's gown and peeped out from behind her at me, bashful, the way they always do. And here comes the white woman running from the house, about forty-five or fifty year old, bareheaded, and her spinning-stick in her hand; and behind her comes her little white children, acting the same way the little niggers was doing. She was smiling all over so she could hardly stand—and says, "It's *you*—at last! *Ain't* it?"

I out with a "Yes'm" before I thought.

She grabbed me and hugged me tight; and then gripped me by both hands and shook and shook; and the tears come in her eyes and run down over; and she couldn't seem to hug and shake enough, and kept saying, "You don't look as much like your mother as I reckoned you would. But law sakes, I don't care for that, I'm *so* glad to see you! Dear, dear, it does seem like I could eat you up! Children, it's your cousin Tom! Tell him howdy."

But they ducked their heads and put their fingers in their mouths and hid behind her. So she run on, "Lize, hurry and get him a hot breakfast right away—or did you get your breakfast on the boat?"

I said I had got it on the boat. So then she started for the house leading me by the hand and the children tagging after. When we got there she set me down in a split-bottomed chair, and set herself down on a little low stool in front of me, holding both of my hands, and says, "Now I can have a *good* look at you; and laws-a-me, I've been hungry for it a many and a many a time, all these long years, and it's come at last! We been expecting you a couple of days and more. What kep' you? Boat get aground?"

"Yes'm—she—"

"Don't say yes'm—say Aunt Sally. Where'd she get aground?"

I didn't rightly know what to say, because I didn't know whether the boat would be coming up the river or down. But I go a good deal on instinct, and my instinct said she would be coming up—from down toward Orleans. That didn't help much, though, for I didn't know the names of bars down that way. I see I'd got to invent a bar, or forget the name of the one we got aground on—or—

Now I struck an idea and fetched it out, "It warn't the grounding—that didn't keep us back but a little. We blowed out a cylinder head."

"Good gracious! Anybody hurt?"

"No'm. Killed a nigger."

Your uncle's been up to the town every day to fetch you. And he's gone again, not more'n an hour ago; he'll be back any minute now. You must 'a' met him on the road, didn't you? Oldish man, with a—"

"No, I didn't see nobody, Aunt Sally. The boat landed just at daylight, and I left my baggage on the wharf boat and went looking around the town and out a piece in the country, to put in the time and not get here too soon; and so I come down the back way."

"Who'd you give the baggage to?"

"Nobody."

"Why, child, it'll be stole!"

"Not where *I* hid it I reckon it won't," I says.

"How'd you get your breakfast so early on the boat?"

It was kinder thin ice, but I says, "The captain see me standing around and told me I better have something to eat before I went ashore. So he took me in the texas to the officers' lunch and give me all I wanted."

I was getting so uneasy I couldn't listen good. I had my mind on the children all the time. I wanted to get them out to one side and pump them a little and find out who I was. But I couldn't get no show, Mrs. Phelps kept it up and run on so.

Pretty soon she made the cold chills streak all down my back, because she says, "But here we're a-running on this way, and you hain't told me a word about Sis, nor any of them. Now I'll rest my works a little, and you start up yourn. Just tell me *everything*-tell me all about 'm all-every one of 'm, and how they are, and what they're doing, and what they told you to tell me; and every last thing you can think of."

Well, I see I was up a stump-and up it good. Providence had stood by me this fur all right, but I was hard and tight aground now. I see it warn't a bit of use to try to go ahead-I'd got to throw up my hand. So I says to myself, here's another place where I got to resk the truth.

I opened my mouth to begin, but she grabbed me and hustled me in behind the bed and says, "Here he comes! Stick your head down lower-there, that'll do. You can't be seen now. Don't you let on you're here. I'll play a joke on him. Children, don't you say a word."

I see I was in a fix now. But it warn't no use to worry; there warn't nothing to do but just hold still.

I had just one little glimpse of the old gentleman when he come in; then the bed hid him. Mrs. Phelps she jumps for him and says, "Has he come?"

"No", says her husband.

"Good-*ness* gracious!" she says. "What in the world *can* have become of him?"

"I can't imagine," says the old gentleman. "And I must say it makes me dreadful uneasy."

"Uneasy!" she says. "I'm ready to go distracted! He *must* 'a' come, and you've missed him along the road. I *know* it's so-something tells me so."

"Why, Sally, I *couldn't* miss him along the road. *You* know that."

"But oh, dear, dear, what *will* Sis say! He must 'a' come! You must 'a' missed him. He-"

"Oh, don't distress me any more'n I'm already distressed. I don't know what in the world to make of it. I'm at my wit's end, and I don't mind acknowledging 't I'm right down scared. But there's no hope that he's come, for he *couldn't* come and me miss him. Sally, it's terrible–just terrible–something's happened to the boat, sure!"

"Why, Silas! Look yonder! Up the road! Ain't that somebody coming?"

He sprung to the window at the head of the bed, and that give Mrs. Phelps the chance she wanted. She stooped down quick at the foot of the bed and give me a pull, and out I come. And when he turned back from the window, there she stood, a-beaming and a-smiling like a house afire, and I standing pretty meek and sweaty alongside.

The old gentleman stared and says, "Why, who's that?"

"Who do you reckon 'tis?"

"I hain't no idea. Who *is* it?"

"It's *Tom Sawyer!*"

By jings, I most slumped through the floor! But there warn't no time to swap knives. The old man grabbed me by the hand and shook, and kept on shaking, and all the time how the woman did dance around and laugh and cry. And then how they both did fire off questions about Sid and Mary and the rest of the tribe.

But if they was joyful, it warn't nothing to what I was, for it was like being born again, I was so glad to find out who I was. Well, they froze to me for two hours. At last, when my chin was so tired it couldn't hardly go any more, I had told them more about my family–I mean the Sawyer family–than ever happened to any six Sawyer families. And I explained all about how we blowed out a cylinder head at the mouth of White River, and it took us three days to fix it. Which was all right, and worked first-rate, because they don't know but what it would take three days to fix it. If I'd 'a' called it a bolt head it would 'a' done just as well.

Now I was feeling pretty comfortable all down one side, and pretty uncomfortable all up the other. Being Tom Sawyer was easy and comfortable, and it stayed easy and comfortable till by and by I hear a steamboat coughing along down the river. Then I says to myself, s'pose Tom Sawyer comes down on that boat? And s'pose he steps in here any minute and sings my name right out before I can throw him a wink to keep quiet? Well, I could'nt *have* it that way; it wouldn't do at all. I must go up the road and waylay him. So I told the folks I reckoned I would go up to the town and fetch down my baggage. The old gentleman was for going along with me, but I said no, I could drive the horse myself, and I druther he wouldn't take no trouble about me.

CHAPTER XXII

A nigger stealer–Southern hospitality–A pretty long blessing–
Tar and feathers

So I started for town in the wagon, and when I was halfway I see a wagon coming, and sure enough it was Tom Sawyer, and I stopped and waited till he come along. I says, "Hold on!" And it stopped alongside, and his mouth opened up like a trunk, and stayed so; and he swallowed two or three times like a person that's got a dry throat.

Then he says, "I hain't ever done you no harm. You know that. So, then, what you want to come back and ha'nt *me* for?"

I says, "I hain't come back–I hain't been *gone*."

When he heard my voice it righted him up some, but he warn't quite satisfied yet. He says, "Don't you play nothing on me. Honest injun, you ain't a ghost?"

"Honest injun, I ain't," I says.

"Well–I–I–well, that ought to settle it, of course; but I can't somehow seem to understand it no way. Looky here, warn't you ever murdered *at all*?"

"No. I warn't ever murdered at all–I played it on them. You come in here and feel of me if you don't believe me."

So he done it, and it satisfied him; and he was that glad to see me again he didn't know what to do. And he wanted to know all about it right off, because it was a grand adventure, and mysterious, and so it hit him where he lived. But I said, leave it alone till by and by, and told his driver to wait, and we drove off a little piece, and I told him the kind of a fix I was in, and what did he reckon we better do? He said, let him alone a minute and don't disturb him.

So he thought and thought, and pretty soon he says, "It's all right. I've got it. Take my trunk in your wagon and let on it's yourn, and you turn back and fool along slow, so as to get to the house about the time you ought to. And I'll go toward town a piece, and take a fresh start, and get there a quarter or a half an hour after you. And you needn't let on to know me at first."

I says, "All right, but wait a minute. There's one more thing–a thing that *nobody* don't know but me. And that is, there's a nigger here that I'm a-trying to steal out of slavery, and his name is *Jim*–old Miss Watson's Jim."

He says, "What! Why, Jim is–"

He stopped and went to studying.

I says, "*I* know what you'll say. You'll say it's dirty, low-down business; but what if it is? *I'm* low-down, and I'm a-going to steal him, and I want you to keep mum and not let on. Will you?"

His eye lit up, and he says, "I'll *help* you steal him!"

Well, I let go all holts then, like I was shot. It was the most astonishing speech I ever heard–and I'm bound to say Tom Sawyer fell considerable in my estimation. Only I couldn't believe it. Tom Sawyer a *nigger-stealer*!

"Oh, shucks!" I says. "You're joking."

"I ain't joking, either."

"Well, then", I says, "joking or no joking, if you hear anything said about a runaway nigger, don't forget to remember that *you* don't know nothing about him, and *I* don't know nothing about him."

Then we took the trunk and put it in my wagon, and he drove off his way and I drove mine. But of course I forgot all about driving slow on accounts of being glad and full of thinking. So I got home a heap too quick for that length of a trip.

The old gentleman was at the door, and he says, "Why, this is wonderful! Whoever would 'a' thought it was in that mare to do it? I wish we'd 'a' timed her. And she hain't sweated a hair–not a hair. It's wonderful. Why, I wouldn't take a hundred dollars for that horse now–I wouldn't, honest. And yet I'd 'a' sold her for fifteen before and thought 'twas all she was worth."

That's all he said. He was the innocentest, best old soul I ever see. But it warn't surprising; because he warn't only just a farmer, he was a preacher, too, and had a little one-horse log church down back of the plantation, which he built it himself at his own expense, for a church and schoolhouse, and never charged nothing for his preaching, and it was worth it, too. There was plenty other farmers-preachers like that, and done the same way, down South.

In about half an hour Tom's wagon drove up to the front stile, and Aunt Sally, she see it through the window, because it was only about fifty yards, and says, "Why, there's somebody come! I wonder who 'tis? Why, I do believe it's a stranger. Jimmy" (that's one of the children), "run and tell Lize to put on another plate for dinner."

Everybody made a rush for the front door, because, of course, a stranger don't come *every* year, and so he lays over the yaller-fever, for interest, when he does come. Tom was over the stile and starting for the house, the wagon was spinning up the road for the village, and we was all bunched in the front door.

Tom had his store clothes on, and an audience–and that was always nuts for Tom Sawyer. In them circumstances it warn't no trouble to him to throw in an amount of style that was suitable. He warn't a boy to meeky along up that yard like a sheep. No, he come ca'm and important, like the ram. When he got a-front of us he lifts his hat ever so gracious and dainty, like it was the lid of a box that had butterflies asleep in it and he didn't want to disturb them, and says, "Mr. Archibald Nichols, I presume?"

"No, my boy," says the old gentleman. "I'm sorry to say 't your driver has deceived you. Nichols's place is down a matter of three mile more. Come in, come in."

Tom he took a look back over his shoulder and says, "Too late—he's out of sight."

"Yes, he's gone, my son, and you must come in and eat your dinner with us, and then we'll hitch up and take you down to Nichols's."

"Oh, I *can't* make you so much trouble. I couldn't think of it. I'll walk —I don't mind the distance."

"But we won't *let* you walk—it wouldn't be Southern hospitality to do it. Come right in."

"Oh, *do*", says Aunt Sally. "It ain't a bit of trouble to us, not a bit in the world. You *must* stay. It's a long, dusty three mile, and we *can't* let you walk. Besides, I've already told 'em to put on another plate when I see you coming; so you mustn't disappoint us. Come right in and make yourself at home."

So Tom, he thanked them very hearty and handsome, and let himself be persuaded, and come in; and when he was in, he said he was a stranger from Hicksville, Ohio, and his name was William Thompson—and he made another bow.

Well, he run on, and on, and on, making up stuff about Hicksville and everybody in it he could invent, and I getting a little nervous, and wondering how he was going to help me out of my scrape. And at last, still talking along, he reached over and kissed Aunt Sally right on the mouth and then settled back again in his chair and was going on talking.

But she jumped up and wiped it off with the back of her hand and says, "You owdacious puppy!"

He looked kind of hurt and says, "I'm surprised at you, m'am."

"You're s'rp—Why, what do you reckon *I* am? I've a good notion to take and—Say, what do you mean by kissing me?"

He looked kind of humble and says, "I didn't mean nothing, m'am. I didn't mean no harm. I—I—thought you'd like it."

"Why, you born fool!" She took up the spinning-stick, and it looked like it was all she could do to keep from giving him a crack with it. "What made you think I'd like it?"

"Well, I don't know. Only, they—they—told me you would."

"*They* told you I would. Whoever told you's *another lunatic.* I never heard the beat of it. Who's *they?*"

"Why, everybody. They all said so, m'am."

It was all she could do to hold in, and her eyes snapped, and her fingers worked like she wanted to scratch him; and she says, "Who's 'everybody'? Out with their names, or there'll be an idiot short."

He got up and looked distressed and fumbled his hat and says, "I'm sorry, and I warn't expecting it. They told me to. They all told me to. They all said, kiss her; and said she'd like it. They all said it—every one of them. But I'm sorry, m'am, and I won't do it no more—I won't, honest."

"You won't, won't you? Well, I sh'd *reckon* you won't!"

"No'm, I'm honest about it. I won't ever do it again—till you ask me."

102

"Till I *ask* you! Well, I never see the beat of it in my born days! I lay you'll be the Methusalem-numskull of creation before ever *I* ask you—or the likes of you."

"Well," he says, "it does surprise me so. I can't make it out, somehow. They said you would, and I thought you would. But—" He stopped and looked around slow, like he wished he could run across a friendly eye somewheres, and fetched up on the old gentleman's and says, "Didn't *you* think she'd like me to kiss her, sir?"

"Why, no. I—I—well, no, I b'lieve I didn't."

Then he looks on around the same way to me and says, "Tom, didn't *you* think Aunt Sally'd open out her arms and say, 'Sid Sawyer—' "

"My land!" she says, breaking in and jumping for him.

"You impudent young rascal, to fool a body so—" and was going to hug him, but he fended her off and says, "No, not till you've asked me first."

So she didn't lose no time, but asked him, and hugged him and kissed him over and over again, and then turned him over to the old man, and he took what was left.

And after they got a little quiet again she says, "Why, dear me, I never see such a surprise. We warn't looking for *you* at all, but only Tom. Sis never wrote about anybody coming but him."

"It's because it warn't *intended* for any of us to come but Tom," he says. "But I begged and begged, and at the last minute she let me come, too. So coming down the river, me and Tom thought it would be a first-rate surprise for him to come here to the house first, and for me to by and by tag along and drop in and let on to be a stranger. But it was a mistake, Aunt Sally. This aint' no healthy place for a stranger to come."

"No—not impudent whelps, Sid. You ought to had your jaws boxed. I hain't been so put out since I don't know when. But I don't care, I don't mind the terms—I'd be willing to stand a thousand such jokes to have you here. Well, to think of that performance! I don't deny it, I was most putrified with astonishment when you give me that smack."

Tom and me went up to bed right after supper, and clumb out of the window and down the lightning rod, and shoved for the town. For I didn't believe anybody was going to give the king and the duke a hint, and so if I didn't hurry up and give them one they'd get into trouble sure.

On the road, Tom, he told me all about how it was reckoned I was murdered, and how Pap disappeared pretty soon, and didn't come back no more, and what a stir there was when Jim run away. And I told Tom all about our "Royal Nonesuch" rapscallions, and as much of the raft voyage as I had time to.

As we struck into the town and up through the middle of it—it was as much as half after eight then—here comes a raging rush of people with torches, and an awful whooping and yelling and banging tin pans and blowing horns. We jumped to one side to let them go by, and as they went by I see they had the king and the duke astraddle of a rail—I knowed it *was* the king and the duke, though they was all over tar and feathers, and they didn't look like nothing in the world that was human–just looked like a couple of monstrous big soldier plumes. Well, it made me sick to see it, and I was sorry for them poor pitiful rascals; it seemed I couldn't ever feel any hardness against them any more in the world. It was a dreadful thing to see. Human beings *can* be awful cruel to one another.

CHAPTER XXIII

The hut by the ash-hopper–Outrageous–Climbing the lightning rod–
Troubled with witches

WE STOPPED talking and got to thinking. By and by Tom says, "Looky here, Huck, what fools we are to not think of it before! I bet I know where Jim is."

"No! Where?"

"In that hut down by the ash-hopper. Why, looky here. When we was at dinner, didn't you see a nigger man go in there with some vittles?"

"Yes."

"What did you think the vittles was for?"

"For a dog."

"So'd I. Well, it wasn't for a dog."

"Why?"

"Because part of it was watermelon."

"So it was–I noticed it. Well, it does beat all that I never thought about a dog not eating watermelon. It shows how a body can see and don't see at the same time."

"Well, the nigger unlocked the padlock when he went in, and he locked it again when he came out. He fetched uncle a key about the time we got up from table–same key, I bet. Watermelon shows man, lock shows prisoner; and it ain't likely there's two prisoners on such a little plantation, and where the people's all so kind and good. Jim's the prisoner. All right –I'm glad we found it out detective fashion; I wouldn't give shucks for any other way. Now you work your mind, and study out a plan to steal Jim, and I will study out one, too; and we'll take the one we like the best."

What a head for just a boy to have! If I had Tom Sawyer's head I wouldn't trade it off to be a duke nor mate of a steamboat nor clown in a circus nor nothing I can think of. I went to thinking out a plan, but only just to be doing something. I knowed very well where the right plan was coming from.

Pretty soon Tom says, "Ready?"

"Yes," I says.

"All right–bring it out."

"My plan is this", I says. "We can easy find out if it's Jim in there.

Then get up my canoe tomorrow night and fetch my raft over from the island. Then the first dark night that comes steal the key out of the old man's britches after he goes to bed, and shove off down the river on the raft with Jim, hiding daytimes and running nights, the way me and Jim used to do before. Wouldn't that plan work?"

"*Work?* Why, cert'nly it would work, like rats a-fighting. But it's too blame' simple; there ain't nothing *to* it. What's the good of a plan that ain't no more trouble than that? It's as mild as goosemilk. Why, Huck, it wouldn't make no more talk than breaking into a soap factory."

I never said nothing, because I warn't expecting nothing different; but I knowed mighty well that whenever he got *his* plan ready it wouldn't have none of them objections to it.

And it didn't. He told me what it was, and I see in a minute it was worth fifteen of mine for style, and would make Jim as free a man as mine would, and maybe get us all killed besides. So I was satisfied and said we would waltz in on it. I needn't tell what it was here, because I knowed it wouldn't stay the way it was. I knowed he would be changing it around every which way as we went along and heaving in new bullinesses wherever he got a chance. And that is what he done.

Well, one thing was dead sure, and that was that Tom Sawyer was in earnest, and was actuly going to help steal that nigger out of slavery. That was the thing that was too many for me. Here was a boy that was respectable and well brung up, and had a character to lose, and folks at home that had characters, and was bright and not leather-headed, and knowing and not ignorant, and not mean, but kind; and yet here he was, without any more pride or rightness or feeling than to stoop to this business and make himself a shame, and his family a shame, before everybody. I *couldn't* understand it no way at all. It was outrageous, and I knowed I ought to just up and tell him so, and so be his true friend and let him quit the thing right where he was and save himself.

And I *did* start to tell him. But he shut me up and says, "Don't you reckon I know what I'm about? Don't I generly know what I'm about?"

"Yes."

"Didn't I *say* I was going to help steal the nigger?"

"Yes."

"*Well*, then."

That's all he said, and that's all I said. It warn't no use to say any more, because when he said he'd do a thing, he always done it. But *I* couldn't make out how he was willing to go into this thing. So I just let it go, and never bothered no more about it. If he was bound to have it so, *I* couldn't help it.

When we got home the house was all dark and still; so we went on down to the hut by the ash-hopper for to examine it. We went through the yard so as to see what the hounds would do. They knowed us and didn't make no more noise than country dogs is always doing when anything comes by in the night. When we got to the cabin we took a look at the front and the two sides, and on the side I warn't acqainted with –which was the north side– we found a square window-hole, up tolerable high, with one stout board nailed across it.

I says, "Here's the ticket. This hole's big enough for Jim to get through if we wrench off the board."

Tom says, "It's as simple as tit-tat-toe, three-in-a-row, and as easy as playing hooky. I should *hope* we can find a way that's a little more complicated than *that*, Huck Finn."

"Well, then," I says, "how'll it do to saw him out, the way I done before I was murdered that time?"

"That's more *like*," he says. "It's real mysterious and troublesome and good," he says. "But I bet we can find a way that's twice as long. There ain't no hurry; le's keep on looking around."

Betwixt the hut and the fence, on the back side, was a lean-to that joined the hut at the eaves and was made out of plank. It was as long as the hut, but narrow–only about six foot wide. The door to it was at the south end and was padlocked. Tom, he went to the soap-kettle and searched around, and fetched back the iron thing they lift the lid with; so he took it and prized out one of the staples. The chain fell down, and we opened the door and went in, and shut it, and struck a match, and see the shed was only built against the cabin and had no connection with it. And there warn't no floor to the shed, nor nothing in it but some old rusty played-out hoes and spades and picks and a crippled plow.

The match went out, and so did we, and shoved in the staple again, and the door was locked as good as ever. Tom was joyful. He says, "Now we're all right. We'll *dig* him out. It'll take about a week!"

Then we started for the house, and I went in the back door–you only have to pull a buckskin latchstring; they don't fasten the doors–but that warn't romantical enough for Tom Sawyer. No way would do him but he must climb up the lightning rod. But after he got up halfway about three times and missed fire and fell every time, and the last time most busted his brains out, he thought he'd got to give it up. But after he was rested he allowed he would give her one more turn for luck, and this time he made the trip.

In the morning we was up at break of day, and down to the nigger cabins to pet the dogs and make friends with the nigger that fed Jim–if it *was* Jim that was being fed. The niggers was just getting through breakfast and starting for the fields, and Jim's nigger was piling up a tin pan with bread and meat and things. Whilst the others was leaving, the key come from the house.

The nigger had a good-natured, chuckle-headed face, and his wool was all tied up in little bunches with thread. That was to keep witches off. He said the witches was pestering him awful these nights and making him see all kinds of strange things and hear all kinds of strange words and noises, and he didn't believe he was ever witched so long before in his life. He got so worked up, and got to running on so about his troubles, he forgot all about what he'd been a-going to do.

So Tom says, "What's the vittles for? Going to feed the dogs?"

The nigger kind of smiled around gradual over his face, like when you heave a brick bat in a mud puddle, and he says, "Yes, Mars Sid, *a* dog. Cur'us dog, too. Does you want to go en look at 'im?"

"Yes."

I hunched Tom and whispers, "You going, right here in the daybreak? *That* warn't the plan."

"No, it warn't; but it's the plan *now*."

So, drat him, we went along, but I didn't like it much. When we got in we couldn't hardly see anything, it was so dark. But Jim was there, sure enough, and could see us.

He sings out, "Why, *Huck*! En good *lan'*! Ain' dat Misto Tom?"

I just knowed how it would be. I just expected it. *I* didn't know nothing to do, and if I had I couldn't 'a' done it, because that nigger busted in and says, "Why, de gracious sakes! Do he know you genlmen?"

We could see pretty well now. Tom he looked at the nigger, steady and kind of wondering, and says, "Does *who* know us?"

"Why, dis-yer runaway nigger."

"I don't reckon he does; but what put that into your head?"

"What *put* it dar? Didn't he jis' dis minute sing out like he knowed you?"

Tom says, in a puzzled-up kind of way, "Well, that's mighty curious. *Who* sung out? *When* did he sing out? *What* did he sing out?" And turns to me, perfectly ca'm, and says, "Did *you* hear anybody sing out?"

Of course there warn't nothing to be said but the one thing; so I says, "No. *I* ain't heard nobody say nothing."

Then he turns to Jim and looks him over like he never see him before, and says, "Did you sing out?"

"No, sah," says Jim. "I hain't said nothing, sah."

"Did you ever see us before?"

"No, sah, not as *I* knows on."

Jim only had time to grab us by the hand and squeeze it. Then the nigger come back and we said we'd come again sometime if the nigger wanted us to. And he said he would, more particular if it was dark, because the witches went for him mostly in the dark, and it was sure enough good to have folks around then.

CHAPTER XXIV

Escaping properly–Dark schemes–Discrimination in stealing–A deep hole

IT WOULD be most an hour yet till breakfast, so we left and struck down into the woods, because Tom said we got to have *some* light to see how to dig by, and a lantern makes too much and might get us into trouble. What we must have was a lot of them rotten chunks that's called fox fire and just make a soft kind of a glow when you lay them in a dark place. We fetched an armful and hid it in the weeds and set down to rest.

Tom says, kind of dissatisfied, "Blame it, this whole thing is just as easy and awkward as it can be. And so it makes it so rotten difficult to get up a difficult plan. There ain't no watchman to be drugged–now there *ought* to be a watchman. There ain't even a dog to give a sleeping-mixture to. And there's Jim chained by one leg with a ten-foot chain to the leg of his bed. Why, all you got to do is to lift up the bedstead and slip off the chain. And Uncle Silas he trusts everybody; sends the key to the punkin-headed nigger, and don't send nobody to watch the nigger. Jim could 'a' got out of that window-hole before this, only there wouldn't be no use trying to travel with a ten-foot chain on his leg.

"Why, drat it, Huck, it's the stupidest arrangement I ever see. You got to invent *all* the difficulties. Well, we can't help it. We got to do the best we can with the materials we've got. Anyhow, there's one thing–there's more honor in getting him out through a lot of difficulties and dangers, where there warn't one of them furnished to you by the people who it was their duty to furnish them, and you had to contrive them all out of your own head. Now look at just that one thing of the lantern. When you come down to the cold facts, we simply got to *let on* that a lantern's resky. Why, we could work with a torchlight procession if we wanted to, *I* believe. Now, whilst I think of it, we got to hunt up something to make a saw out of the first chance we get."

"What do we want of a saw?"

"What do we *want* of a saw? Hain't we got to saw the leg of Jim's bed off, so as to get the chain loose?"

"Why, you just said a body could lift up the bedstead and slip the chain off."

"Well, if that ain't just like you, Huck Finn. You *can* get up the infant-schooliest ways of going at a thing."

Along during the morning I borrowed a sheet and a white shirt off of the clothesline. I found an old sack and put them in it, and we went down and got the fox fire, and put that in, too. I called it borrowing, because that was what Pap always called it, but Tom said it warn't borrowing, it was stealing. He said we was representing prisoners, and prisoners don't care how they get a thing so they get it, and nobody don't blame them for it, either. It ain't no crime in a prisoner to steal the thing he needs to get away with, Tom said; it's his right. And so, as long as we was representing a prisoner, we had a perfect right to steal anything on this place we had the least use for to get ourselves out of prison with. He said if we warn't prisoners it would be a very different thing, and nobody but a mean, ornery person would steal when he warn't a prisoner.

So we allowed we would steal everything there was that come handy. And yet he made a mighty fuss one day after that when I stole a watermelon out of the nigger patch and eat it, and he made me go and give the niggers a dime without telling them what it was for. Tom said that what he meant was, we could steal anything we *needed*. Well, I says I needed the watermelon. But he said I didn't need it to get out of prison with; there's where the difference was. He said if I'd 'a' wanted it to hide a knife in, and smuggle it to Jim to kill the seneskal with, it would 'a' been all right. So I let it go at that, though I couldn't see no advantage in my representing a prisoner if I got to set down and chaw over a lot of gold leaf distinctions like that every time I see a chance to hog a watermelon.

Well, as I was saying, we waited that morning till everybody was settled down to business and nobody in sight around the yard. Then Tom, he carried the sack into the lean-to whilst I stood off a piece to keep watch. By and by he come out, and we went and set down on the woodpile to talk.

He says, "Everything's all right now except tools; and that's easy fixed."

"Tools?" I says.

"Yes."

"Tools for what?"

"Why, to dig with. We ain't a-going to *gnaw* him out!"

"Ain't them old crippled picks and things in there good enough to dig a nigger out with?" I says.

He turns on me, looking pitying enough to make a boy cry, and says, "Huck Finn, did you *ever* hear of a prisoner having picks and shovels and all the modern conveniences in his wardrobe to dig himself out with? Now I want to ask you—if you got any reasonableness in you at all—what kind of a show would *that* give him to be a hero? Why, they might as well lend him the key and done with it. Picks and shovels—why, they wouldn't furnish 'em to a king."

"Well, then," I says, "if we don't want the picks and shovels, what do we want?"

"A couple of case knives."

"To dig the foundations out from under that cabin with?"

"Yes."

"Confound it, it's foolish, Tom."

"It don't make no difference how foolish it is, it's the *right* way—and it's the regular way. And there ain't no *other* way that ever *I* heard of, and I've read all the books that gives any information about these things. They always dig out with a case knife—and not through dirt, mind you;

109

generly it's through solid rock. And it takes them weeks and weeks and weeks, and for ever and ever. Why, look at one of them prisoners in the bottom dungeon of the Castle Deef, in the harbor of Marseilles, that dug himself out that way: How long was *he* at it, you reckon?"

"I don't know."

"Well, guess."

"I don't know. A month and a half."

"*Thirty-seven year*–and he come out in China. *That's* the kind. I wish the bottom of *this* fortress was solid rock."

"*Jim* don't know nobody in China."

"What's *that* go to do with it? Neither did that other fellow. But you're always a-wandering off on a side issue. Why can't you stick to the main point?"

"All right–*I* don't care where he comes out, so he *comes* out, and Jim don't, either, I reckon. But there's one thing, anyway–Jim's too old to be dug out with a case knife. He won't last."

"Yes he will *last*, too. You don't reckon it's going to take thirty-seven years to dig out through a *dirt* foundation, do you?"

"How long will it take, Tom?"

"Well, we can't resk being as long as we ought to, because it mayn't take long for Uncle Silas to hear from down there by New Orleans. He'll hear Jim ain't from there. Then his next move will be to advertise Jim, or something like that. So we can't resk being as long digging him out as we ought to. By rights I reckon we ought to be a couple of years, but we can't. Things being so uncertain, what I recommend is this; that we really dig right in, as quick as we can; and after that, we can *let on*, to ourselves, that we was at it thirty-seven years. Then we can snatch him out and rush him away the first time there's an alarm. Yes, I reckon that'll be the best way."

"Now, there's *sense* in that," I says. "Letting on don't cost nothing. Letting on ain't no trouble, and if it's any object, I don't mind letting on we was at it a hundred and fifty year. It wouldn't strain me none, after I got my hand in. So I'll mosey along now, and smouch a couple of case knives."

"Smouch three," he says. "We want one to make a saw out of."

"Tom, if it ain't unregular and irreligious to sejest it," I says, "there's an old rustry saw blade around yonder sticking under the weather-boarding behind the smokehouse."

He looked kind of weary and discouraged-like, and says, "It ain't no use to try to learn you nothing, Huck. Run along and smouch the knives–three of them." So I done it.

CHAPTER XXV

The lightning rod–His level best–A bequest to posterity–A high figure

As soon as we reckoned everybody was asleep that night we went down the lightning rod, shut ourselves up in the lean-to, got out our pile of fox fire, and went to work.

We cleared everything out of the way, about four or five foot along the middle of the bottom log. Tom said we was right behind Jim's bed now, and we'd dig in under it, and when we got through there couldn't nobody in the cabin ever know there was any hole there, because Jim's counterpin hung down most to the ground, and you'd have to raise it up and look under to see the hole. So we dug and dug with the case knives till most midnight; and then we was dog-tired, and our hands was blistered, and yet you couldn't see we'd done anything hardly.

At last I says, "This ain't no thirty-seven-year job. This is a thirty-eight-year job, Tom Sawyer."

He never said nothing. But he sighed, and pretty soon he stopped digging, and then for a good little while I knowed that he was thinking.

Then he says, "It ain't no use, Huck, it ain't a-going to work. If we was prisoners it would, because then we'd have as many years as we wanted, and no hurry; and we wouldn't get but a few minutes to dig, every day, while they was changing watches, and so our hands wouldn't get blistered, and we could keep it up right along, year in and year out, and do it right and the way it ought to be done. But *we* can't fool along; we got to rush; we ain't got no time to spare. If we was to put in another night this way we'd have to knock off for a week to let our hands get well–couldn't touch a case knife with them sooner."

"Well, then, what we going to do, Tom?"

"I'll tell you. It ain't right, and it ain't moral, and I wouldn't like it to get out, but there ain't only just the one way. We got to dig him out with the picks, and *let on* it's case knives."

"*Now*, you're *talking!*" I says. "Your head gets leveler and leveler all the time, Tom Sawyer," I says. "Picks is the thing, moral or no moral, and as for me, I don't care shucks for the morality of it, nohow. When I start in to steal a nigger or a watermelon or a Sunday-school book, I ain't no ways particular how it's done so it's done. What I want is my nigger; or what I want is my watermelon; or what I want is my Sunday-school book. And if a pick's the handiest thing, that's the thing. I'm a-going to dig that nigger or that watermelon or that Sunday-school book out with, and I don't give a dead rat what the authorities thinks about it nuther."

"Well," he says, "there's excuse for picks and letting on in a case like this. If it warn't so, I wouldn't approve of it, nor I wouldn't stand by and see the rules broke–because right is right and wrong is wrong, and a body ain't got no business doing wrong when he ain't ignorant and knows better. It might answer for *you* to dig Jim out with a pick, *without* any letting on, because you don't know no better. But it wouldn't for me, because I do know better. So, gimme a case knife."

He hid his own by him, but I handed him mine. He flung it down, and says, "Gimme a *case knife*."

I didn't know just what to do—but then I thought. I scratched around amongst the old tools, and got a pickax and give it to him, and he took it and went to work and never said a word.

He was always just that particular. Full of principle.

So then I got a shovel, and then we picked and shoveled, turn about, and made the fur fly. We stuck to it about a half an hour, which was as long as we could stand up; but we had a good deal of a hole to show for it.

When I got upstairs I looked out at the window and see Tom doing his level best with lightning rod, but he couldn't come it, his hands was so sore. At last he says, "It ain't no use, it can't be done. What you reckon I better do? Can't you think of no way?"

"Yes," I says, "but I reckon it ain't regular. Come up the stairs, and let on it's a lightning rod."

So he done it.

Next day Tom stole a pewter spoon and a brass candlestick in the house, for to make some pens for Jim out of, and six tallow candles; and I hung around the nigger cabins and laid for a chance and stole three tin plates. Tom says it wasn't enough, but I said nobody wouldn't ever see the plates that Jim throwed out, because they'd fall in the dog fennel and jimpson weeds under the window-hole. Then we could tote them back and he could use them over again. So Tom was satisfied about the plates.

Then he says, "Now, the thing to study out is, how to get the things to Jim."

"Take them in through the hole," I says.

He only just looked scornful and said something about nobody ever heard of such an idiotic idea, and then he went to studying. By and by he had ciphered out two or three ways, but there warn't no need to decide on any of them yet. Said we'd got to post Jim first.

That night we went down the lightning rod a little after ten, and took one of the candles along, and listened under the window-hole, and heard Jim snoring. So we pitched it in, and it didn't wake him. Then we whirled in with the pick and shovel, and in about two hours and a half the job was done. We crept in under Jim's bed and into the cabin, and pawed around and found the candle and lit it and stood over Jim awhile, and found him looking hearty and healthy, and then we woke him up gentle and gradual.

He was so glad to see us he most cried, and called us honey, and all the pet names he could think of, and was for having us hunt up a cold chisel to cut the chain off of his leg with right away, and clearing out without losing any time. But Tom he showed him how unregular it would be, and set down and told him all about our plans, and how we could alter them in

112

a minute any time there was an alarm; and not to be the least afraid, because we would see he got away, *sure*. So Jim he said it was all right, and we set there and talked over old times awhile, and then Tom asked a lot of questions, and when Jim told him Uncle Silas come in every day or two to pray with him, and Aunt Sally come in to see if he was comfortable and had plenty to eat, and both of them was kind as they could be, Tom says, "*Now* I know how to fix it. We'll send you some things by them."

I said, "Don't do nothing of the kind; it's one of the most jackass ideas I ever struck." But he never paid no attention to me—went right on. It was his way when he'd got his plans set.

So he told Jim how we'd have to smuggle in the rope-ladder pie and other large things by Nat, the nigger that fed him, and he must be on the lookout, and not be surprised, and not let Nat see him open them. And we would put small things in Uncle's coat pockets and he must steal them out; and we would tie things to Aunt's apron strings or put them in her apron pocket, if we got a chance; and told him what they would be and what they was for. And told him how to keep a journal on the shirt with his blood, and all that. He told him everything. Jim he couldn't see no sense in the most of it, but he allowed we was white folks and knowed better than him. So he was satisfied and said he would do it all just as Tom said.

Jim had plenty corn-cob pipes and tobacco; so we had a right down good sociable time. Then we crawled out through the hole, and so home to bed, with hands that looked like they'd been chawed. Tom was in high spirits. He said it was the best fun he ever had in his life, and the most intellectual, and said if he only could see his way to it we would keep it up all the rest of our lives and leave Jim to our children to get out; for he believed Jim would come to like it better and better the more he got used to it. He said that in that way it could be strung out to as much as eighty year, and would be the best time on record. And he said it would make us all celebrated that had a hand in it.

In the morning we went out to the woodpile and chopped up the brass candlestick into handy sizes, and Tom put them and the pewter spoon in his pocket. Then we went to the nigger cabins, and while I got Nat's notice off, Tom shoved a piece of candlestick into the middle of a corn pone that was in Jim's pan, and we went along with Nat to see how it would work, and it just worked noble. When Jim bit into it, it most mashed all his teeth out, and there warn't ever anything could 'a' worked better; Tom said so himself. Jim, he never let on but what it was only just a piece of rock or something like that's always getting into bread, you know. But after that he never bit into nothing but what he jabbed his fork into it in three or four places first.

And whilst we was a-standing there in the dimmish light, here comes a couple of the hounds bulging in from under Jim's bed; and they kept on piling in till there was eleven of them, and there warn't hardly room in there to get your breath. By jings, we forgot to fasten that lean-to door! The nigger Nat he only just hollered "Witches" once and keeled over onto the floor amongst the dogs, and begun to groan like he was dying. Tom jerked the door open and flung out a slab of Jim's meat, and the dogs went for it, and in two seconds he was out himself and back again and shut the door, and I knowed he'd fixed the other door, too. Then he went to work on the nigger, coaxing him and petting him, and asking him if he'd been imagining he saw something again.

He raised up, and blinked his eyes around, and says, "Mars Sid, you'll say I's a fool, but if I didn't b'lieve I see most a million dogs, er devils, er some'n, I wisht I may die right heah in dese tracks. I did, mos' sholy. Mars Sid, I *felt* um—I *felt* um, sah; dey was all over me. Dad fetch it, I jis' wisht I could git my han's on one er dem witches jis' wunst—on'y jis' wunst—it's all *I'd* ast. But mos'ly I wisht dey'd lemme 'lone, I does."

Tom says, "Well, I tell you what *I* think. What makes them come here just at this runaway nigger's breakfast-time? It's because they're hungry; that's the reason. You make them a witch pie. That's the thing for *you* to do."

"But my lan', Mars Sid, how's I gwyne to make 'm a witch pie? I doan' know how to make it. I hain't ever hearn er sich a thing b'fo'."

"Well, then, I'll have to make it myself."

"Will you do it, honey? Will you? I'll wusshup de groun' and' yo' foot, I will!"

"All right, I'll do it, seeing it's you, and you've been good to us and showed us the runaway nigger. But you got to be mighty careful. When we come around, you turn your back, and then whatever we've put in the pan, don't let on you see it at all. And don't you look when Jim unloads the pan—something might happen, I don't know what. And above all, don't you *handle* the witch things."

"*Hannel* 'm, Mars Sid? What *is* you a-talkin' about? I wouldn't lay de weight er my finger on um, not f'r ten hund'd thous'n billion dollars, I wouldn't."

CHAPTER XXVI

The last shirt—Mooning around—Sailing orders—The witch pie

THAT was all fixed. So then we went away and went to the rubbage pile in the back yard, where they kept the old boots and rags and pieces of bottles and wore-out tin things and all such truck, and scratched around and found an old tin washpan, and stopped up the holes as well as we could, to bake the pie in. We took it down cellar and stole it full of flour and started for breakfast, and found a couple of shingle nails that Tom said would be handy for a prisoner to scrabble his name and sorrows on the dungeon walls with, and dropped one of them in Aunt Sally's apron pocket which was hanging on a chair, and t'other we stuck in the band of Uncle Silas's hat, which was on the bureau, because we heard the children say their pa and ma was going to the runaway nigger's house this morning. Then we went to breakfast, and Tom dropped the pewter spoon in Uncle Silas's coat pocket, and Aunt Sally wasn't come yet, so we had to wait a little while.

And when she come she was hot and red and cross, and couldn't hardly wait for the blessing. Then she went to sluicing out coffee with one hand and cracking the handiest child's head with her thimble with the other, and says, "I've hunted high and I've hunted low, and it does beat all what *has* become of your other shirt."

My heart fell down amongst my lungs and livers and things, and a hard piece of corn-crust started down my throat after it and got met on the road with a cough, and was shot across the table, and took one of the children in the eye and curled him up like a fishing worm. He let a cry out of him the size of a war whoop, and Tom, he turned kinder blue around the gills, and it all amounted to a considerable state of things for about a quarter of a minute or as much as that, and I would 'a' sold out for half price if there was a bidder. But after that we was all right again—it was the sudden surprise of it that knocked us so kind of cold.

Uncle Silas, he says, "It's most uncommon curious, I can't understand it. I know perfectly well I took it *off*, because—"

"Because you hain't got but one *on*. Just *listen* at the man! *I* know you took it off, and know it by a better way than your woolgethering memory, too, because it was on the clo'sline yesterday—I see it there myself. But it's gone, that's the long and the short of it, and you'll just have to change to a red flann'l one till I can get time to make a new one. And it'll be the third I've made in two years. It just keeps a body on the jump to keep you in shirts, and whatever you do manage to *do* with 'm all is more'n *I* can make out. A body'd think you *would* learn to take some sort of care of 'em at your time of life."

"I know it, Sally, and I do try all I can. But it oughtn't to be altogether my fault, because, you know, I don't see them nor have nothing to do with them except when they're on me; and I don't believe I've ever lost one of them *off* of me."

"Well, it ain't *your* fault if you haven't, Silas. You'd 'a' done it if you could, I reckon. And the shirt ain't all that's gone, nuther. Ther's a spoon gone, and *that* ain't all. There was ten, and now ther's only nine. The calf got the shirt, I reckon, but the calf never took the spoon, *that's* certain."

"Why, what else is gone, Sally?"

"Ther's six *candles* gone—that's what. The rats could 'a' got the candles, and I reckon they did. I wonder they don't walk off with the whole place, the way you're always going to stop their holes and don't do it; and if they warn't fools they'd sleep in your hair, Silas—*you'd* never find it out.

But you can't lay the *spoon* on the rats, and that I *know*," declared Aunt Sally.

"Well, Sally, I'm in fault, and I acknowledge it. I've been remiss. But I won't let tomorrow go by without stopping up them holes."

"Oh, I wouldn't hurry; next year 'll do. Matilda Angelina Araminta *Phelps!*"

Whack comes the thimble, and the child snatches her claws out of the sugar bowl without fooling around any. Just then the nigger woman steps onto the passage, and says, "Missus, dey's a sheet gone."

"A *sheet* gone! Well, for land's sake!"

"I'll stop up them holes today," says Uncle Silas, looking sorrowful.

"Oh, *do* shet up! S'pose the rats took the *sheet?* *Where's* it gone, Lize?"

"Clah to goodness I hain't no notion, Miss' Sally. She wuz on de clo'sline yistiddy, but she done gone. She ain' dah now."

"I reckon the world *is* coming to an end. I *never* see the beat of it in all my born days. A shirt and a sheet and a spoon and six can–"

"Missus," comes a young yaller wench, "deys a brass candlestick miss'n."

"Cler out from here, you hussy, er I'll take a skillet to ye!"

Well, she was just a-biling. I begun to lay for a chance; I reckoned I would sneak out and go for the woods till the weather moderated. She kept a-raging right along, running her insurrection all by herself, and everybody else mighty meek and quiet. And at last Uncle Silas, looking kind of foolish, fishes up that spoon out of his pocket. She stopped, with her mouth open and her hands up, and as for me, I wished I was in Jerusalem or somewheres. But not lang, because she says, "It's *just* as I expected. So you had it in your pocket all the time, and like as not you've got the other things there, too. How'd it get there?"

"I reely don't know, Sally," he says, kind of apologizing, "or you know I would tell. I was a-studying over my text in Acts Seventeen before breakfast, and I reckon I put it in there, not noticing, meaning to put my Testament in, and it must be so, because my Testament ain't in. But I'll go and see; and if the Testament is where I had it, I'll know I didn't put it in, and that will show that I laid the Testament down and took up the spoon, and–"

"Oh, for the land's sake! Give a body a rest! Go 'long now, the whole kit and biling of ye; and don't come nigh me again till I've got back my peace of mind."

I'd 'a' heard her if she'd 'a' said it to herself, let alone speaking it out, and I'd 'a' got up and obeyed her if I'd 'a' been dead. As we was passing through the setting room the old man he took up his hat, and the shingle nail fell out on the floor, and he just merely picked it up and laid it on the mantel shelf, and never said nothing, and went out.

Tom see him do it, and remembered about the spoon, and says, "Well, it ain't no use to send things by *him* no more, he ain't reliable." Then he says, "But he done us a good turn with the spoon, anyway, without knowing it, and so we'll do him one without *him* knowing it–stop up his rat holes."

There was a noble good lot of them down cellar, and it took us a whole hour, but we done the job tight and good and shipshape. Then we heard steps on the stairs, and blowed out our light and hid. And here comes the old man, with a candle in one hand and a bundle of stuff in t'other, looking as absentminded as year before last. He went a-mooning around, first to one rat hole and then another, till he'd been to them all. Then he stood about five minutes, picking tallow-drip off his candle and thinking.

Then he turns off slow and dreamy towards the stairs, saying, "Well, for the life of me I can't remember when I done it. I could show her now that I warn't to blame on account of the rats. But never mind–let it go. I reckon it wouldn't do no good."

And so he went on a-mumbling upstairs, and then we left. He was a mighty nice old man. And always is.

Tom was a good deal bothered about what to do for a spoon, but he said we'd got to have it; so he took a think. When he had ciphered it out he told me how we was to do. Then we went and waited around the spoon basket till we see Aunt Sally coming, and then Tom went to counting the spoons and laying them out to one side, and I slid one of them up my sleeve, and Tom says, "Why, Aunt Sally, there ain't but nine spoons *yet.*"

She says, "Go 'long to your play and don't bother me. I know better, I counted 'm myself."

"Well, I've counted them twice, Aunty, and *I* can't make but nine."

She looked out of patience, but of course she come to count–anybody would.

"I declare to gracious ther' *ain't* but nine!" she says. "Why, what in the world–plague *take* 'em, I'll count 'em again."

So I slipped back the one I had, and when she got done counting, she says, "Hang the troublesome rubbage, ther's *ten* now!" and she looked huffy and bothered both.

But Tom says, "Why, Aunty, *I* don't think there's ten."

"You numskull, didn't you see me *count* 'm?"

"I know, but–"

"Well, I'll count 'em again."

So I smouched one, and they come out nine, same as the other time. Well, she *was* in a tearing way–just a-trembling all over, she was so mad. But she counted and counted till she got that addled she'd start to count in the *basket* for a spoon sometimes; and so, three times they come out right, and three times they come out wrong.

Then she grabbed up the basket and slammed it across the house and knocked the cat galley-west. And she said cler out and let her have some peace, and if we come bothering around her again betwixt that and the dinner she'd skin us. So we had the odd spoon and dropped it in her apron pocket whilst she was a-giving us our sailing orders, and Jim got it all right, along with her shingle nail, before noon.

We was very well satisfied with this business, and Tom allowed it was worth twice the trouble it took, because he said *now* she couldn't ever count them spoons twice alike again to save her life; and wouldn't believe she'd counted them right if she *did;* and said that after she'd about counted her head off for the next three days he judged she'd give it up and offer to kill anybody that wanted her to ever count them any more.

So we put the sheet back on the line that night and stole one out of her closet; and kept on putting it back and stealing it again for a couple of days till she didn't know how many sheets she had any more, and she didn't *care,* and warn't a-going to bullyrag the rest of her soul out about it, and wouldn't count them again, not to save her life; she druther die first.

So we was all right now, as to the shirt and the sheet and the spoon and the candles, by the help of the calf and the rats and the mixed-up counting; and as to the candlestick, it warn't no consequence, it would blow over by and by.

But that pie was a job. We had no end of trouble with that pie. We fixed it up away down in the woods, and cooked it there. And we got it done at last, and very satisfactory, too, but not all in one day. And we had to use up three washpans full of flour before we got through, and we got burnt pretty much all over, in places, and eyes put out with the smoke; because, you see, we didn't want nothing but a crust, and we couldn't prop it up right, and she would always cave in. But of course we thought of the right way at last—which was to cook the ladder, too, in the pie. So then we laid in with Jim the second night, and tore up the sheet all in little strings and twisted them together, and long before daylight we had a lovely rope that you could 'a' hung a person with. We let on it took nine months to make it.

And in the forenoon we took it down to the woods, but it wouldn't go into the pie. Being made of a whole sheet, that way, there was rope enough for forty pies if we'd 'a' wanted them, and plenty left over for soup, or sausage, or anything you choose. We could 'a' had a whole dinner.

But we didn't need it. All we needed was just enough for the pie, so we throwed the rest away. We didn't cook none of the pies in the washpan—afraid the solder would melt. But Uncle Silas, he had a noble brass warming pan which he thought considerable of, because it belonged to one of his ancestors with a long wooden handle that come over from England with William the conqueror in the *Mayflower* or one of them early ships and was hid away up in the garret with a lot of other old pots and things that was valuable, not on account of being any account, because they warn't, but because of them being relics, you know, and we snaked her out, private, and took her down there. But she failed on the first pies, because we didn't know how, but she come up smiling on the last one.

We took and lined her with dough, and set her in the coals, and loaded her up with rag rope, and put on a dough roof, and shut down the lid, and put hot embers on top, and stood off five foot, with the long handle, cool and comfortable, and in fifteen minutes she turned out a pie that was a satisfaction to look at. But the person that et it would want to fetch a couple of kags of toothpicks along, for if that rope ladder wouldn't cramp him down to business I don't know nothing what I'm talking about, and lay him in enough stomach-ache to last him till next time, too.

Nat didn't look when we put the witch pie in Jim's pan, and we put the three tin plates in the bottom of the pan under the vittles; and so Jim got everything all right, and as soon as he was by himself he busted into the pie and hid the rope ladder inside of his straw tick, and scratched some marks on a tin plate and throwed it out the window-hole.

CHAPTER XXVII

The coat of arms—A skilled superintendent
Unpleasant glory—A tearful subject

MAKING them pens was a distressid tough job, and so was the saw, and Jim allowed the inscription was going to be the toughest of all. That's the one which the prisoner has to scrabble on the wall. But he had to have it. Tom said he'd *got* to. There warn't no case of a state prisoner not scrabbling his inscription to leave behind, and his coat of arms.

"Look at Lady Jane Grey," he says. "Look at Gilford Dudley; look at old Northumberland! Why, Huck, s'pose it *is* considerable trouble? What you going to do? How you going to get around it? Jim's *got* to do his inscription and coat of arms. They all do."

Jim says, "Why, Mars Tom, I hain't got no coat o' arms; I hain't got nuffn but dish yer ole shirt, en you knows I got to keep de journal on dat."

"Oh, you don't understand, Jim; a coat of arms is very different."

"Well," I says, "Jim's right, anyway, when he says he hain't got no coat of arms, because he hain't."

"I reckon *I* knowed that," Tom says. "But you bet he'll have one before he goes out of this—because he's going out *right*, and there ain't going to be no flaws in his record."

So whilst me an Jim filed away at the pens on a brickbat apiece, Jim a-making his'n out of the brass and I making mine out of the spoon. Tom set to work to think out the coat of arms. By and by he said he'd struck so many good ones he didn't hardly know which to take, but there was one which he reckoned he'd decide on.

He says, "On the scutcheon we'll have a bend *or* in the dexter base, a saltire *murrey* in the fess, with a dog, couchant, for common charge, and under his foot a chain embattled, for slavery, with a chevron *vert* in a

119

chief engrailed, and three invected lines on a field *azure*, with the nombril points rampant on a dancette indented; crest, a runaway nigger, *sable*, with his bundle over his shoulder on a bar sinister; and a couple of gules for supporters, which is you and me; motto, *Maggiore fretta, minore atto.* Got it out of a book—means the more haste the less speed."

"Geewhillikins!" I says. "But what does the rest mean?"

"We ain't got no time to bother over that," he says.

"Well, anyway," I says, "what's *some* of it? What's a fess?"

"A fess—a fess is—*you* don't need to know what a fess is. I'll show him how to make it when he gets to it."

"Shucks, Tom," I says, "I think you might tell a person. What's a bar sinister?"

"Oh, *I* don't know. But he's got to have it. All the nobility does, and he's got to."

That was just his way. If it didn't suit him to explain a thing to you, he wouldn't do it. You might pump at him a week, it wouldn't make no difference.

He'd got all that coat-of-arms business fixed, so now he started in to finish up the rest of that part of the work, which was to plan out a mournful inscription—said Jim got to have one, like they all done. He made up a lot and wrote them out on a paper and read them off, so:

> "Onc. Here a captive heart busted.
>
> "Two. Here a poor prisoner, forsook by the world and friends, fretted out his sorrowful life.
>
> "Three. Here a lonely heart broke and a worn spirit went to its rest, after thirty-seven years of solitary captivity.
>
> "Four. Here, homeless and friendless, after thirty-seven years of bitter captivity, perished a noble stranger, natural son of Louis XIV."

Tom's voice trembled whilst he was reading them, and he most broke down. When he got done he couldn't no way make up his mind which one for Jim to scrabble onto the wall, they was all so good; but at last he allowed he would let him scrabble them all on. Jim said it would take him a year to scrabble such a lot of truck onto the logs with a nail, and he didn't know how to make letters, besides. But Tom said he would block them out for him, and then he wouldn't have nothing to do but just follow the lines. Then pretty soon he says, "Come to think, the logs ain't a-going to do; they don't have log walls in a dungeon. We got to dig the inscriptions into a rock. We'll fetch a rock."

Jim said the rock was worse than the logs; he said it would take such a pison long time to dig them into a rock he wouldn't ever get out. But Tom said he would let me help him do it. Then he took a look to see how me and Jim was getting along with the pens. It was most pesky tedious hard work and slow, and didn't give my hands no show to get well of the sores, and we didn't seem to make no headway, hardly.

So Tom say's, "I know how to fix it. We got to have a rock for the coat of arms and mournful inscriptions, and we can kill two birds with that same rock. There's a gaudy big grindstone down at the mill, and we'll smouch it, and carve the things on it, and file out the pens and the saws on it, too."

It warn't no slouch of an idea; and it warn't no slouch of an grindstone nuther. But we allowed we'd tackle it. It warn't midnight yet, so we cleared out for the mill, leaving Jim at work. We smouched the grindstone, and set out to roll her home, but it was a most nation tough job. Sometimes, do what we could, we couldn't keep her from falling over, and she come mighty near mashing us every time. Tom said she was going to get one of us, sure, before we got through. We got her halfway; and then we was plumb played out and most drownded with sweat. We see it warn't no use; we got to go and fetch Jim. So he raised up his bed and slid the chain off the bed leg, and wrapt it round and round his neck, and we crawled out through our hole and down there, and Jim and me laid into that grindstone and walked her along like nothing; and Tom superintended. He could out-superintend any boy I ever see. He knowed how to do everything.

Our hole was pretty big, but it warn't big enough to get the grindstone through; but Jim he took the pick and soon made it big enough. Then Tom marked out them things on it with the nail, and set Jim to work on them, with the nail for a chisel and an iron bolt from the rubbage in the lean-to for a hammer, and told him to work until the rest of his candle quit on him, and then he could go to bed and hide the grindstone under his straw tick and sleep on it. Then we helped him fix his chain on the bed leg, and was ready for bed ourselves.

But Tom thought of something and says, "You got any spiders in here, Jim?"

"No, sah, thank to goodness I hain't, Mars Tom."

"All right, we'll get you some."

"But bless you, honey, I doan' *want* none. I's afeard un um. I jis' 's soon have rattlesnakes aroun'."

Tom thought a minute or two and says, "It's a good idea. And I reckon it's been done. It *must* 'a' been done; it stands to reason. Yes, it's a prime good idea. Where could you keep it, Jim?"

"Keep what, Mars Tom?"

"Why, a rattlesnake."

"De goodness gracious alive, Mars Tom! Why, if dey was a rattlesnake to come in heah I'd take en bust right out thoo dat log wall, I would, wid my head."

"Why, Jim, you wouldn't be afraid of it after a little. You could tame it."

"*Tame* it!"

"Yes—easy enough. Every animal is grateful for kindness and petting, and they wouldn't *think* of hurting a person that pets them. Any book will tell you that. You try—that's all I ask; just try for two or three days. Why, you can get him so in a little while that he'll love you; and sleep with you; and won't stay away from you a minute; and will let you wrap him around your neck and put his head in your mouth."

"*Please,* Mars Tom—*doan'* talk so! I can't *stan'* it! He'd *let* me shove his head in my mouf—fer a favor, hain't it? I lay he'd wait a pow'ful long time 'fo' I *ast* him. En mo' en dat, I doan' *want* him to sleep wid me."

"Jim, don't act so foolish. A prisner's *got* to have some kind of a dumb pet, and if a rattlesnake hain't ever been tried, why, there's more glory to be gained in your being the first to ever try it than any other way you could ever think of to save your life."

"Why, Mars Tom, I doan' *want* no sich glory. Snake take n' bite Jim's chin off, den *whah* is de glory? No, sah, I doan' want no sich doin's."

"Blame it, can't you try? I only *want* you to try—you needn't keep it up if it don't work!"

"But de trouble all *done* ef de snake bite me while I's a-tryin' him. Mars Tom, I's willin' to tackle mos' anything 'at ain't onreasonable, but ef you en Huck fetches a rattlesnake in heah for me to tame, I's gwyne to *leave,* dat's *shore.*"

"Well, then, let it go, let it go, if you're so bullheaded about it. We can get some garter snakes, and you can tie some buttons on their tail, and let on they're rattlesnakes, and I reckon that'll have to do."

"I k'n stan' *dem,* Mars Tom, but blame' 'f I couldn't get along widout um, I tell you dat. I never knowed b'fo' twas so much bother and trouble to be a prisoner."

"It *always* is when it's done right. You got any rats?"

"No, sah, I hain't seed none."

"Well, we'll get you some rats."

"Why, Mars Tom, I doan' *want* no rats. Dey's de dadblamedest creturs to 'sturb a body, en rustle roun' over 'im, en bite his feet, when he's tryin' to sleep, I ever see. No, sah, gimme g'yarter snakes 'f I's got to have 'm, but doan' gimme no rats. I hain' got no use f'r um, skasely."

"But, Jim, you *got* to have 'em—they all do. So don't make no more fuss about it. Prisoners ain't ever without rats. There ain't no instance of it. And they train them and pet them and learn them tricks, and they get to be as sociable as flies. But you got to play music to them. You got anything to play music on?"

"I ain't got nuffn but a coarse comb en a piece o' paper, en a juice harp; but I reck'n dey wouldn't take no stock in a juice harp."

"Yes, they would. *They* don't care what kind of music 'tis. A jew's harp's plenty good enough for a rat. All animals like music—in a prison

122

they dote on it. Specially, painful music; and you can't get no other kind
out of a jew's harp. It always interests them; they come out to see what's
the matter with you. Yes, you're all right; you're fixed very well. You
want to set on your bed nights before you go to sleep, and early in the
mornings, and play your jew's harp. Play 'The Last Link Is Broken'—that's
the thing that 'll scoop a rat quicker 'n anything else. And when you've
played about two minutes, you'll see all the rats and the snakes and
spiders and things begin to feel worried about you, and come. And they'll
just fairly swarm over you and have a noble good time."

"Yes, *dey* will, I reck'n, Mars Tom, but what kine er time is *Jim* havin'?
Blest if I kin see de pint. But I'll do et ef I got to. I reck'n I better keep
de animals satisfield, en not have no trouble in de house."

Tom waited to think it over, and see if there wasn't nothing else; and
pretty soon he says, "Oh, there's one thing I forgot. Could you raise a
flower here, do you reckon?"

"I doan' know but maybe I could, Mars Tom; but it's tolable dark in
heah, en I ain' got no use f'r no flower, nohow, en she'd be a pow'ful
sight o' trouble."

"Well, you try it, anyway. Some other prisoners has done it."

"One er dem big cat-tail-lookin' mullen stalks would grow in heah,
Mars Tom, I reck'n, but she wouldn't be wuth half de trouble she'd
coss."

"Don't you believe it. We'll fetch you a little one, and you plant it in
the corner over there, and raise it. And don't call it mullen, call it
Pitchiola—that's its right name when it's in a prison. And you want to
water it with your tears."

"Why, I got plenty spring water, Mars Tom."

"You don't *want* spring water; you want to water it with your tears.
It's the way they always do."

"Why, Mars Tom, I lay I kin raise one er dem mullen stalks twyste wid
spring water whiles another man's *start'n* one wid tears."

"That ain't the idea. You *got* to do it with tears."

"She'll die on my han's, Mars Tom, she sholy will; kase I doan' skasely
ever cry."

So Tom was stumped. But he studied it over, and then said Jim would
have to worry along the best he could with an onion. He promised he
would go to the nigger cabins and drop one, private, in Jim's coffeepot,
in the morning. Jim said he would "jis' 's soon have tobacker in his
coffee", and found so much fault with it, and with the work and bother
of raising the mullen, and jew's-harping the rats, and petting and flatte-
ring up the snakes and spiders and things, on top of all the work he had
to do on pens and inscriptions and journals and things, which made it
more trouble and worry and responsibility to be a prisoner than anything
he ever undertook, that Tom most lost all patience with him; and said
he was just loadened down with more gaudier chances than a prisoner

ever had in the world to make a name for himself, and yet he didn't know enough to appreciate them, and they was just about wasted on him.

So Jim, he was sorry, and said he wouldn't behave so no more, and then me and Tom shoved for bed.

CHAPTER XXVIII
Rats—Lively bedfellows—The straw dummy

IN THE morning we went up to the village and bought a wire rattrap and fetched it down and unstopped the best rat hole, and in about an hour we had fifteen of the bulliest kind of ones; and then we took it and put it in a safe place under Aunt Sally's bed. But while we was gone for spiders little Thomas Franklin Benjamin Jefferson Elexander Phelps found it there, and opened the door of it to see if the rats would come out, and they did. And Aunt Sally she come in, and when we got back she was a-standing on top of the bed raising Cain, and the rats was doing what they could to keep off the dull times for her.

So she took and dusted us both with the hickry, and we was as much as two hours catching another fifteen or sixteen, drat that meddlesome cub, and they warn't the likeliest, nuther, because the first haul was the pick of the flock. I never see a likelier lot of rats than what that first haul was.

We got a splendid stock of sorted spiders and bugs and frogs, and catterpillars and one thing or another; and we like to got a hornet's nest, but we didn't. The family was at home. We didn't give it right up, but stayed with them as long as we could, because we allowed we'd tire them out or they'd got to tire us out, and they done it. Then we got allycumpain and rubbed on the places, and was pretty near all right again, but couldn't set down convenient. And so we went for the snakes, grabbed a couple of dozen, put them in a bag, and put it in our room, and by that time it was supper-time, and a rattling good honest day's work. And hungry? Oh, no, I reckon not! And there warn't a blessed snake up there when we went back—we didn't half tie the sack, and they worked out somehow and left. But it didn't matter much, because they was still on the premises somewheres. So we judged we could get some of them again. No, there warn't no real scarcity of snakes about the house for a considerable spell. You'd see them dripping from the rafters and places every now and then, and they generly landed in your plate, or down the back of your neck, and most of the time where you didn't want them. Well, they was handsome and striped, and there warn't no harm in a million of them, but that never made no difference to Aunt Sally. She despised snakes, be the breed what they might, and she couldn't stand them no way you could fix it. And every time one of them flopped down on her, it didn't make no difference what she was doing, she would just lay that work down and light out. I never see such a woman. And you could hear her whoop to Jericho. You couldn't get her to take a-holt of one of them with the tongs. And if she turned over and found one in bed she would scramble out and lift a howl that you would think the house was afire.

She disturbed the old man so that he could most wish there hadn't ever been no snakes created. Why, after every last snake had been gone clear out the house for as much as a week Aunt Sally warn't over it yet, she warn't near over it; when she was setting thinking about something you could touch her on the back of her neck with a feather and she would jump right out of her stockings. It was very curious. But Tom said all women was just so. He said they was made that way for some reason or other.

We got a licking every time one of our snakes come in her way, and she allowed these lickings warn't nothing to what she would do if we ever loaded up the place again with them. I didn't mind the lickings, because they didn't amount to nothing; but I minded the trouble we had to lay in another lot. But we got them laid in, and all the other things; and you never see a cabin as blithesome as Jim's was when they'd all swarm out for music and go for Jim. Jim didn't like spiders, and the spiders didn't like Jim, and so they'd lay for him and make it mighty warm for him. And he said that between the rats and the snakes and the grindstone there warn't no room in bed for him, skasely. And when there was a body couldn't sleep, it was so lively, and it was always lively, he said, because *they* never all slept at one time, bot took turn about, so when the rats turned in the snakes come on watch, so he always had one gang under him, in his way, and t'other gang having a circus over him, and if he got up to hunt a new place the spiders would take a chance at him as he crossed over.

He said if he ever got out this time he wouldn't ever be a prisoner again, not for a salary.

Well, by the end of three weeks everything was in pretty good shape. The shirt was sent in early in a pie, and every time a rat bit Jim he would get up and write a line in his journal whilst the ink was fresh. The pens was made, the inscriptions and so on was all carved on the grindstone. The bed leg was sawed in two, and we had et up the sawdust, and it give us a most amazing stomach-ache. We reckoned we was going to die, but didn't. It was the most undigestable sawdust I ever see, and Tom said the same.

But as I was saying, we'd got all the work done now, at last; and we was all pretty much fagged out, too, but mainly Jim. The old man had wrote a couple of times to the plantation below Orleans to come and get their runaway nigger, but hadn't got no answer, becouse there warn't no such plantation. So he allowed he would advertise Jim in the St. Louis and New Orleans papers. When he mentioned the St. Louis ones, it give me the cold shivers, and I see we hadn't no time to lose.

So Tom said, now for the nonnamous letters.

"What's them?" I says.

"Warnings to the people that something is up. Sometimes it's done one way, sometimes another. But there's always somebody spying around that gives notice to the governor of the castle. When Louis XVI was going to light out of the Tooleries, a servant-girl done it. It's a very good way, and so is the nonnamous letters. We'll use them both. And it's usual for the prisoner's mother to change clothes with him, and she stays in, and he slides out and gets away in her clothes. We'll do that, too."

"But looky here, Tom, what do we want to *warn* anybody for that something's up? Let them find it out for themselves—it's their lookout."

"Yes, I know, but you can't depend on them. It's way they've acted from the very start—left us to do *everything*. They're so confiding and mullet-headed they don't take notice of nothing at all. So if we don't *give* them notice there won't be nobody nor nothing to interfere with us, and so after all our hard work and trouble this escape'll go off perfectly flat; won't amount to nothing—won't be nothing *to* it if we don't watch out."

"Well, as for me, Tom, that's the way I'd like."

"Shucks!" he says and looked disgusted.

So I says, "But I ain't going to make no complaint. Any way that suits you suits me. What you going to do about the servant girl?"

"You'll be her. You slide in, in the middle of the night, and hook that yaller girl's frock."

"Why, Tom, that'll make trouble next morning, because, of course, she prob'bly hain't got any but that one."

"I know; but you don't want it but fifteen minutes, to carry the nonnamous letter and shove it under the front door."

"All right, then, I'll do it; but I could carry it just as handy in my own togs."

"You wouldn't look like a servant-girl *then*, would you?"

"No, but there won't be nobody to see what I look like, *anyway*."

"That ain't got nothing to do with it. The thing for us to do is just to do our *duty*, and not worry about whether anybody *sees* us do it or not. Hain't you got no principle at all?"

"All right, I ain't saying nothing; I'm the servant-girl. Who's Jim's mother?"

"I'm his mother. I'll hook a gown from Aunt Sally."

"Well, then, you'll have to stay in the cabin when me and Jim leaves."

"Not much. I'll stuff Jim's clothes full of straw and lay it on his bed to represent his mother in disguise, and Jim'll take the nigger woman's gown off of me and wear it, and we'll all evade together. When a prisoner of style escapes it's called an evasion. It's always called so when a king escapes, f'rinstance. And the same with a king's son; it don't make no difference whether he's a natural one or an unnatural one."

So Tom he wrote the nonnamous letter, and I smouched the yaller wench's frock that night, and put it on, and shoved it under the front door, the way Tom told me to. It said:

Beware. Trouble is brewing. Keep a sharp lookout.

Unknown Friend

Next night we stuck a picture, which Tom drawed in blood, of a skull and crossbones to the front door; and next night another one of a coffin on the back door. I never see a family in such a sweat. They couldn't 'a' been worse scared if the place had 'a' been full of ghosts laying for them behind everything and under the beds and shivering through the air. If a door banged, Aunt Sally, she jumped and said "Ouch!" If anything fell, she jumped and said "Ouch!" If you happened to touch her when she warn't noticing, she done the same. She couldn't face no way and be satisfied, because she allowed there was something behind her every time—so she was always a-whirling around sudden, and saying "Ouch!" And before she'd got two-thirds around she'd whirl back again and say it again. And she was afraid to go to bed, but she dasn't set up. So the thing was working very well, Tom said; he said he never see a thing work more satisfactory. He said it showed it was done right.

So he said, now for the grand bulge! So the very next morning at the streak of dawn we got another letter ready, and was wondering what we better do with it, because we heard them say at supper they was going to have a nigger on watch at both doors all night. Tom he went down the lightning rod to spy around; and the nigger at the back door was asleep, and he stuck it in the back of his neck and come back. This letter said:

Don't betray me, I wish to be your friend. There is a desprate gang of cutthroats from over in the Indian Territory going to steal your runaway nigger tonight, and they have been trying to scare you so as you will stay in the house and not bother them. I am one of the gang, but have got relligion and wish to quit it and lead an honest life again, and will betray the helish design. They will sneak down from northards, along the fence, at midnight exact, with a false key, and go in the nigger's cabin to get him. I am to be off a piece and blow a tin horn if I see any danger; but stead of that I will BA like a sheep soon as they get in and not blow at all. Then whilst they are getting his chains loose, you slip there and lock them in, and can kill them at your leisure. Don't do anything but just the way I am telling you. If you do they will suspicion something and raise whoop-jambooreehoo. I do not wish any reward but to know I have done the right thing.

Unknown Friend

CHAPTER XXIX

Fishing–The vigilance committee–A lively run–Jim advises a doctor

HE WAS feeling pretty good after breakfast, and took my canoe and went over the river a-fishing, with a lunch, and had a good time, and took a look at the raft and found her all right, and got home late for supper. We found them in such a sweat and worry they didn't know which end they was standing on, and made us go right off to bed the minute we was done supper, and wouldn't tell us what the trouble was, and never let on a word about the new letter, but didn't need to, because we knowed as much about it as anybody did. As soon as we was half upstairs and her back was turned we slid for the cellar cupboard and loaded up a good lunch and took it up to our room and went to bed. We got up about half past eleven, and Tom put on Aunt Sally's dress that he stole.

He was going to start with the lunch, but he says, "Where's the butter?"

"I laid out a hunk of it," I says, "on a piece of a corn pone."

"Well, you *left* it laid out, then–it ain't here."

"We can get along without it," I says.

"We can get along *with* it, too," he says. "Just you slide down cellar and fetch it. And then mosey right down the lightning rod and come along. I'll go stuff the straw into Jim's clothes to represent his mother in disguise, and be ready to *ba* like a sheep and shove as you get there."

So out he went, and down cellar went I. The hunk of butter, big as a person's fist, was where I had left it, so I took up the slab of corn pone with it on, and blowed out my light, and started upstairs very stealthy, and got to the main floor all right. But here comes Aunt Sally with a candle, and I clapped the truck in my hat, and clapped my hat on my head, and the next second she see me. And she says, "You been down cellar?"

"Yes'm."

"What you been doing down there?"

"Noth'n."

"*Noth'n!*"

"No'm."

"Well, then, what possessed you to go down there this time of night?"

"I don't know 'm."

"You don't *know?* Don't answer me that way. Huck, I want to know what you been *doing* down there."

"I hain't been doing a single thing, Aunt Sally, I hope to gracious if I have."

I reckoned she'd let me go now, and as a generl thing she would; but I s'pose there was so many things going on she was just in a sweat about every little thing that warn't yardstick straight. So she says, very decided, "You just march into that setting room and stay there till I come. You been up to something you no business to, and I lay I'll find out what it is before *I'm* done with you."

So she went away as I opened the door and walked into the setting room. My, but there was a crowd there! Fifteen farmers, and every one of them had a gun. I was most powerful sick, and slunk to a chair and set down. They was setting around, some of them talking a little in a low voice, and all of them fidgety and uneasy, but trying to look like they warn't; but I knowed they was, because they was always taking off their hats and putting them on and scratching their heads and changing their seats and fumbling with their buttons. I warn't easy myself, but I didn't take my hat off, all the same.

I did wish Aunt Sally would come, and get done with me, and lick me if she wanted to, and let me get away and tell Tom how we'd overdone this thing, and what a thundering hornets' nest we'd got ourselves into, so we could stop fooling around straight off and clear out with Jim before these rips got out of patience and come for us.

At last she come and begun to ask me questions, but I *couldn't* answer them staight, I didn't know which end of me was up; because these men was in such a fidget now that some was wanting to start right *now* and lay for them desperadoes, and saying it warn't but a few minutes to midnight; and others was trying to get them to hold on and waid for the sheep signal. And here was Aunty pegging away at the questions, and me a-shaking all over and ready to sink down in my tracks I was that scared, and the place getting hotter and hotter, and the butter beginning to melt and run down my neck and behind my ears. Pretty soon, when one of them says, "*I'm* for going and getting in the cabin *first* and right *now*, and catching them when they come," I most dropped, and a streak of butter come a-trickling down my forehead, and Aunt Sally, she see it and turns white as a sheet and says, "For the land's sake, what *is* the matter with the child? He's got the brain fever as shore as you're born, and they're oozing out!"

And everybody runs to see, and she snatches off my hat, and out comes the bread and what was left of the butter, and she grabbed me and hugged me and says, 'Oh, what a turn you did give me! And how glad and grateful I am it ain't no worse; for luck's against us, and it never rains but it pours, and when I see that truck I thought we'd lost you, for I knowed by the color and all it was just like your brains would be if—Dear, dear, whyd'n't you *tell* me that was what you'd been down there for, *I* wouldn't 'a' cared. Now cler out to bed, and don't lemme see no more of you till morning!"

I was upstairs in a second and down the lightning rod in another one and shinning through the dark for the lean-to. I couldn't hardly get my words out, I was so anxious; but I told Tom as quick as I could we must jump for it now, and not a minute to lose—the house full of men, yonder, all of 'em with guns!

His eyes just blazed, and he says, "No! Is that so? *Ain't* it bully! Why,

Huck, if it was to do over again, I bet I could fetch two hundred! If we could put it off till–"

"Hurry! *Hurry!*" I says. "Where's Jim?"

"Right at your elbow. If you reach your arm you can touch him. He's dressed, and everything's ready. Now we'll slide out and give the sheep signal."

But then we heard the tramp of men coming to the door, and heard them begin to fumble with the padlock, and heard a man say, "I *told* you we'd be too soon. They haven't come–the door is locked. Here, I'll lock some of you into the cabin, and you lay for 'em in the dark and kill 'em when they come; and the rest scatter around a piece, and listen if you can hear 'em coming."

So in they come, but couldn't see us in the dark, and most trod on us whilst we was hustling to get under the bed. But we got under all right, and out through the hole, swift but soft–Jim first, me next, and Tom last, which was according to Tom's orders. Now we was in the lean-to, and heard trampings close by outside. So we crept to the door, and Tom stopped us there and put his eye to the crack, but he couldn't make out nothing, it was so dark; and whispered and said he would listen for the steps to get further, and when he nudged us Jim must glide out first, and him last. So he set his ear to the crack and listened and listened and listened, and the steps a-scraping around out there all the time; and at last he nudged us, and we slid out and stooped down, not breathing and not making the last noise, and slipped stealthy toward the fence in Injun file and got to it all right, and me and Jim over it; but Tom's britches catched fast on a splinter on the top rail, and then he heard the steps coming, so he had to pull loose, which snapped the splinter and made a noise. And as he dropped in our tracks and started, somebody sings out, "Who's that? Answer, or I'll shoot!"

But we didn't answer. We just unfurled our heels and shoved. Then there was a rush, and a *bang, bang, bang!* And the bullets fairly whizzed around us! We heard them sing out, "Here they are! They've broke for the river! After 'em, boys, and turn loose the dogs!"

So here they come, full tilt. We could hear them because they wore boots and yelled, but we didn't wear no boots and didn't yell. We was in the path to the mill; and when they got pretty close onto us we dodged into the bush and let them go by, and then dropped in behind them. They'd had all the dogs shut up, so they wouldn't scare off the robbers. But by this time somebody had let them loose, and here they come, making pow-wow enough for a million. But they was our dogs, so we stopped in our tracks till they catched up; and when they see it warn't nobody but us, and no excitement to offer them, they only just said howdy and tore right ahead toward the shouting and clattering. And then we up steam again, and whizzed along after them till we was nearly to the mill, and then struck up through the bush to where my canoe was tied, and hopped in and pulled for dear life toward the middle of the river, but didn't make no more noise than we was obleeged to. Then we struck out, easy and comfortable, for the island where my raft was; and we could hear them yelling and barking at each other all up and down the bank, till we was so far away the sounds got dim and died out.

And when we stopped onto the raft I says, "Now, old Jim, you're a free man again, and I bet you won't ever be a slave no more."

"En a mighty good job it wuz, too, Huck. It 'uz planned beautiful, en it 'uz done beautiful; en dey ain't nobody kin git up a plans dat's mo' mixed up en splendid den what dot one wuz. An' Jim's mighty glad."

We was all glad as we could be, but Tom was the gladdest of all because he had a bullet in the calf of his leg.

When me and Jim heard that, we didn't feel as brash as what we did before. It was hurting him considerable, and bleeding; so we laid him in the wigwam and tore up one of the duke's shirts for to bandage him, but he says, "Gimme the rags; I can do it myself. Don't stop now. Don't fool around here, and the evasion booming along so handsome; man the sweeps, and set her loose! Boys, we done it elegant—'deed we did! I wish we'd 'a' had the handling of Louis XVI; there wouldn't 'a' been no 'Son of Saint Louis, ascend to heaven!' wrote down in his biography. No, sir, we'd 'a' whooped him over the border—that's what we'd 'a' done with him—and done it just as slick as nothing at all, too. Man the sweeps—man the sweeps!"

But me and Jim was consulting—and thinking. And after we'd thought a minute, I says, "Say it, Jim."

So he says, "Well, den, dis is de way it look to me, Huck. Ef it wuz him dat 'uz bein' sot free, en one er de boys wuz to git shot, would he say, 'Go on en save me, nemmine 'bout a doctor f'r to save dis one'? Is dat like Mars Tom Sawyer? Would he say dat? You bet he wouldn't! Well, den, is Jim gwyne to say it? No, sah—I doan' budge a step out'n dis place 'dout a doctor, not if it's forty year!"

I knowed he was white inside, and I reckoned he'd say what he did say—so it was all right now, and I told Tom I was a-going for a doctor. He raised considerable row about it, but me and Jim stuck to it and wouldn't budge; so he was for crawling out and setting the raft loose himself, but we wouldn't let him. Then he give us a piece of his mind, but it didn't do no good.

So when he sees me getting the canoe ready, he says, "Well, then, if you're bound to go, I'll tell you the way to do when you get to the village. Shut the door and blindford the doctor tight and fast, and make him swear to be silent as the grave, and put a purse full of gold in his hand, and then take and lead him all around the back alleys and everywheres in the dark, and then fetch him here in the canoe, in a roundabout way amongst the islands, and search him and take his chalk away from him, and don't give it back to him till you get him back to the village, or else he will chalk this raft so he can find it again. It's the way they all do."

So I said I would, and left, and Jim was to hide in the woods when he see the doctor coming till he was gone again.

CHAPTER XXX

The doctor—Uncle Silas—Sister Hotchkiss—Aunt Sally in trouble

The doctor was an old man, a very nice, kind-looking old man when I got him up. I told him me and my brother was over on Spanish Island hunting yesterday afternoon, and camped on a piece of raft we found, and about midnight he must 'a' kicked his gun in his dreams, for it went off and shot him in the leg, and we wanted him to go over there and fix it and not say nothing about it, nor let anybody know, because we wanted to come home this evening and surprise the folks.

"Who is your folks?" he says.

"The Phelpses, down yonder."

"Oh," he says. And after a minute, he says, "How'd you say he got shot?"

"He had a dream," I says, "and it shot him."

"Singular dream," he says.

So he lit up his lantern and got his saddlebags, and we started. But when he see the canoe he didn't like the look of her—said she was big enough for one, but didn't look pretty safe for two.

I says, "Oh, you needn't be afeard, sir, she carried the three of us easy enough."

"What three?"

"Why, me and Sid, and—and—and *the guns;* that's what I mean."

"Oh," he says.

But he put his foot on the gunnel and rocked her, and shook his head, and said he reckoned he'd look around for a bigger one. But they was all locked and chained. So he took my canoe and said for me to wait till he come back, or I could hunt around further, or maybe I better go down home and get them ready for the surprise if I wanted to. But I said I didn't; so I told him just how to find the raft, and then he started.

I struck an idea pretty soon. I says to myself, spos'n he can't fix that leg just in three shakes of a sheep's tail, as the saying is? Spos'n it takes him three or four days? What are we going to do? Lay around there till he lets the cat out of the bag? No, sir; I know what *I'll* do. I'll wait, and when he comes back if he says he's got to go any more I'll get down there, too, if I swim. And we'll take and tie him, and keep him and shove out down the river. And when Tom's done with him, we'll give him what it's worth, or all we got, and then we'll let him get ashore.

So then I crept into a lumber pile to get some sleep; and next time I waked up the sun was away up over my head! I shot out and went for the doctor's house, but they told me he'd gone away in the night sometime or other, and warn't back yet. Well, thinks I, that looks powerful bad for Tom, and I'll dig out for the island right off.

So away I shoved, and turned the corner, and nearly rammed my head into Uncle Silas's stomach! He says, "Why, *Tom!* Where you been all this time, you rascal?"

"*I* hain't been nowheres," I says, "only just hunting for the runaway nigger—me and Sid."

"Why, where ever did you go?" he says. "Your aunt's been mighty uneasy."

"She needn't," I says, "because we was all right. We followed the men and dogs, but they outrun us, and we lost them. But we thought we heard them on the water, so we got a canoe and took out after them and crossed over, but couldn't find nothing of them. So we cruised along upshore till we got kind of tired and beat out, and tied up the canoe and went to sleep and never waked up till about an hour ago. Then we paddled over here to hear the news, and Sid's at the post office to see what he can hear, and I'm a-branching out to get something to eat for us, and then we're going home."

So then we went to the post office to get "Sid," but just as I suspicioned, he warn't there. So the old man, he got a letter out of the office, and we waited awhile longer, but Sid didn't come. So the old man said, come along, let Sid foot it home, or canoe it, when he got done fooling around—but we would ride. I couldn't get him to let me stay and wait for Sid. He said there warn't no use in it, I must come along and let Aunt Sally see we was all right.

When we got home, Aunt Sally was that glad to see me she laughed and cried both, and hugged me, and give me one of them lickings of hern that don't amount to shucks, and said she'd serve Sid the same when he come.

And the place was plum full of farmers and farmers' wives, to dinner, and such another clack a body never heard. Old Mrs. Hotchkiss was the worst; her tongue wa a-going all the time, fast and loud.

She says, "Well, Sister Phelps, I've ransacked that-air cabin over, an' I b'lieve the nigger was crazy. I says to Sister Damrell—didn't I, Sister Damrell?—s'I, he's crazy, s'I—them's the very words I said. You all hearn me: he's crazy, s'I. Everything shows it, s'I. Look at that-air grindstone, s'I. Want to tell *me* any cretur 't's in his right mind 's a-goin' to scrabble all them crazy things onto a grindstone? s'I. Here sich 'n' sich a person busted his heart; 'n' here so 'n' so pegged along for thirty-seven year, 'n' all that—natcherl son o' Louis somebody, 'n' sich everlast'n rubbage. He's plumb crazy, s'I; it's what I says in the fust place, it's what I says in the middle, 'n' it's what I says last 'n' all the time—the nigger's crazy—crazy's Nebokoodneezer, s'I."

"An' look at that-air ladder made out'n rags, Sister Hotchkiss," says old Mrs. Damrell. "What in the name o' goodness *could* he ever want of—"

"The very words I was a-sayin' no longer ago th'n this minute to Sister Utterback, 'n' she'll tell you so herself. Sh-she, look at that-air rag ladder, sh-she; 'n' s'I, yes, *look* at it, s'I—what *could* he 'a' wanted of it? s'I. Sh-she, Sister Hotchkiss, sh-she—"

"But how in the nation'd they ever git that grindstone *in* there, *anyway*? 'N' who dug that-air *hole*? 'N' who—"

"My very *words*, Brer Penrod! I was a-sayin'—pass that-air sasser o' m'lasses, won't ye?—I was a-sayin' to Sister Dunlap, jist this minute, how *did* they git that grindstone in there? s'I. Without *help*, mind you—'thout *help*! Thar's where 'tis. Don't tell *me*, s'I; there *wuz* help, s'I; 'n' ther' wuz a *plenty* help, too, s'I; ther's ben a *dozen* a-helpin' that nigger; 'n' I lay I'd skin every last nigger on this place but *I'd* find out who done it, s'I; 'n' moreover, s'I—"

"A *dozen* says you! *Forty* couldn't 'a' done everything that's been done. Look at them case-knife saws and things, how tedious they've been made; look at that bed leg sawed off with 'm, a week's work for six men; look at that nigger made out'n straw on the bed; and look at—"

"You may *well* say it, Brer Hightower! It's jist as I was a-sayin' to Brer Phelps, his own self. S'e, what do *you* think of it, Sister Hotchkiss? s'e. Think o' what, Brer Phelps? s'I. Think o' that bed leg sawed off that a way? s'e. *Think* of it? s'I. I lay it never sawed *itself* off. s'I—somebody *sawed* it, s'I; that's my opinion take it or leave it, it mayn't be no 'count, s'I, but sich as 't is. it's my opinion, s'I, 'n' if anybody k'n start a better one, s'I, let him *do* it, s'I, that's all. I says to Sister Dunlap, s'I—"

"Why, dog my cats, they must 'a' ben a house-full o' niggers in there every night for four weeks to 'a' done all that work, Sister Phelps. Look at that shirt—every last inch of it kivered over with secret African writ'n done with blood! Must 'a' ben a raft uv 'm at it right along, all the time, a'most. Why, I'd give two dollars to have it read to me; 'n' as for the niggers that wrote it, I 'low I'd take 'n' lash 'm t'll—"

"People to *help* him, Brother Marples! Well, I reckon you'd *think* so if you'd 'a' been in this house for a while back. Why, they've stole everything they could lay their hands on—and we a-watching all the time, mind you. They stole that shirt right off o' the line! And as for that sheet they made the rag ladder out of, ther' ain't no telling how many times they *didn't* steal that; and flour and candles and candlesticks and spoons and the old warming pan and most a thousand things that I risremember now, and my new calico dress. And me and Silas and my Sid and Tom on the constant watch day *and* night, as I was a-telling you, and not a one of us could catch hide nor hair nor sight nor sound of them. And here at the last minute, lo and behold you, they slides right in under our noses and fools us, and not only fools *us* but the Injun Territory robbers, too, and actuly gets *away* with that nigger safe and sound, and that with sixteen men and twenty-two dogs right on their very heels at that very time! I tell you, it just bangs anything I ever *heard* of.

"Why, *sperits* couldn't 'a' done better and been no smarter. And I reckon they must 'a' *been* *s*perits—because, *you* know our dogs, and ther' ain't no better. Well, them dogs never even got on the *track* of 'm once! You explain *that* to me if you can!"

"Well, it does beat—"

"Laws alive, I never—"

"So help me, I wouldn't 'a' be—"

"*House* thieves as well as—"

"Goodnessgracioussakes, I'd 'a' ben afeard to *live* in a—"

"'Fraid to *live!* Why, I was that scared I dasn't hardly go to bed or get up or lay down or *set* down, Sister Ridgeway. Why, they'd steal the very—why, goodness sakes, you can guess what kind of a fluster *I* was in by the time midnight come last night. I hope to gracious if I warn't afraid they'd steal some o' the family! I was just to that pass I didn't have no reasoning faculties no more. It looks foolish enough *now*, in the daytime; but I says to myself, there's my two poor boys asleep, 'way upstairs in that lonesome room, and I declare to goodness I was that uneasy 't I crep' up there and locked 'em in! I *did*. And anybody would. Because, you know, when you get scared that way, and it keeps running on, and getting worse and worse all the time, and your wits get to addling, and you get to doing all sorts o' wild things, and by and by you think to yourself, spos'n *I* was a boy, and was away up there, and the door ain't locked, and you—"

She stopped, looking kind of wondering, and then she turned her head around slow, and when her eye lit on me—I got up and took a walk.

Says I to myself, I can explain better how we come to not be in that room this morning if I go out to one side and study over it a little. So I done it. But I dasn't go fur, or she'd 'a' sent for me. And when it was late in the day the people all went, and then I come in and told her the noise and shooting waked up me an "Sid," and the door was locked, and we wanted to see the fun, so we went down the lightning rod, and both of us got hurt a little, and we didn't never want to try *that* no more.

And then I went on and told her all what I told Uncle Silas before; and then she said she'd forgive us, and maybe it was all right enough anyway, and about what a body might expect of boys, for all boys was a pretty harum-scarum lot as fur as she could see. And so, as long as no harm hadn't come of it, she judged she better put in her time being grateful we was alive and well and she had us still, stead of fretting over what was past and done. So then she kissed me and patted me on the head and dropped into a kind of a brown study, and pretty soon jumps up and says, "Why, lawsamercy, it's most night, and Sid not come yet! What you reckon *has* become of that boy?"

I see my chance; so I skips up and says, "I'll run right up to town and get him," I says.

"No, you won't," she says. "You'll stay right wher' you are, *one's* enough to be lost at a time. If he ain't here to supper, your uncle 'll go."

Well, he warn't there to supper. So right after supper Uncle Silas went.

He come back about ten a little bit uneasy; hadn't run across Tom's track. Aunt Sally was a good *deal* uneasy, but Uncle Silas, he said there warn't no occasion to be—boys will be boys, he said, and you'll see this one turn up in the morning all sound and right. So she had to be satisfied. But she said she'd set up fo him awhile anyway, and keep a light burning so he could see it.

And then when I went up to bed she come with me and fetched her candle and tucked me in and mothered me so good I felt mean, and like I couldn't look her in the face. And she set down on the bed and talked with me a long time, and said what a splendid boy Sid was, and didn't seem to want to ever stop talking about him, and kept asking me every now and then if I reckoned he could 'a' got lost or hurt or maybe drownded, and might be laying at this minute somewheres suffering or dead, and she not by him to help him, and so the tears would drip down silent. And I would tell her that Sid was all right and would be home in the morning, sure; and she would squeeze my hand and tell me to keep on saying it, because it done her good and she was in so much trouble.

And when she was going away she looked down in my eyes so steady and gentle, and says, "The door ain't going to be locked, Tom, and there's the window and the rod; but you'll be good, *won't* you? And you won't go? For *my* sake."

Laws knows I *wanted* to go bad enough to see about Tom, and was all intending to go; but after that I wouldn't 'a' went, not for kingdoms.

But she was on my mind and Tom was on my mind, so I slept very restless. And twice I went down the rod away in the night, and slipped around front, and see her setting there by her candle in the window with her eyes towards the road and the tears in them. And I wished I could do something for her, but I couldn't, only to swear that I wouldn't never do nothing to grieve her any more. And the third time I waked up at dawn and slid down, and she was there yet, and her candle was most out, and her old gray head was resting on her hand, and she was asleep.

CHAPTER XXXI

*Tom Sawyer wounded—The doctor's story—Tom confesses
Aunt Polly arrives—Hand out them letters*

THE old man was uptown again before breakfast, but couldn't get no track of Tom; and both of them set at the table thinking, and not saying nothing, and looking mournful, and their coffee getting cold, and not eating anything. And by and by the old man says, "Did I give you the letter?"

"What letter?"

"The one I got yesterday out of the post office."

"No, you didn't give me no letter."

"Well, I must 'a' forgot it."

So he rummaged his pockets and then went off somewheres where he had laid it down, and fetched it, and give it to her. She says, "Why, it's from St. Petersburg—it's from Sis."

I allowed another walk would do me good, but I couldn't stir. But before she could break it open she dropped it and run—for she see something. And so did I. It was Tom Sawyer on a mattress, and that old doctor, and Jim in *her* calico dress with his hands tied behind him, and a lot of people. I hid the letter behind the first thing handy, and rushed.

She flung herself at Tom, crying, and says, "Oh, he's dead, he's dead, I know he's dead!"

And Tom he turned his head a little and muttered something or other, which showed he warn't in his right mind. Then she flung up her hands and says, "He's alive, thank God! And that's enough!" And she snatched a kiss of him, and flew for the house to get the bed ready, and scattering orders right and left at the niggers and everybody else, as fast as her tongue could go, every jump of the way.

I followed the men to see what they was going to do with Jim, and the old doctor and Uncle Silas followed after Tom into the house. The men was very huffy, and some of them wanted to hang Jim for an example to all the other niggers around there, so they wouldn't be trying to run away like Jim done, and making such a raft of trouble, and keeping a whole family scared most to death for days and nights. But the others said, don't do it, it wouldn't answer at all; he hain't our nigger, and his owner would turn up and make us pay for him, sure. So that cooled them down a little, because the people that's always the most anxious for to hang a nigger that hain't done just right is always the very ones that ain't the most anxious to pay for him when they've got their satisfaction out of him.

They cussed Jim considerable, though, and give him a cuff or two side the head once in a while, but Jim never said nothing, and he never let on to know me, and they took him to the same cabin and put his own clothes on him, and chained him again, and not to no bed leg this time, but to a big staple drove into the bottom log, and chained his hands, too, and both legs, and said he warn't to have nothing but bread and water to eat after this till his owner come, or he was sold at auction because he didn't come in a certain length of time, and filled up our hole, and said a couple of farmers with guns must stand watch around about the cabin every night, and a bulldog tied to the door in the daytime.

About this time they was through with the job and was tapering off with a kind of generl good-bye cussing, and then the old doctor comes and takes a look and says, "Don't be no rougher on him than you're obleeged to because he ain't a bad nigger. When I got to where I found the boy, I see I couldn't cut the bullet out without some help, and he warn't in no condition for me to leave to go and get help. And he got a little worse and a little worse, and after a long time he went out of his head, and wouldn't let me come a-nigh him any more, and said if I chalked his raft he'd kill me, and no end of wild foolishness like that, and I see I couldn't do anything at all with him. So I says, I got to have *help* somehow; and the minute I says it, out crawls this nigger from somewheres and says he'll help, and he done it, too, and done it very well.

"Off course I judged he must be a runaway nigger, and there I *was!* And there I had to stick right straight along all the rest of the day and all night. It was a fix, I tell you! I had a couple of patients with the chills, and of course I'd of liked to run up to town and see them, but I dasn't, because the nigger might get away, and then I'd be to blame; and yet never a skiff come close enough for me to hail. So there I had to stick plumb until daylight this morning. And I never see a nigger that was a better nuss or faithfuler, and yet he was risking his freedom to do it, and was all tired out, too, and I see plain enough he'd been worked main hard lately. I liked the nigger for that. I tell you, gentlemen, a nigger like that is worth a thousand dollars—and kind treatment, too. I had everything I needed, and the boy was doing as well there as he would 'a' done at home—better, maybe, because it was so quiet; but there I *was* with both of 'm on my hands, and there I had to stick till about dawn this morning.

"Then some men in a skiff come by, and as good luck would have it the nigger was setting by the pallet with his head propped on his knees sound asleep; so I motioned them in quiet, and they slipped up on him and grabbed him and tied him before he knowed what he was about, and we never had no trouble. And the boy being in a kind of flighty sleep, too, we muffled the oars and hitched the raft on, and towed her over very nice and quiet, and the nigger never made the least row nor said a word from the start. He ain't no bad nigger."

Somebody says, "Well, it sounds very good, doctor, I'm obleeged to say."

Then the others softened up a little, too, and I was mighty thankful to that old doctor for doing Jim that good turn, and I was glad it was according to my judgement of him, too; because I thought he had a good heart in him and was a good man the first time I see him. Then they all agreed that Jim had acted very well, and was deserving to have some notice took of it, and reward. So every one of them promised, right out and hearty, that they wouldn't cuss him no more.

Then they come out and locked him up. I hoped they was going to say he could have one or two of the chains took off, because they was rotten heavy, or could have meat and greens with his bread and water. But they didn't think of it, and I reckoned it warn't best for me to mix in, but I judged I'd get the doctor's yarn to Aunt Sally somehow or other as soon as I'd got through the breakers that was laying just ahead of me–explanations, I mean, of how I forgot to mention about Sid being shot when I was telling how him and me put in that dratted night paddling around hunting the runaway nigger.

But I had plenty time. Aunt Sally she stuck to the sickroom all day and all night, and every time I see Uncle Silas mooning around I dodged him.

Next morning I heard Tom was a good deal better, and they said Aunt Sally was gone to get a nap. So I slips to the sickroom, and if I found him awake I reckoned we could put up a yarn for the family that would wash. But he was sleeping, and sleeping very peaceful, too; and pale, not fire-faced the way he was when he come. So I set down and laid for him to wake. In about half an hour Aunt Sally comes gliding in, and there I was, up a stump again! She motioned me to be still, and set down by me, and begun to whisper, and said we could all be joyful now, because all the symptoms was first-rate, and he'd been sleeping like that for ever so long, and looking better and peacefuler all the time, and ten to one he'd wake up in his right mind.

So we set there watching, and by and by he stirs a bit, and opened his eyes very natural, and takes a look, and says, "Hello! Why, I'm at *home!* How's that? Where's the raft?"

"It's all right," I says.

"And *Jim?*"

"The same," I says, but couldn't say it pretty brash. But he never noticed, but says, "Good! Splendid! *Now* we're all right and safe! Did you tell, Aunty?"

I was going to say yes, but she chipped in and says, "About what, Sid?"

"Why, about the way the whole thing was done."

"What whole thing?"

"Why, *the* whole thing. There ain't but one; how we set the runaway nigger free–me and Tom."

"Good land! Set the run–What *is* the child talking about! Dear, dear, out of his head again!"

"*No,* I ain't out of my *head;* I know all what I'm talking about. We *did* set him free–me and Tom. We laid out to do it, and we *done* it. And we done it elegant, too." He'd got a start, and she never checked him up, just set and stared and stared, and let him clip along, and I see it warn't no for *me* to put in.

"Why, Aunty, it cost us a power of work–weeks of it–hours and hours, every night, whilst you was all asleep. And we had to steal candles and the sheet and the shirt and your dress and spoons and tin plates and case knives and the warming pan and the grindstone, and flour, and just no end of things, and you can't think what work it was to make the saws and pens and inscriptions and one thing or another, and you can't think *half* the fun it was. And we had to make up the pictures of coffins and things, and nonnamoüs letters from the robbers, and get up and down the lightning rod, and dig the hole into the cabin, and make the rope ladder and send it in cooked up in a pie, and send in spoons and things to work with in your apron pocket—"

"Mercy sakes!"

"—and load up the cabin with rats and snakes and so on, for company for Jim; and then you kept Tom here so long with the butter in his hat that you come near spiling the whole business, because the men come before we was out of the cabin, and we had to rush, and they heard us and let drive at us, and I got my share, and we dodged out of the path and let them go by, and when the dogs come they warn't interested in us, but went for the most noise, and we got our canoe and made for the raft, and was all safe, and Jim was a free man, and we done it all by ourselves, and *wasn't* it bully, Aunty?"

"Well, I never heard the likes of it in all my born days! So it was *you,* you little rapscallions, that's been making all this trouble, and turned everybody's wits clean inside out and scared us all to death. I've as good a notion as ever I had in my life to take it out o' you this very minute. To think, here I've been, night after night, a—*you* just get well once, you young scamp, and I lay I'll tan the Old Harry out o' both o' ye!"

But Tom, he *was* so proud and joyful, he just *couldn't* hold in, and his tongue just *went* it—she a-chipping in and spitting fire all along, and both of them going it at once, like a cat convention.

She says, "*Well,* you get all the enjoyment you can out of it *now,* for mind, I tell you if I catch you meddling with him again—"

"Meddling with *who?*" Tom says, dropping his smile.

"With *who?* Why, the runaway nigger. Who'd you reckon?"

Tom looks at me very grave and says, "Tom didn't you just tell me he was all right? Hasn't he got away?"

"*Him?*" says Aunt Sally. "The runaway nigger? 'Deed he hasn't. They've got him back, safe and sound, and he's in that cabin again, on bread and water, and loaded down with chains, till he's claimed or sold!"

Tom rose square up in the bed, with his eye hot, and his nostrils opening and shutting like gills, and sings out to me, "They hain't no *right* to shut him up! *Shove*—and don't you lose a minute! Turn him loose! He ain't no slave; he's as free as any cretur that walks this earth!"

"What *does* the child mean?"

"I mean every word I *say,* Aunt Sally, and if somebody don't go, *I'll* go. I've known him all his life, and so has Tom, there. Old Miss Watson died two months ago, and she was ashamed she ever was going to sell him down the river, and *said* so. And she set him free in her will."

"Then what on earth did *you* want to set him free for?"

"Well, that *is* a question, I must say! And *just* like women! Why, I wanted the *adventure* of it, and I'd 'a' waded neck-deep in blood to—goodness alice, *Aunt Polly!*"

If she warn't standing right there, just inside the door, looking as sweet and contented as an angel half full of pie, I wish I may never!

Aunt Sally jumped for her, and most hugged the head off of her, and cried over her, and I found a good enough place for me under the bed, for it was getting pretty sultry for *us*, seemed to me. And I peeped out, and in a little while Tom's Aunt Polly shook herself loose and stood there looking across at Tom over her spectacles—kind of grinding him into the earth, you know.

And then she says, "Yes, you *better* turn y'r head away—I would if I was you, Tom."

"Oh, deary me!" says Aunt Sally. *Is* he changed so? Why, that ain't *Tom*, it's Sid. Tom's—Tom's—why, where is Tom? He was here a minute ago."

"You mean wheres Huck *Finn*—that's what you mean! I reckon I hain't raised such a scamp as my Tom all these years not to know him when I *see* him. That *would* be a pretty howdy-do. Come out from under that bed, Huck Finn."

So I done it. But not feeling brash.

Aunt Sally, she was one of the mixed-upest-looking persons I ever see—except one, and that was Uncle Silas, when he come in and they told it all to him. It kind of made him drunk, as you may say, and he didn't know nothing at all the rest of the day, and preached a prayer-meeting sermon that night that gave him a rattling reputation, because the oldest man in the world couldn't 'a' understood it.

So Tom's Aunt Polly, she told all about who I was, and what. And I had to up and tell how I was in such a tight place that when Mrs. Phelps took me for Tom Sawyer—she chipped in and says, "Oh, go on and call me Aunt Sally. I'm used to it now, and 'tain't no need to change"—that when Aunt Sally took me for Tom Sawyer, I had to stand it. There warn't no other way, and I knowed he wouldn't mind, because it would be nuts for him, being a mystery, and he'd make an adventure out of it, and be perfectly satisfied.

And so it turned out, and he let on to be Sid, and made things as soft as he could for me.

And his Aunt Polly, she said Tom was right about old Miss Watson setting Jim free in her will, and so, sure enough, Tom Sawyer had gone and took all that trouble and bother to set a free nigger free! And I couldn't ever understand before, until that minute and that talk, how he *could* help a body set a nigger free with his bringing-up.

Well, Aunt Polly, she said that when Aunt Sally wrote to her that Tom and *Sid* had come all right and safe, she says to herself, "Look at that, now! I might have expected it, letting him go off that way without anybody to watch him. So now I got to go and trapse all the way down the river, eleven hundred mile, and find out what that creetur's up to *this* time, as long as I couldn't seem to get any answer out of you about it."

"Why. I never heard nothing from you," says Aunt Sally.

"Well, I wonder! Why, I wrote you twice to ask you what you could mean by Sid being here."

"Well, I never got 'em, Sis."

Aunt Polly, she turns arount slow and severe, and says, "You, Tom!"

"Well—*what?*" he says, kind of pettish.

"Don't you what *me*, you impudent thing—hand out them letters."

"What letters?"

"*Them* letters. I be bound, if I have to take a-holt of you I'll—"

"They're in the trunk. There, now. And they're just the same as they was when I got them out of the office. I hain't looked into them. I hain't touched them. But I knowed they'd make trouble, and I thought if you warn't in no hurry, I'd—"

"Well, you *do* need skinning, there ain't no mistake about it. And I wrote another one to tell you I was coming, and I s'pose he—"

"No, it come yesterday. I ain't read it yet, but *it's* all right. I've got that one."

I wanted to offer to bet two dollars she hadn't, but I reckoned maybe it was just as safe to not to. So I never said nothing.

CHAPTER THE LAST

Out of bondage—Paying the captive—Yours truly, Huck Finn

THE first time I catched Tom private I asked him what was his idea, time of the evasion? What it was he'd planned to do if the evasion worked all right and he managed to set a nigger free that was already free before? And he said what he had planned in his head from the start, if we got Jim out all safe, was for us to run him down the river on the raft, and have adventures plumb to the mouth of the river, and then tell him about his being free, and take him back up home an a steamboat, in style, and pay him for his lost time, and write word ahead and get out all the niggers around, and have them waltz him into town with a torchlight procession and a brass band. Then he would be a hero, and so would we. But I reckoned it was about as well the way it was.

We had Jim out of the chains in no time, and when Aunt Polly and Uncle Silas and Aunt Sally found out how good he helped the doctor nurse Tom, they made a heap of fuss over him and fixed him up prime and give him all he wanted to eat, and a good time and nothing to do. And we had him up to the sickroom, and had a high talk; and Tom give Jim forty dollars for being prisoner for us so patient, and doing it up so good.

And then Tom, he talked along and talked along, and he says le's all three slide out of here one of these nights and get an outfit and go for howling adventures amongst the Injuns over in the territory for a couple of weeks or two. And I says right, that suits me, but I ain't got no money for to buy the outfit, and I reckon I couldn't get none from home, because it's likely Pap's been back before now and got it all away from Judge Thatcher and drunk it up.

"No, he hain't," Tom says. "It's all there yet—six thousand dollars and more. And your pap hain't ever been back since. Hadn't when I come away, anyhow."

Jim says, kind of solemn, "He hain't a-comin' back no mo', Huck."

I says, "Why, Jim?"

"Nemmine why, Huck—but he ain't comin' back no mo'."

But I kept at him. So at last he says, "Doan' you 'member de house dat was float'n down the river, en dey wuz a man in dah, kivered up, en I went in en unkivered him and didn't let you come in? Well, den, you kin git yo' money when you wants it, kase dat wuz him."

Tom's most well now, and got his bullet around his neck on a watch-guard for a watch, and is always seeing what time it is, and so there ain't nothing more to write about, and I am rotten glad of it, because if I'd 'a' knowed what a trouble it was to make a book I wouldn't 'a' tackled it, and ain't a-going to no more. But I reckon I got to light out for the territory ahead of the rest, because Aunt Sally, she's going to adopt me and sivilize me, and I can't stand it. I been there before.